ON THE FREE

COERT VOORHEES

ON THE FREE

carolrhoda LAB
MINNEAPOLIS

Carolrhoda Lab™ is a trademark of Lerner Publishing Group, Inc.

Carolrhoda Lab™
An imprint of Carolrhoda Books
A division of Lerner Publishing Group, Inc.
241 First Avenue North
Minneapolis, MN 55401 USA

For reading levels and more information, look up this title at
www.lernerbooks.com.

Front cover and interior images: © Ethan Welty/Aurora/Getty Images.
Back cover: © Seleneos/photocase.com.
Foilstamp: Chinch/Shutterstock.com.

Main body text set in Janson Text LT Std 10.5/15.
Typeface provided by Linotype AG.

Library of Congress Cataloging-in-Publication Data

Names: Voorhees, Coert, author.
Title: On the free / Coert Voorhees.
Description: Minneapolis : Carolrhoda Lab, [2017] | Summary: When a mudslide
    wipes out multiple members of a wilderness therapy trip, the three surviving
    teenagers must survive the elements, their demons, and one another.
Identifiers: LCCN 2016036266 (print) | LCCN 2016058537 (ebook) |
    ISBN 9781512429138 (lb : alk. paper) | ISBN 9781512448597 (eb pdf)
Subjects: | CYAC: Survival—Fiction. | Wilderness areas—Fiction. | Camping—
    Fiction. | Juvenile delinquency—Fiction. | Hispanic Americans—Fiction.
Classification: LCC PZ7.V943 On 2017 (print) | LCC PZ7.V943 (ebook) |
    DDC [Fic]—dc23

LC record available at https://lccn.loc.gov/2016036266

Manufactured in the United States of America
1-41568-23393-3/6/2017

For all of you on unit.
The next chapter is one only you can write.

SANTIAGO

1

When you're built like Santiago Rivas, you learn to deal with pain. Gaunt and gangly gets you practice. Repetition. You hang with pain on weekends. See each other at school and mix it up on the way home. But this is different. Not blinding like a pop to the nose, or shocking like a kidney blow. Not even unexpected, like that one time at the McDonald's on Osuna, when that pendejo from Belen ambushed Santi with a Little League bat.

Pain like that, he's used to. Pain like that happens in an instant. But not this. This is a slow, building kind of pain. Inevitable, like a thundercloud on the horizon.

Santi stays barefoot in his tent for just one second more. Just one minute longer. His sleeping bag and pad all stuffed and rolled and ready to go. He stares at his boots, a size too large, the tread worn smooth, the thin leather like cardboard compared to what everyone else is wearing.

And now his heels, which look like someone went after them with a blowtorch: open wounds, deep red beneath flaps of bloody skin, shredded from days of popped blisters.

The wool socks fit. The tent doesn't leak. The sleeping bag is warm enough. And even though his air mattress has a hole, it's small; he only has to refill the pad once a night. Everything is fine except the boots.

It could be worse, of course. It could always be worse. He could be back in juvie, lying on a three-inch mattress, leaning against the wall, his legs straight, ankles crossed, his undamaged feet sheathed in Sandoval County–issued cotton tube socks.

"Let's go, Santi. We need the oatmeal."

"In my pack," he says. "Top pouch, Ziploc bag."

Jerry unzips the tent door and sticks his head inside. A cool orange tint covers what little of his face isn't swallowed by a thick black beard. "Did it sound like I was asking for directions?"

It did not. Santi ties the laces together, slings the boots over his shoulder, and emerges from the tent carrying his sleeping bag and mattress.

"Good morning, Mary Sunshine. Why did you wake so soon?" Santi's tentmate sits next to the small campfire, drinking something hot from a mug. "You frightened off the little stars and scared away the moon."

"Victor," Jerry says.

"I'm just messing with him. Kid let the rest of us set up breakfast."

"That's not the point. We've got to focus on treating one another with respect."

"Santi-San can take it," Victor says. "He's hardcore, remember? So hardcore."

Santi ignores him and continues past the fire to where his pack dangles from a length of nylon rope he'd tossed over a branch. Twenty feet high or higher, Jerry had told them. Company policy, on the off-chance that a bear happened by the camp in the middle of the night.

Rico Salazar wanders up as Santi unties the knot. Rico,

youngest of them, a wiry little punk, just barely fifteen. "Why do you let Victor talk to you that way?"

Santi stares at him. The last thing he needs is a voice like this in his ear.

Rico blinks. Blinks again. His whole face commits, like eye-blink Tourette's. Even his cheeks get involved.

"What does it matter?" Santi finally says.

More blinking. The little dude is stumped. "It matters."

Santi lowers his backpack, which hits the ground with a satisfying thud. "Here." He hands Rico the big Ziploc of instant oatmeal pouches. "Jerry wanted this."

"Are you eating?"

"I'm eating. The hell is it to you?"

"You should put your shoes on," Rico says, nodding at Santi's feet. "You could step on something."

He watches Rico bound across the campground, short and spindly and full of shit.

It's starting to come back to him, with every breath of mountain air that passes through his lungs, every piece of dirt that crunches between his teeth at mealtime. As though Santi's been given a week's pass to his former life. Just glimpses, but they're becoming more frequent and more detailed each time. Maybe when the trip is over, he'll even remember who he was before the move to his uncle Ray's.

He takes a deep breath and tries to clear his head. Another to slow his pulse. The air is so thin up here that his heart is racing from the simple effort of lowering his backpack.

They're higher than ten thousand feet this morning, day three of the weeklong hike through southern Colorado's Weminuche Wilderness. "*Wem-in-ooch*," Rico whispered to Santi at orientation, "like 'screw-the-pooch.'"

They've basically done nothing but climb since they left the trailhead, and the elevation profile of the hike looks like the outline of a mountain itself: starting at 7,000 feet, then three days of a jagged rise to Bonfire Pass at almost 12,000, followed by an equally jagged three-day descent to the wilderness exit at 8,000.

Hiking uphill is bad enough, the blisters grinding against the back of his boots with every step, but at least uphill he can try to walk flat-footed. Santi knows downhill will be worse. There's no way he can avoid his heel hitting the ground, his body weight scraping it against the ruthless leather.

His feet aren't even the only problem; his lower back, just above his waist, feels like someone took a sledgehammer to it. His own fault, because he's probably carrying food for half the group, but he'd wanted it that way. Every time Jerry asked for a volunteer, Santi raised his hand. Yes, I can take the oatmeal. Yes, I can take the Bisquick. I've got the rice. It's heavy, I know. I've got it.

Once you've known what it's like to be hungry, you don't let food out of your sight unless you have to.

"Oh my God, Santi. What happened to your feet?"

The concern belongs to Amelia Something. The assistant leader, a volunteer from somewhere in Texas. Houston? He should know by now, but soon he'll be back in Albuquerque and she'll go back to Houston—Dallas, or wherever—and the amazing boyfriend she can't stop talking about and then her freshman year at the amazing college she also can't stop talking about. It's easier not to care.

"I'm cool," Santi says. "Just letting them breathe."

"I got certified in first aid last week," she says. "My skills are fresh."

She orders him to stay where he is, her arm outstretched like a traffic cop. Then she turns around, springing to her backpack in a supple-looking pair of new hiking boots.

Santi follows her, barefoot, tiptoeing as he avoids the minefield of pointed rocks. He'd rather do it himself, but he doesn't even have a Band-Aid, much less a first-aid kit. Amelia sits on the ground and gestures for him to take a seat on the log in front of her.

The only other girl on the trip is Celeste, a sixteen-year-old from Colorado Springs whose only goal seems to be winning the *Who's the Most Messed Up?* competition.

In all, they're a fearsome foursome of theft (Santi), rebelliousness (Rico), emotional distress (Celeste), and—as far as Santi can tell—being a gigantic asshole (Victor). Entrusted into the care of the Bear Canyon Wilderness Therapy Program under the all-star leadership team of Jerry and Amelia.

"That's just nasty," Celeste says now, faking a gag.

Amelia scissors a large donut out of a thick piece of moleskin. "You should have asked for better boots."

"Budget cuts, I guess," Santi says.

"It's because your pack is so heavy," Amelia says. "You don't have to impress anyone."

"That's not why," Santi says. "Besides, there's nobody here to impress."

"That's a little harsh."

Santi grins. Amelia is slight, with brown, shoulder-length hair and a set of wide green eyes that take up more of her face than they should. But she's cute enough, and cuter every day they spend in the wilderness. "Are you saying you think there's a future for us?"

Victor laughs from across the campsite. Dudes like

Victor. Rich kids playing badass. Full swagger right up until the moment of impact.

Santi closes his eyes for a moment and lets the scene unfold. His fist will work just fine. Or maybe a fallen branch. Or that rock, just a foot away, which could obliterate Victor's nose in an instant.

But there are some things you can't unsee, Santi knows. And the tweaker next to him in his holding cell at County pulling a little baggie of meth out of his ass and snorting it on the bench? That's one of those things.

So Santi does not pick up that rock. This time will be different. The straight and narrow. No more fighting, no more lifting cars. He'll make it to the end of the trip, only four days away, and the felony larceny charge will be dropped, and he'll spend the two years until his eighteenth birthday as a choirboy. Then, once his juvie record is expunged, he can start fresh.

"Good as new," Amelia says. "Well, maybe not *as new*."

White athletic tape now covers the moleskin over Santi's heels. If he's lucky, it will last until the evening, at which point he'll have to wander barefoot across Amelia's line of sight again.

Thick smoke from the morning campfire drifts his way, and his face broadens into a smile when he remembers his dad's old nickname for him: smoke magnet.

Before the weight of the pack, before the agony of the blisters, before the lunchtime ice-breakers and team-building exercises—as if Jerry and Amelia really believe that a trust fall is going to trigger some anti-delinquency feature in their young brains—before all of that, there is the morning. The sun creeping over the ridge, showering warmth on the valley below. The breeze. And the birds, too many to count, tweeting and singing and completely unaware that Santi's day is about to go to shit.

"Gather 'round, everybody," Jerry says, clapping twice. Next he'll ask how they feel, encouraging them to "dig a little deeper." Jerry's heart is probably in the right place, but it's almost worse that way. He wouldn't be as condescending if he didn't care so much.

Santi perches himself on a rock in front of the fire as Rico passes around the bag of oatmeal pouches. Santi takes one Apples & Cinnamon and one Maple & Brown Sugar and rips the tops off both at the same time. A little cloud of powder billows up from his bowl when he dumps the pouches inside.

Celeste follows Rico with the pot of boiling water, her arms trembling slightly as she grips the handle with both hands. "Nobody to impress?" she says.

Santi bounces his eyebrows up and down. "You know I like 'em crazy."

He notices her jaw tighten, and for a second he thinks she might dump the water on him. She seems to catch herself, and her face relaxes. She tilts the pot and begins to pour. "Say when."

"When," Santi says, but she keeps pouring. "When!"

Celeste shrugs at the extra water in his bowl. "Oops."

"We've got a difficult ten miles today," Jerry says, groats of oatmeal burrowed into the thicket on his chin, as if hiding from his mouth. "We'll break every ninety minutes for water and snack. If we make it over Bonfire Pass in time, I want to stop for lunch at an abandoned gold mine in the ghost town of Felton."

"Gold mine?" Rico says. "Like real gold?"

"Hope you brought your pick and shovel!" Victor's voice drips with fake enthusiasm.

Jerry ignores him. "It's been abandoned for over seventy years, Rico, but yes, there was real gold there. And everyone, make sure you have easy access to your rain gear. We may run into some weather before we get to camp tonight."

While the rest of them finish eating, Jerry pulls Santi aside and whispers, "If you lag again today, we're going to have to redistribute the food—"

"It's not the food. My feet are—"

"I'm just saying, if we need to make it easier for you, we can do that."

Santi gulps the last of his oatmeal and checks to see if any of the others have noticed their discussion. He gives Jerry a nod and goes up to help Victor break down their tent.

But Victor sits on a log ten feet away, his sleeping bag and pad already packed at his feet. He whittles with a long knife, scattering curled ribbons of wood across the ground.

"A little help?" Santi says, motioning to the tent.

"Nah, that's okay. You let us set up breakfast, right? I'm gonna sit this one out."

Santi shoots Victor double birds before unclipping the tent poles from their anchors and sliding them through the little sleeves at the top of the tent.

"We're not waiting for you today," Victor says. "If you're slow, you're slow."

"Like I need you to wait for me."

"Just remember to keep up. Mountain lions always go after the stragglers."

Santi laughs. "I thought Boy Scouts were supposed to be Good Samaritans. Helping old ladies across the street and all that."

"It's Eagle Scout, first of all," Victor says. "And are you

seriously comparing yourself to an old lady? I know how much you like to waddle at the back of the line, but still."

Santi says nothing, trying to mask how close Victor is to the truth. Santi is not meant for the front of the line, on the trail or off it. Never has been. It's how he found himself in this position in the first place.

Victor just keeps talking, though his eyes never move up from the spike as he whittles. Cut. Cut. Cut. "You've had a hard life, we know. So sad. But stop blaming people. Jesus."

Santi turns back to the tent, closing his eyes and concentrating on the cold aluminum in his hands. Collapse the pole. Pull the section apart, fold it, pull another section. Pretend Victor isn't using what Santi said in his group "sharing" session against him.

"I've got to admit, I didn't know real people used the term *broken family*. I thought it was just in the movies. What the hell is that, anyway?"

Santi can't help it. He tosses the collapsed pole onto the dirt and spins around, sprinting the ten feet to Victor. No pain in his feet. He could be walking on broken glass and it wouldn't matter.

Victor is ready, standing before Santi even reaches him. He's a year older, four inches taller, and a good twenty pounds heavier, but Santi figures Victor's extra bulk will slow him down just enough. A couple punches before Victor can react, and it will be over.

"I know how bad you think you are," Victor says, his arms relaxed at his sides, a spike in one hand, knife in the other. "You're welcome to give it a shot."

"Guys!" Jerry yells from across the campsite. He jogs over. "Guys!"

The straight and narrow, Santi thinks. *The straight and narrow.*

Jerry's beard is almost upon them. "Let's get past this, okay?" the counselor says. "Let's apologize."

"I've got two words for you," Victor says under his breath. "And I think you can guess they're not 'I'm sorry.'"

2

The knock came in the early evening. A quick rap against the metal of his uncle's front door. Santi had been expecting it, in a sense, in the same way that a field mouse expects the shadow of an owl.

Eric Ayala stood at the front door, his hands in the back pockets of jean shorts that went halfway down his calves. An array of tats snaked up his arms and disappeared beneath the bleached white beater: an eagle with a snake in its talons, the Virgen de Guadalupe, a rose, a bullet.

Two words: "You ready?"

Two more words: *Not tonight*. Santi could have said, *Not tonight*. Would have been so easy. Instead, he came up with two other words: "I guess."

Santi yelled inside to his sister that he'd be back later and followed Eric down the uneven South Valley sidewalk. In the six years he and Marisol had been with Ray, the neighborhood had hardly changed at all. Same neighbors behind the same thick doors. Same cars in the same driveways. Same painted dirt and rocks trying to pass for lawns. Same dogs. Same barking.

It was late evening, a Tuesday night. There was no reason for him to go out, he thought even then. Eric reached the driver-side door of his Cutlass Supreme and yanked it open. He must have noticed Santi's hesitation.

"Let's go," Eric said across the top of the car.

There was no plan, really. There never was. Cruise around, see what happened. Make something out of nothing.

Santi opened the door. A full 40 oz. lay on the passenger floorboard; another, half-empty one leaned against the armrest in the front seat. The Cutlass groaned slightly when Eric got in, while Santi stood with one hand on the roof and one hand on the door.

"You coming?" Eric said.

Santi got in the car and slammed the door behind him.

Days later, the prosecutor would put a deal on the table. Easy choice, he'd say. Santi wasn't the driver, was clearly just along for the ride, so how did probation sound? No record, no juvie, no reason this had to destroy Santi's life. Give us a name, he would say, and you walk out that door. Just a name. First and last. Two simple words.

Two simple words: *Eric Ayala.*

3

The drizzle is constant. More mist than rain, as though they're stranded in a cloud. They stop an hour into the hike to put on rain gear and cover their backpacks with plastic garbage bags, even though each pack is already lined with a garbage bag inside. Better safe than sorry!

Rico, Celeste, and Santi wear Bear Canyon–issued "waterproof" ponchos that leave their forearms exposed and funnel rivulets of water directly to their thighs, but Victor sports a rich-kid Eagle Scout jacket: seam-sealed Gore-Tex, bright red and form-fitting. Top-of-the-line, like everything else in his pack. He even brought an actual climbing rope with him, as opposed to the nylon the others use to hang their packs.

"Your feet okay?" Rico asks when they start again.

Santi ignores him.

"Yo, I said are your heels okay?"

This will go on all day long, Santi knows, if he doesn't at least humor the kid. He nods and tells Rico that he's trying not to think about it, but the truth is that he can't stop. The wet poncho slips against the garbage bag covering his pack, which slides from side to side no matter how tight Santi pulls the waist belt, and the weight of it means he can't walk flat-footed to keep his heels from rubbing.

He tries anyway, taking smaller steps, keeping his ankles flexed so that the boot lands flat on the slope. Doing this puts more pressure on his thighs and lower back, but it's better than the alternative. Better than using his toes to step. At least the foot stays flat inside the boot.

The weather gets worse all morning, and they summit Bonfire Pass in the middle of a gray storm, stopping at the top for handfuls of trail mix and sips of water.

"This is the halfway point and the highest we'll go," Jerry says. He snaps a couple of pictures, but the fact that they can only see about a hundred feet in front of them takes a little pizzazz out of the celebration. "Eleven thousand six hundred feet is an accomplishment you should all be proud of."

Gusts of wind roar up the valley and over the pass, and Jerry cuts the break short in order to get downhill as quickly as possible, just in case the thick clouds are packing lightning inside.

Santi is fucked. By hiking uphill as though he had stumps for feet, he managed to fatigue every muscle in his legs to the point of involuntary twitching, and the descent is twice as bad as he'd feared. The athletic tape unpeels with the wetness of his socks, causing the moleskin to bunch on top of the blisters. It gets so bad that Jerry finally sends Amelia to bring up the rear.

"You know what's crazy?" she says after a few minutes, as if by ignoring the obvious pain on Santi's face, she can take his mind off it.

Santi smiles at her through gritted teeth. "I know a lot of things that are crazy."

"We have no idea what's going on out in the world. There could have been a bombing or a death in the family or whatever."

"There probably wasn't a bombing."

"You know what I mean. Parties, friends. So-and-so hooked up with so-and-so. Life, right?"

She has a point. Even during his first stint in juvie, a month on unit for being caught with someone else's weed, he didn't feel this cut off. There was a set schedule: weekdays were school days, movies at night if all went well. The outside world wasn't exactly accessible, but at least he had the sense that it existed. His sister visited once a week.

"There's a flip side, too," Santi says. "The real world has no idea what's going on here, either."

"It's creepy, is all I'm saying. It feels weird not knowing what happened yesterday, what my friends were up to."

"Your boyfriend, too?" Santi says.

Amelia doesn't answer at first.

"I can hear you blushing from back here."

"Yes, him too," she says.

"Check out this scat," Jerry yells back to them.

He's waiting in the middle of the trail, and when they've all caught up, he squats down close to a long tube of crap and pokes at it with a stick. "Mountain lion scat. Cougar. See the little white flecks in there? That's bone."

Uncle Ray had a cat for a while. A stray from the neighborhood that used to come inside the house to eat and take shits on Marisol's bed. That's what this looks like, only bigger, and with more bones in it.

"Cat shit's a tourist attraction now?" Victor says.

"Is that hair?" Celeste says.

Rico adds, "Why did it take a crap in the middle of the trail?"

"Because if it had gone in the woods," Jerry says, "we wouldn't have seen it."

Santi notices a white flash in the distance, and he instinctively begins counting to himself. One. Two. Three. Four. Five. Thunder rumbles before he makes it to six. The lightning is about a mile away.

"Let's go, guys," Jerry says. He leads the way up the trail, followed by Celeste and Victor.

"Wait," Rico says to nobody in particular, "what did he mean about the shit in the trail? Why would the mountain lion want us to see it?"

Santi shrugs into the padded shoulder straps and feels the pack slip against his poncho. He yanks the waist strap tighter, moving even more weight from his upper back, then winces at the sharp pinch on his hipbones. He convinces himself to start moving. One foot in front of the other.

The trail emerges from the forest and makes a scar across the side of the mountain. Jerry is hustling, pushing the pace even as the trail gets sketchier.

In the distance, a thin sliver of sunlight pierces the cloud cover, and while the clouds are still thick above them, the rain has regressed to its earlier mist.

"Don't look down, bro," Rico says.

Of course, the first thing Santi does is look down. The muddy trail cuts directly across a steep barren slope, probably a slide path in the winter, judging by the lack of trees and bushes. The mountainside uphill, to his left, is steep enough, but the right side is worse, the slope becoming more and more vertical and finally ending at a littered heap of avalanche debris. To make matters worse, long stretches of the trail are only slightly wider than the sole of Santi's boot.

"What the hell, Rico?"

"You're not afraid of heights, are you?"

17

"Not heights," Santi says. "I'm afraid of what's at the bottom."

His legs are so tired that he stubs his toe on a little rock as he steps forward. The pack lurches up his back, and he reaches for the muddy uphill slope with his left arm, flailing to regain his balance.

This is it. Tonight he'll give in to Jerry. He'll have to figure out a way to save face, though. Maybe he can talk to Jerry before they get to camp, and they'll come up with a plan. He'll get Jerry to make a big deal of *forcing* Santi to give up the food, like Santi's doing a disservice to the others by carrying everything. This trip is all about individual responsibility, after all. "Órale," Rico says. "Santi. You got a lady back home?"

Santi wipes his hand on his thigh, leaving a thick brown smear on the wet jeans. He doesn't even know how to answer that one. It depends on what happens when he gets back home. Depends on what Diana says. Depends on if she even says anything.

He should have a girlfriend, and if it had been up to him, he would. If it had been up to him, he wouldn't even be here now. He'd be with Diana instead. But it hadn't been up to him, no matter what anybody said.

"I do," Rico says proudly. "She's hot, too."

"What's her name?"

Rico's answer is immediate. "Lucy."

Santi lets a smile come to his face. The kid hasn't learned how to lie right yet. If you're *that* fast with the name, it sounds too fake. "Good name."

"Yeah, bro," Rico says. "She's all sorts of hot."

"All sorts of hot?" He finds himself actually laughing, but not in a mean way, and he makes the decision to believe. He imagines Rico on a date, holding Lucy's hand in the park or at the movies. Rico's face twitching as he tries to muster up the balls to kiss her. Santi suddenly wants to know more. What does she look like? How did they meet? How long have they been together?

But he's falling.

One wrong step is all it takes. His left foot plants itself on a wide, flat rock that slips out from under him like a banana peel, pitching his foot forward. His boot's leather folds over at the heel and digs into Santi's raw skin, and he has just enough time to squeal in pain before he crashes to the ground. Hard.

The momentum of his backpack takes over from there, spinning him so that his head is pointing straight downhill. All that weight and no solid ground for it to rest on.

For a moment, he's like a turtle on its back, limbs flailing, his pack sliding down the hill as if greased. Santi looks between his legs as he slides, and Rico's terrified face uphill tells him everything he needs to know.

"Santi!" Rico says.

He watches Rico's face get smaller and smaller, and then, in his mind's eye, sees the rocks below coming up behind him.

His muscles go limp for another five feet of sliding, and then something in him triggers movement. As if his body finally realizes what his mind already knows. If he doesn't do something, he's going to die.

He'll die, and Marisol will be alone.

4

A full year before Santi even met Eric Ayala, he did a month for possession. Hours of mandated alone time in what passed for his cell: a bed, a shelf, a waist-high wall cutting halfway across the open end instead of a door, and a thick yellow line across the threshold that no other detainees could cross. It was different enough from what he'd thought his cell would be that he took to calling it his room instead.

Even when he wasn't in his room, he kept to himself as much as possible, trying not to get into shit with anyone, trying not to piss off any of the guards. Stressful as hell, but when he was in his room, he was fine.

The unit had twelve cells just like his, six on either side of a long rectangular room, with a series of picnic tables in between. A television hung on the wall at one end, but they only got to watch it if things went well on unit. That only happened twice in the four weeks and three days he spent inside.

On the afternoon of his third Saturday, Santi lay on the thin mattress, working his way through an article about tree ants in *Discover* magazine, waiting for Marisol to come make him laugh.

Officer Vazquez appeared in the open doorway. Thick shoulders, big forehead, one long eyebrow across the top of his face. "Rivas," he said, knocking on the wall inside his room.

Santi tossed the magazine on the bed and put on his slippers and followed Officer Vasquez along a red line to the unit's exit, where they both looked up at the surveillance camera in the corner and waited for the door to buzz open. More steps along the red line on the linoleum floor, down the beige hallway. Another door, another buzz, and into the visitation room.

The long table in the center of the room was completely full, but his sister was waiting at one of the small circular tables that lined the walls, her long black hair draped over her head like a hood. Only three years younger than he was but ten times smarter. Math prize, History prize, Outstanding Attitude prize. Make Your Brother Seem Like a Piece of Shit in Comparison prize. That last one took no effort.

This time she didn't get up to hug him, and when he sat down, she wouldn't meet his gaze.

"Marisol?" he said. "Are you okay?"

She nodded slowly.

He reached across the table, and she flinched slightly but let him push the curtain of hair away, revealing the purple shadow of a bruise.

Santi could hardly breathe. He bit his bottom lip until he was able to speak without yelling. "What happened? Who did this?"

"Nobody," she said softly. "It was an accident. I tripped."

A rising panic quickly overtook his anger. "Mari, please tell me."

"It was just some girls after school. I should have been more careful." She looked at him, and he saw the sadness in her eyes and the swelling on her cheek and the twin scratches down the side of her face, and he almost threw up.

"I wasn't going to come," she said quietly. "I didn't want you to be worried about me."

"I should have been there," he said. "This wouldn't have happened if I had been there."

"Maybe. You know how it is."

That was the problem. He knew exactly how it was.

"What about the science thing?" he said with forced cheer, trying to pretend that this was a normal visit. "Your project or whatever."

Marisol hesitated for a moment, and then a smile fought its way onto her face. "It was good. Really good."

"I bet you got an A."

"Duh," she said. There was a long pause. Santi looked down at his feet, the plastic slippers, the white socks. Over the murmurs of the other visitors came the newly familiar sounds of the facility in the distance: a buzz to open the doors, a deep metallic thud when the doors closed.

"I only have a week left," he said.

She nodded. "I'm going to be fine."

"I know you are. I'll make sure of it."

"Yeah." She nodded again. "Okay."

"I promise," he said, but when he said the word *promise*, he couldn't help but notice that she winced.

5

Sliding faster now, Santi flails to get off his back, lurching to the left, scraping his arms against the wet mud. His elbow catches first, spins him around so that his legs whip down below him.

On his chest now but still falling. He digs both elbows into the mud, jamming them deeper. His skin grating away.

His foot hits something, knocks his right knee up and into his chest, slows him just enough for his right hand to grab onto an exposed root. The other hand now. His body swings like a pendulum against the scree, first to the right of the root, then the left.

And he stops. And the world returns.

"Santi!" Amelia's voice.

He tries to pull himself up, but the pack is too heavy. He can see all of them up there, twenty feet above him. Too far to reach out for a hand. Too far to chain themselves together. Santi recognizes the fear on Jerry's face.

"Should have shared the food," Santi manages. "You guys are probably going to starve."

Jerry does not laugh. "Hold on. We'll figure something out!"

For some reason, Santi allows himself a peek downhill—a little glimpse to see exactly how far he still has to go—and he immediately regrets it. Shards of broken trees stick up amid the rocks and boulders another thirty feet below. It's like some-thing out of a horror movie.

"Ditch your backpack," Amelia says.

"No," Jerry says. "Santi, hold on. We're going to get you up."

"There's kind of a little drop-off here," Santi shouts.

"Are you sure you can't scramble up on all fours?"

"I look like a goat to you?" he screams. "My feet are dangling."

When Jerry speaks again, there's resignation in his voice, like a TV doctor calling out time of death. "Amelia, get out the radio in case we have to call in a rescue."

"Do something!" The root is slick from all the rain, and Santi's hands are slipping. It's only a matter of time. "My arms are cramping up!"

"Just hold on a little longer, okay?" This is Victor, and his voice is all business. Santi sees him take off his pack. He pulls out his blue climbing rope and ties a quick loop at the end.

"You're not going to die," Rico says. "Maybe get mangled or something, but not die. So don't worry about that."

"Rico!" Jerry and Santi yell at the same time.

"I'm just saying."

Victor clips an orange carabiner through the loop and begins to feed the rope down the cliff. "Take off your pack and clip it to the rope," he says. "We'll pull it up and then get you."

"How do I know you're not going to leave me once you get the food?"

"No promises."

Jerry quickly says, "He's kidding!"

The carabiner dangles in front of Santi's face, but he can only stare at it. His shoulders twitch with fatigue, and he can't feel the fingers of either hand anymore.

"Come on, Santi," Amelia says. "Clip it to your backpack."

"I can't take my backpack off."

Now they're yelling. Every one of them with a different suggestion at the same time, and all reminding him to hurry, as if he hadn't already thought of that. He reaches his left arm above and behind him, to the top of his pack, but the damn thing is still covered by the garbage bag, and even though the fall tore up the plastic, the bag's still too slick to grab onto.

They won't shut the hell up and they're all still looking at him and suddenly this crazy feeling of shame hits him so hard. Shame that he can't help himself. Shame that he fell. Shame that Victor was the one to throw him a damned rope.

"Shut up!" he screams. "Just shut up!"

His feet will hit the rocks first, the shoddy boots no protection. His ankles will twist instantly, tendons popping before the bones shatter. His legs will come next, the weight of all his gear and four days of food driving them down. Then his spine, his chest, his arms, his head. He can already feel the impact.

Santi clenches his teeth as the nausea rolls over him. He opens his eyes, and the solution is right there, so simple he's even more embarrassed that he didn't think of it right away.

Keeping his stronger hand on the root, Santi snatches the carabiner with his left and quickly clips it across his chest, onto to the pack's right shoulder strap. Then he unbuckles his waist belt. With the full weight of the pack now resting on his shoulders, the muscles in his right arm flare in pain.

"Pull up!" Santi screams. "Just a little! Take some weight off me."

Above him, they pull slack from the rope, and the backpack lightens. Santi sneaks his free arm underneath the left shoulder strap, and with the pack on one shoulder, he grips the root with his left hand and quickly unshoulders his right.

The second he's no longer supporting his pack, the rope stretches, and the pack drops a foot. It careens into him, knocking one arm off the root.

"I said pull up!" he yells.

"Sorry!" Jerry says. "We've got it now!"

"Jesus, your pack is heavy!" Victor says. "You got a dead guy in there?"

Free of the pack's weight now, Santi grabs the root with both hands again, pulling up so that his elbows are completely bent. He presses his cheek into the rough bark of the tree like he's cuddling a pillow. His hands are still cramping; he needs to hurry. When the rope comes down again, Santi takes his left hand off the root and grabs the carabiner.

He makes a loop by clipping the carabiner back onto the rope about three feet up. After threading his head and left arm through, he holds onto the root with his left hand and he snakes his right hand against his body and through. Now the rope is under his arms, wrapped around his back, with the carabiner at his chest. His forearms start to twitch and his hands are cramping and his fingers are now losing their grip. He has nothing left.

"I hope you got me," he yells, letting go of the root.

The rope tightens around him instantly, digging into his armpits, but he doesn't fall to his death, so they must have him. Santi scrambles up the slope until he reaches the path, and three sets of arms grasp at him.

Santi collapses. The rain pelts his back, mixing with the blood from his elbows, pooling where his hands press into the muddy trail. He's trembling on all fours. But he's alive.

Amelia says, "Are you okay?"

"That was good, Victor," Jerry says. "That was really good."

Santi struggles to catch his breath. "Thanks."

"Hmm?" Victor says as he coils the rope back up. "I didn't get that."

Pushing himself to his feet, his chest still heaving, Santi glares at him.

"Are you okay?" Jerry says. "Because we really should get going."

Santi nods. The adrenaline is trickling out of him now, and his legs feel tired and heavy. Soon, he knows, the pain will come, but there's nothing he can do about that. "I'm fine."

They shoulder their packs and continue on the trail. Victor hangs back, motioning for Santi to move ahead of him. "We got a connection now," Victor says with a chuckle Santi can't exactly figure out. "Me saving your life and all. A lot of cultures think that means you owe me your allegiance."

Allegiance. The word rolls through his head. Allegiance is complicated.

6

The week after Santi got into Eric's car, he sat alone on the small hill overlooking the El Real High School football field. Spring practices were underway but far enough down the hill that the sounds of the coaches' screaming and the crush of helmets against pads were only a distant soundtrack.

There'd been no space for him in the system, no place to hold him until the adjudication, so he'd come back to school. Gone to his classes as if it hadn't happened. Eric Ayala seated behind him in third period English. But the clock was ticking. It was his second offense, after all, and the clock was most definitely ticking.

Everyone knew it, and they were all waiting to see what Santi would do.

Diana came up behind him and sat at his side on the grass without saying a word, and Santi's skin began to tingle. He knew her smell like a deer knows the smell of a hunter. The blend of shampoo and perfume that was her hallmark, like honey and peaches and some sort of mint.

Marisol once described Diana Martinez as "the blondest, whitest Martinez you're ever going to see." After the move from Santa Fe to Albuquerque, when Santi'd had to live with Ray, when he'd had to change schools, Diana had been the first person to talk to him. His first friend. Weeks of keeping to himself, just trying to get through without crying in public, and then one day at lunch this white chick Martinez was sitting across from him in the lunchroom, asking what his name was. Back then, ten years old, with some baby fat still on her, she was just another girl.

But she didn't stay that way forever. One day Santi looked up and flinched, frightened of how beautiful she had become. Whenever they talked, he tried to arrange it so that they were next to each other, not facing each other, taking eye contact out of the equation. That way he was less likely to make an ass out of himself.

That's how they sat now, thankfully, both surveying the field in front of them, silent for a long while. Santi figured that since Diana was the one to sit down next to him, she would have to speak first, but she refused to break the silence, and he finally cracked.

"I don't have a choice," Santi said.

"Why does Eric get away with it? What makes him the lucky one?"

"He didn't wear a seat belt," Santi said with a rueful shake of his head.

"What is that supposed to mean—"

"Never mind."

"Santi," she said. This time it was almost a whisper. She reached her hand toward his knee, a gesture that Santi only later realized must have been a risk for her. A signal that she felt the way he'd always prayed she would.

He knocked the hand away and stood up. "What do you expect me to do?"

She flushed, but that didn't stop him. "There's no witness

protection for juvie felonies, right? So where am I supposed to go? It's easy for you to act like you have all the answers, but you're not the one who has to deal with what happens when the shit goes down."

Her eyes went cold halfway through his speech, and by the time he'd finished, he was talking to the back of her head.

7

Santi's jeans scour the bloody scratches on his knees when he steps; his elbows stick against the poncho when he swings his arms. His heels. His back. It's a miracle he can move at all. Even though every footfall brings a fresh blast of hurt, he says nothing. No grunting, no wincing. Just him and his swallowed pain.

When they finally stop to rest, Santi catches a glimpse of something sharp on the hillside next to the trail. A spike, maybe? A big nail? Sticking up from underneath the muddy earth. Rain has washed the dirt away from the tip, but the rest is buried deep enough that he has to wedge it back and forth to get it out.

It's heavy, about four inches long and at least a half-inch thick at one end. A deep orange rust cakes most of the surface, but when Santi scrapes it off, he can see the black iron beneath.

"Santi found a nail," Rico says.

"That makes sense," Jerry says. "We're almost to Felton."

"We're stopping there, right?" Rico says. "For lunch?"

"Think about how hard it must have been back then," Jerry says. "Coming over the passes, no protection from the elements. No Gore-Tex, no lightweight backpacks. The people here had to work for everything. Nothing was given to them."

"Oh, man," Victor says. "You were this close."

"This close to what?"

"To actually being interesting. I was learning. And then you had to go and ruin it with 'nothing was given to them.'"

Jerry shrugs but then says, "When you have to chop wood all summer in order to have enough fuel to get through the winter, fuel for cooking, fuel for heating, then I think it's pretty fair to say that nothing is given to you."

"Yes, sir," Victor says, giving Jerry an exaggerated salute. "Got it, sir."

For a moment it looks like Jerry is going to say something else, but instead he closes his eyes, like an extra-long blink, and turns away.

They've only gone a few steps when Rico points at the trail ahead of him. "Check it out. More scat."

"Since when are we on the Discovery Channel?" Victor says. "It's cat shit. That's all it is. Cat shit, so can we please just call it that?"

He kicks the scat off the trail with the side of his boot and trudges ahead.

"What did I do?" Rico gives Santi an anxious look, but Santi doesn't have the energy to do anything but shrug.

A collapsed outhouse is the first sign of the ghost town. Its small square roof lies in the middle of a pile of snapped and rotting boards splayed out in every direction as if the whole thing was crushed by the foot of an angry giant.

They slog through more trees until the path opens up to reveal a clearing. Small wooden cabins are scattered around the edges, all in various states of decay. Some have four walls but no roof; others look more like lean-tos. Some are just piles of logs, any vertical surface having fallen down long ago.

The trail cuts past the rock-strewn entrance of a mine shaft on the side of the hill, about five feet tall by four feet wide. Thick wooden beams frame the opening, and the rusted ends of some sort of railroad track poke out of the ground before disappearing into a jumbled heap of boulders, broken logs, and packed earth a few steps into the shaft.

Jerry motions for them to gather around the mine's entrance as the rain falls harder. The garbage bag covering Santi's backpack channels every drop directly onto his neck and shoulders, which are now so drenched that he wonders why he's wearing any rain gear at all.

They're all soaked. All of them except Victor, of course, the rain being no match for his million-dollar jacket.

"This was operational until the early 1930s," Jerry says. "The miners followed a vein about a half-mile deep, but the easy pickings were gone by the beginning of the Great Depression, when the price of gold went down by almost twenty percent. Some miners kept at it for a few years, but it didn't make financial sense to keep digging much longer."

Victor breaks from the group and ducks into the mine shaft.

"Careful," Amelia says, "you don't know how stable that is."

Victor ignores her, sitting on the edge of a boulder inside the shaft. His pack rides up on his shoulders, pitching him forward so that he has to rest his elbows on his legs. "This is cool," he says. "I'm going to hang out here for a sec."

"There's no more gold in there," Santi says.

Victor smirks. "Oh, Santi-San. You so funny."

The mine isn't big enough for all of them, so Jerry points to a small cabin across the clearing, the only one that still seems to have a roof. "We'll be in there," he says. "You're going to need to eat, so don't dawdle."

"I never dawdle," Victor says, his eyes on Santi.

Jerry shakes his head as he trudges toward the cabin. Off the trail now, pushing through thick grass more than two feet high, they might as well be wading through a stream. Santi's socks squish inside his boots with every footstep.

"Best not to lean against the walls," Jerry says when they arrive at the small cabin's doorway. "It may not take much for them to cave in on us."

They follow him inside, but the benefit of shelter from the rain is almost entirely negated by the stench of decaying flesh that greets them as soon as they step over the threshold.

"What *is* that?" Celeste says through her elbow.

About half of the floorboards are missing, most of them on the far corner of the room. A combination of rot and animal panic has seen to that; long teeth marks scar the remaining boards. "Probably a marmot got trapped underneath," Jerry says, covering his nose. "You'll get used to it."

"I don't want to get used to it," Celeste says. "I want to puke."

Santi gags once, then steps back outside for a cleansing breath of fresh air. It's no use. The reek has burrowed into his nostrils. A thick smell. Mildewed. Rotten. Syrupy.

White flashes light up the clouds. One. Two. Three. The thunder rolls slowly toward them, building on itself until it fills Santi's head, until he can't even hear the rain cascading off the cabin roof.

"Storm's getting closer," Jerry says once the thunder ebbs. "Come back in. I promise you'll get over it."

Santi reluctantly steps inside and takes off his pack and poncho. He unties the pack's outer garbage bag and then the inner one. He pulls out a bag of bagels, a jar of peanut butter, and their last block of cheese. The cheese and peanut butter are heavy, and he's looking forward to losing a couple of pounds.

He lays his pack on its side and sits on it, leaning against the wall with his legs outstretched.

"I should probably do something about those, huh?" Amelia says, appearing above him with a bagel sandwich in one hand and the first-aid kit in the other.

"Nah," Santi says, cringing as he brings his arms up to look at one elbow, then the other. It's like someone attacked him with a weed whacker: long scrapes down the underside of his forearms, a complete lack of skin at the elbows. "Skin is overrated."

Amelia smiles and sits at his side anyway, and he lets her clean and dress his wounds. First his elbows. Then his heels. It's like they're in a war movie, like she's a nurse in a makeshift infirmary tent. Rain beats against the metal roof like machine gun fire, the thunder like distant explosions.

"You're pretty good at beating yourself up," she says when she's finished.

"You're pretty good at fixing me." He winks, but she's already packing up the first-aid kit and doesn't notice.

Jerry is right about the stench, at least, which evolves from noxious to merely disgusting. Eventually, Santi doesn't even mind eating. Celeste, on the other hand, spends the whole time by one of the open windows, still in full rain gear as she leans to keep her upper body outside the room. Every time she needs a bite of her bagel, she leans back inside, chomps down quickly, and then sticks her head outside again.

The rain starts to come down in sheets, the wind gusting, rattling the unsteady walls, enough so that Celeste finally moves away from the window. Santi leans his head against the splintered wall and closes his eyes.

It's the rotting marmot, of all things, that makes him think of his first day on unit.

He'd only caught the stench once, as he was walking toward the main building for the first time. Past the control tower, underneath the razor wire on the perimeter fence. One breath, but one breath was enough. A sweet, stale smell with a hint of burning hair underneath. He'd asked what it was, but nobody had been able to tell him. For the rest of his time there, he kept expecting it. Whenever he walked outside, whenever he hit the yard, he'd braced himself. But the smell never returned.

"Have you guys seen Victor?" Jerry says.

"What do you mean?" Rico says. "He's not there?"

Santi opens his eyes and looks around. He's still in the mining shack. Rain still rattles against the roof. Jerry stands in the doorway with his hands on his hips.

"How long was I out for?" Santi asks.

"Thirty minutes, maybe?" Amelia says. "Victor never came in to eat."

"I guess I sleep better when that dude's not around." Santi takes his own peek out the window. There's no movement, no red rain jacket. Nobody in the abandoned mine at all, at least not that he can see. "Maybe he's taking a leak."

Amelia says, "He must have had some food in his pack."

"I don't think so," Santi says. "Not lunch, anyway."

Jerry cups his hands around his mouth. "Victor!"

No response. Jerry unfolds the topo map from his back pocket and spreads it out on the uneven wooden floor. Their route is traced in red marker, with a big *X* at every planned campsite. "If we don't leave soon, there's no way we'll make it to camp tonight, and if we don't make it to camp tonight, we're behind schedule for tomorrow and the next day."

"We can't leave without him," Amelia says.

"You and I could go ahead," Santi says to her. "Set up camp so that it's ready when the rest of them get there."

"I'll go with you guys," Rico says.

Jerry runs his fingertips through the thicket of his beard. "You could get dinner started. Maybe come back on the trail without your packs if we take too long."

Amelia looks outside instead of responding right away. A thunderclap rattles the metal roof. She clearly wants no part of Santi's plan, which makes him wonder what the hell she's doing out here in the first place.

"It's no big deal," Santi says, pointing at the map. "It's one trail, a little hump near Fall Creek, then down, right?"

Jerry shakes his head. "We need to stick together, especially if it starts raining harder. Thanks for offering, Santi, and no offense, but I'm not comfortable sending you out there without any wilderness experience."

Santi has to stop himself from chuckling. The way he'd figured it, if they all thought he sucked at making fires, nobody would expect him to make them. Let Victor the Eagle Scout pick up the slack. But just because you don't brag about how much experience you have doesn't mean you don't have experience at all.

8

Weekends, when everyone else was off singing hymns, Santi was learning how to make a compass out of a pine needle, how to weave a bracelet out of paracord, how to build a shelter without tools. He asked once why they didn't go to church. His dad just smiled and said, "Where do you think God really lives?"

Santi was six years old the first time he built a fire in the woods. Not with matches and newspaper but with his hands. Gathered the kindling, made a bow out of string and a bent stick, notched the end of another stick into a small groove in a flat piece of wood.

He went back and forth with the bow, rotating the stick faster and faster until smoke began to rise from the little tinder pile he'd collected at the stick's base.

"I did it!" Santi said. He stopped the bow and looked up triumphantly, but his dad only raised his eyebrows and smiled.

"You sure?"

Santi looked down again. The smoke was gone. He pushed the tinder away, only to find a slightly charred groove in the board. The tears came then, even though he tried to hide them. His dad watched, waiting.

"I can help you if you want."

Santi waved him away and wrapped the string back around the stick. Jammed the stick in the little smoke-stained indentation. Back and forth once more with the bow. Smoke appeared again, but just smoke, so he kept at it. He piled more tinder at the base of the stick, blowing gently, still working the bow.

When the little tuft burst into flame, Santi did not look up. He tossed the bow and stick to the side and placed kindling over the fire in a small teepee. He blew again, stoking the fire, then added bigger sticks, and still bigger. For five minutes, he worked. Silently. His dad said nothing.

When he finally backed away from the fire, the sticks of the teepee were the width of his arm. Flames danced before them, over two feet tall. He felt his dad's hand on his head. Tender at first, then a full-on mussing of his hair.

"The time will come, Santiago, when there's nobody else. That time comes sooner for some people than for others, but it always comes." His dad grabbed a big log and tossed it onto Santi's fire. The teepee crashed, but the flames rose, and soon the log was crackling.

9

Santi notices the jacket first, a brief glimpse of red among the trees in the distance, moving steadily toward the ghost town. Soon they're all yelling, and then Victor emerges in the clearing. Meandering through the tall grass with his hood covering his head. Finally he looks up and waves, but he doesn't walk any faster.

"Where the hell were you?" Jerry says—now hoarse and frantic—when Victor reaches the cabin.

"I got lost." His expression is calm. Bewildered, even, as if he's just come back from a quick bathroom break and can't figure out what the big deal is.

"What are you talking about, lost? I told you to join us in here. You promised you wouldn't dawdle."

"I wanted to do some exploring, and I figured, you know, better to ask forgiveness than permission."

Jerry opens his mouth but catches himself, trembling as he struggles to get himself under control. When he finally speaks, his voice is almost a whisper. "You could have asked. You should have told me."

"I'm fine," Victor says. Then, as if sensing that's not quite enough, he offers to shake Jerry's hand. "I'm not lost anymore and I'm not dead. You're not going to get sued or anything."

Amelia steps forward. "That's not what he was worried about, Victor. He was worried about you."

Victor says nothing, and Jerry grunts and moves to his own pack. "We don't have time for this right now."

Jerry stomps out of the cabin and up the trail, followed by Rico, Amelia, and Victor, who ducks into the open mine entrance for his backpack as they pass by. Santi and Celeste bring up the rear.

"What did you mean about Jerry getting sued?" Amelia says. "Why would anyone sue him?"

Victor laughs. "You've never met my stepdad."

"Is he the one who sent you out here?" Santi says.

"Shut up, Santiago. I don't remember including you in this conversation."

"You're next up for sharing tonight. Might as well get it all out right now, don't you think? Try out some lies with us so they're ready for the whole group."

Amelia glares at him with those massive eyes. "Santi."

"Sorry," Santi says. "Please go on about your awesome stepdad."

They hike in silence for a few minutes. Then Victor says, "He's pretty much the baddest-ass lawyer in Colorado. If anything happened to me, he would go apeshit."

"You're lucky he cares so much," Amelia says.

"He's cool. My mom and he got married a couple years ago, and even though he already had some kids in college, he told my mom that he'd been a bad dad before and wanted a second chance."

"You're the worst liar I've ever met," Santi says.

"You've probably met a lot of them, haven't you?"

Santi doesn't really know what that means, but it makes him

hesitate just enough for Victor and Amelia to freeze him out.

"My parents met in college," Amelia says. "Princeton, which is why they were desperate for me to go to an Ivy League school."

"Didn't get in, though, right?"

"Didn't apply."

Victor laughs. "What?"

"I'm sure it would have been awesome, don't get me wrong. But I'm pretty sure the whole thing was all about them."

"No doubt." Victor's right there with her, and their rich kid bonding continues. "My favorite is when they get on you about where all your friends want to go, because all the parents talk about where their kids are going."

His sister will get into a good school. That's what Santi knows. She'll get out of Albuquerque—out of New Mexico, even. Somewhere. She's so much smarter than he is. So much better.

"Everyone's in on it," Amelia says.

"Yep. Why else would there be so much competition for my SAT tutor?"

"You have a tutor for that stuff?" Santi can't help blurting out.

Victor scoffs. "Everyone has tutors for that stuff."

Santi needs a comeback, something about how the world really works. It's going to be a good one, too, so both Victor and Amelia feel nice and guilty. Confidence rises in his chest, and a smile comes to his face.

"What the hell, Santi?" Celeste says, nipping at his heels. "Let's go."

He looks up to see Amelia and Victor twenty feet up the trail.

"Zoned out, I guess." He steps to the side and waves her by. "After you."

Instead of passing completely, she stops next to him and whips a wet strand of purple hair out of her face. "I was kind of worried that nobody on the trip was going to be as messed up as me, but I don't even come close to your sorry ass."

"Thanks."

"I'm just playing," she says with a smile that actually looks genuine. "But you have to admit that you did beat the crap out of yourself today."

Santi returns the smile and gestures up the trail. Amelia and Victor are now a good fifty yards away. "We should go."

She nods and pushes the pace until she almost reaches the others, but then she stops again and waits for him. When Santi finally catches up, Celeste says, "That was a nice little moment we had back there, don't you think?"

He can only shake his head. "Someday, I'm going to figure you out."

"Doubt it." Her eyes widen as she notices something in the forest behind him.

Her pack scrapes against a tree as she pushes past him, dousing them both with a cascade of raindrops from the branches above. Taking a few steps off the trail, she approaches a bush about three feet high, with arrowhead-shaped dark green leaves and clusters of yellow berries the size of Santi's pinky fingernail.

"What are you doing?" he says, flapping the rain off his poncho.

"I'm starving," she says and picks a handful of berries.

"You can't eat those."

"I don't know how you ate anything with that disgusting dead marmot smell filling the cabin." Celeste looks at the berries in her hand and then smiles at him. "I'm a real mountain woman now."

"No!" He lunges forward and knocks the berries from her hand before she can put them in her mouth.

"What the hell?"

"White and yellow, kill a fellow," he says instinctively, quoting part of a rhyme his dad once taught him. "Those are poisonous."

She glares at him. "How do you know that?"

Santi looks away and shrugs. "Jerry told us," he says, trying to mean it.

"I don't think so. I would have remembered."

"Nah. I bet most days you don't even remember your own name."

"Fuck you." She stomps past him.

"No, I'm sorry." He reaches for her, wincing, and spins her around by the shoulder. "Órale, I didn't mean it. That was stupid. Here. There's some trail mix in my bag."

Santi drops his pack and pulls a plastic baggie of trail mix from the side pocket.

Her eyes narrow, and she tilts her head forward slightly, like a bull about to charge. After a few seconds, she lifts her head up again and snatches the bag from his hand. "I'm still pissed at you. But I'm not as pissed as I am hungry."

She opens the baggie and digs her hand inside. Santi feels like he should say something more, but he doesn't know what. "So. Do you have any brothers or sisters?"

"Not gonna happen," she says with her mouth full. "My sharing circle isn't for two more days."

A long pause follows. She lets him take a handful of his own trail mix, at least.

"Okay, fine," she says. "Oldest of four. I'm the worst first child ever."

"What does that mean?"

"Well, if you're the first child, you're supposed to be all responsible, aren't you? That's what everybody keeps telling me."

"I'm pretty sure you're not the worst first child ever," he says, but before he can tell her who is, Jerry's voice rescues him, shouted from a long distance.

"Santi! Are you okay?"

"It was me," Celeste shouts over her shoulder, keeping her eyes on Santi. "I had to tie my shoe!"

Without another word, she twirls away and marches up the trail. She probably wouldn't have died from the berries, but maybe he saved her from getting all sick, so that's something. Santi struggles to put his pack back on, fighting to get his left arm underneath the strap without scraping his elbow.

Belt strap buckled and tightened, he drops his head and leans into the rain, wondering again how the hell his life got this way. Out here in the woods, he knows exactly how to survive, even though he pretends that he doesn't. Back home, it's the opposite. Back home, he has to pretend that he knows—that he's not afraid, that he's hard enough to hang with dudes like Eric Ayala—even though he has no goddamn clue.

10

Santi's first time out with Eric was a blur of nervous excitement and veiled fear. More than the shock of Eric wanting to roll with him. More than the buzz of the 40 oz., or even the thrill every time they passed the cops, that first night out was all about limitless possibility. It didn't matter that they had no plan. Having no plan was the whole point. They'd see what the city had in store for them. Maybe run into some ladies, find a party. Maybe they'd come across a fight, or maybe they'd jump into one.

The last time, though, that excitement was nowhere to be found. They'd been in the car for more than three hours. Darkness crept across the city until it had strangled the red glow of the Sandia Mountains. They hung with a crew over at the McDonald's for a while, but had to jet when the manager called the cops. They hit a parking lot over by a dried-up arroyo, but the dude-to-chick ratio was about twenty to zero. Eric announced that he wasn't in the mood for no damn salchicha party, and he and Santi peeled out, the tires pelting everyone else with bits of gravel and a fine cloud of dust.

At one point, a BMW cut them off at a light, and they spent half an hour following the rich kids inside all over town. Even that got boring, though, and when the kids pulled into a gated community, Eric rolled slowly past and smiled at them, squeezing the trigger of an imaginary gun.

Santi didn't get up to this part of the city very often—the Northeast Heights, where the yards were bigger, the lawns greener, and the streets smoother. Some of the houses even had pillars at the front.

The forty was half gone, and Santi had a nice buzz going when Eric said, out of the blue, "That chick Diana's fine, bro. You better get on that, or someone else I know will, if you know what I mean."

"The hell you will," Santi muttered, looking straight ahead.

"Oooh, look at you, all protective and shit. Something tells me she could take care of herself, though. Those lips on her? She knows how to get down."

Santi ignored him and took his longest pull yet from the forty. A warm sensation spread through his chest, tingling out to his arms.

"Check it," Eric said, swerving the car into a neighborhood street. He pointed out Santi's window as they cruised by a silver Lexus sedan tucked against the curb.

"What are you doing?" Santi said.

"Don't you wonder how that bitch corners?"

"Come on, ese."

"Look at us. Look at you, stuck in that shit house with your uncle. Look at me. Why shouldn't we be the ones to drive a pinche Lexus? Don't we deserve it?"

From the moment Santi had walked out his front door three hours earlier, he should have known this was going to happen.

Sure, he could say no, but he'd have to deal with Eric the next day, and the day after, and forever. Not to mention everyone else.

"Just for a little spin," Eric said, as though the issue had already been decided. "We'll bring it back before anybody notices."

Eric ditched the Cutlass around the block, and from that point forward, everything played out as though Santi were watching it on TV. There he was, getting out of Eric's car, following Eric at a brisk walk down the sidewalk, avoiding the streetlights. There he was, lingering in the shadows as Eric worked the driver's-side door with a slim jim, flinching in the flash of the headlights when the alarm blared. Three seconds later, the alarm went silent, and the door was open.

You'd better get your ass in that car, he thought. And there he was, getting his ass in that car.

The black leather seat felt somehow firm and soft at the same time. The inside still smelled new too. The engine hummed when Eric put it in gear.

"Just a spin, right?" Santi said.

Eric smiled at him and punched it.

They flew down Academy, the engine whining as the RPMs ticked past 8,000. A left on San Mateo, and Santi had to brace himself against the door. When they straightened out again, he strapped on his seat belt, his desire to live past tonight outweighing any concerns about the smirk on Eric's face.

Blue and red lights leapt out from a side street behind them, flashing in the rear view, getting so much closer so fast. "Shit, that's the cops!" Santi said.

"Shut up."

Eric hit the gas through a red light, and Santi's ribs pressed backward into the seat. It was no use. The cops matched their speed. The Lexus clipped the curb as Eric swerved a left turn, and a loud pop filled the air.

"They're shooting at us!" Santi said, but by the time the words were out of his mouth, he knew better. The sound was too loud, too close to have come from the cops. The rear tire was gone, shredded flat.

Eric turned again, fighting the steering wheel. Only half a block away from the cops now, he slammed on the brakes, pressing Santi forward into his seat belt. Eric opened the door and dove out.

Santi tried to follow, but his seat belt buckle was stuck. Jammed. A luxury car, and the seat belt didn't even work. Eric glanced back only once, and the look on his face told Santi everything. Then his friend was gone, disappearing into the shadows. A cop started to give chase, but Eric was too fast.

Santi knew what Eric's look had meant, even as the police opened the door, yelling at him with their guns drawn, even as they dragged him out of the car, as they pressed him face down on the sidewalk, wrenching his arms behind him, a knee in the small of his back. He knew.

11

"We have to stop here," Jerry says at dusk, dropping his pack at the edge of a ravine like a narrow groove chiseled down the side of the mountain. The ravine had at one point been large enough to be labeled *Fall Creek* on the map, but now—even with the rain back to a steady pour—only a faint trickle dribbles down the center. "Tomorrow will just need to be a longer day than we'd planned."

"Thanks a lot, Victor," Celeste says.

Victor scoffs. "I'm not the one who fell down a cliff."

The look in Victor's eyes is different now. Resentful. Maybe he's embarrassed about getting lost. Or maybe he's just tired. Tired of the wilderness, tired of the rain. Tired of having to spend the night in a tent with a juvenile delinquent. Whatever the reason, Santi doesn't like it.

Jerry rigs up a tarp between some trees near the ravine. "We need water, too," he says as he unpacks the camping stove. "Everybody refill their bottles in the stream before dinner, and don't forget to purify. Giardia would ruin your trip."

"Yeah," Victor says. "'Cause it's been a blast so far."

***

Packs finally off, everyone gathers wordlessly under the shelter. It's Celeste's turn to cook, so Santi tosses her a big bag with macaroni, cheese powder, and dehydrated ham. Another pound lost. He can hardly lift his left arm above shoulder level. No matter how exhausted the rest of them are, nobody is remotely as beat up as Santi. His blisters, his elbows, his back, not to mention all the extra bruises from his fall.

He's going to sleep like a dead man tonight, no matter the leaky mattress or his shifty-eyed tentmate.

Night comes too quickly, and they have to set up camp before dinner. Victor tucks their tent and rain fly under his arm, Santi grabs his headlamp and the tent poles, and together they leave the cover of the tarp and trudge back out into the rain.

Santi stops at a flat area about twenty yards from the tarp, close to where Amelia and Rico are setting up their two tents, but Victor continues on, his headlamp bouncing through the trees until it finally settles another fifty yards away.

"What the hell?" Santi says.

"I can't deal with the Beard right now."

Santi shrugs. It doesn't matter. He just wants to set up the tent, eat a quick meal, and go to sleep. There's bound to be some sort of team-building exercise they'll have to endure, but he can suffer through it on autopilot. He starts assembling the poles while Victor kicks rocks away, clearing a spot for the tent.

Thunder rumbles way off in the distance, and Santi shakes his head. "I should have opted for juvie."

"What's the going rate for grand theft auto?"

"You planning on stealing a car?"

"If I stole a car," Victor says, "I wouldn't get caught."

"That's a good plan."

"I'm a good planner." Victor's headlamp blinds him, so Santi can't tell what Victor's expression is.

"You must be. You're out here with me, in the rain, in the middle of nowhere." Santi slides the tent poles through the appropriate sleeves. With the two of them on opposite sides of the tent, he and Victor fix the pole ends into their respective slots, and the tent pops up into a dome.

Victor grunts. He whips the rain fly up over the tent and lets it fall like a bed sheet. "Maybe this is exactly where I wanted to be."

"Yeah, I'm sure it is." Santi clips the ends of the fly to the tent poles and pulls it taut. After staking it down, they're done. He nods toward Jerry and the others. "You ready?"

"Not until he makes me." Victor unzips the rain fly and main tent door. He sits inside with his feet sticking out and his boots still on, the fly's vestibule offering shelter from the rain.

Santi decides to join him. "So," he says, fishing. "Your stepdad."

"Are we bonding now?" Victor scoffs. "The two guys with no dads?"

The rain pelts against the tent, filling the small space with a constant roar. Santi wraps his arms around his knees and breathes in. He can almost count the hours until the trip is over. Three more days, and he'll be done with it. And with all this shit behind him, maybe he'll even talk to Diana. Maybe she'll forgive him.

Victor surprises him by opening his mouth. "He can't help himself, basically, is the deal. My stepdad. Business guys love to manage people, right? It's in their DNA or something. And he falls in love with my mom and decides he's supposed to be the one to manage my discipline, like he's some kind of family home consultant. I had too much autonomy, he said. Hadn't my mom even read the research? The *research*."

"So how'd he manage you? A belt?"

"What?" Victor sounds almost shocked. He shakes his head, then laces his arms behind his head and lies on his back. "A belt? No. I would have kicked his ass if he tried something like that. He's more into intimidation than the physical stuff. Grounds me. Takes away the car."

"What kind of car?"

"Lexus," Victor says. Then, as if catching himself, "An old one, though. Used."

"Nice ride."

"They tell you it's going to get better, the counselors and whatever. You can work on your relationship if you put yourself in his shoes. Like I'm going to take life lessons from some stranger acting like he knows what's going on."

Santi nods like he's interested, even though, what the hell does Victor have to complain about? Private school, tutors, shrinks, and a stepdad who wants to whip him into shape. But Santi listens because what he really needs is ammo. If Victor's going to keep using the material from Santi's sharing circle last night, Santi has to fight back somehow.

"Let's go, guys!" It's Jerry. "Time for dinner!"

Victor closes his eyes, so Santi leaves him lying in the tent and heads back downhill, avoiding the puddles that seem to have multiplied in the twenty minutes it had taken them to set up camp.

Celeste crouches by the small camp stove, aggressively stirring the pot with her aluminum spoon while Amelia and Rico rinse out their mess kits. Jerry sits on the edge of his backpack, writing by headlamp in a small notebook.

"Can I talk to you for a second?" Santi says, pulling Jerry aside. "I was thinking. It's not fair to the others for me to be carrying all the food."

"Not fair?" Jerry adjusts his headlamp so that it points straight up, reflecting off the tarp and bathing them all in a dim blue glow. "How do you mean?"

"It's like I'm robbing them of the satisfaction, the feeling of accomplishment."

Jerry's face is blank behind that beard of his, and then he smiles. "You should probably get rid of some of it, then."

"Just to be fair."

The tarp is just large enough to fit everyone. Victor and Amelia eat standing, but the rest of them sit on their backpacks. An occasional gust lifts the tarp up like a parachute, rattling away any water that has pooled in the center and sending a small river onto the ground.

The old saying that food tastes better when you're camping clearly never went up against Celeste's mac and cheese. The pasta is crunchy, the cheese watery, and the ham tastes like fish for some reason. The only thing more surprising than the taste is the fact that Victor doesn't mention it.

"Sorry about the food," Celeste finally says. "I'm not so good in the kitchen."

"It's fine," Amelia says.

Rico can't help himself. "I thought you guys were against fake praise, or whatever you called it. Look at her. She knows it sucks. Don't lie to her or you're just proving that you can't be trusted. Right?"

"Damn, Rico," Santi says.

"Didn't we promise to be honest to each other?"

"It's okay," Celeste says. She scratches behind her ear and offers an uncharacteristically apologetic shrug.

"No, he's right," Amelia says, turning to Celeste. "I'm sorry I lied to you, Celeste. This is, without a doubt—"

"Oh boy," Rico says.

Amelia starts giggling. "Let me finish."

"I'm waiting." Celeste stands up and latches her hands to her waist, thrusting her hip out to the side. And just like that, she's back!

"I'm sorry," Amelia says. She opens her mouth, but the giggle overwhelms her and she has to cover her face with both hands. Santi is blown away by how out of place she suddenly looks.

"Okay, I'm ready," she says, the strain of keeping a straight face so clearly wearing on her. "Celeste, the powdered cheese was lumpy and dry in chunks, the macaroni was crunchy, and the ham was only partially rehydrated. That was, without a doubt, the worst macaroni and cheese I have ever had."

A long pause. Amelia's smile returns briefly but disappears when Celeste doesn't respond right away. More rain beats against the tarp. Amelia seems to realize that she has gone too far.

"Well," Celeste says softly, looking down at her mac and cheese and then back up to the group. "I guess I should have boiled the water first."

"You didn't boil the water?" Jerry says.

"I'm kidding." Celeste backhands him across the chest, and the tension disappears.

"There's no team building after this, is there?" Rico says with a laugh. "We're still alive, right? Isn't that team building enough?"

"Nothing formal," Jerry says. "And we'll cancel journal time tonight, given the weather. But we do need to talk about what happened today."

"You mean Santi? I told him to be careful," Rico says, turning to Santi. "Didn't I tell you to be careful?"

Jerry shakes his head. "Not Santi. Victor."

"Oh, come on," Victor says. "I already told you. It wasn't my fault."

"That stunt of yours—"

"It wasn't a stunt—"

"The stunt wasn't getting lost. The stunt was leaving in the first place—"

"I—"

"Let me finish." Another crack in Jerry's patient, super-concerned, trip leader persona. The corner of Santi's mouth sneaks upward.

"Finish," Victor says, glancing toward their tent.

"What you did was irresponsible. It was inconsiderate."

"Yeah, but I saved this jack-off's life today too. That should count for something."

Santi points at him. "Don't bring me into this—"

"That's not the point," Jerry says. "You're here because you've—"

Victor sneers. "You have no idea why I'm here."

"*You're here*," Jerry screams, "because you have shown a consistent inability—or straight-out refusal—to think about anybody but yourself. Today that put all of us at risk, including you."

"I could kick your Sasquatch ass right in front of everyone."

Amelia reaches out as if to comfort him, but Victor swats her arm away so hard that she stumbles backward, catching her heel on a small rock. She hits the muddy ground with her legs splayed into the tarp and her upper body outside, in the mud, completely exposed to the rain.

It happens so quickly. Victor freezes, his right fist cocked and ready to strike Jerry, gasping as though he just sprinted up a mountain. Great gulps of air, chest heaving.

Amelia struggles to her feet in a daze. Celeste offers a hand, pulls her back under the shelter, and the two girls step to the far edge of the tarp.

And Jerry snaps. He launches across the space between them, knocking over the pot on the stove, sending watery mac and cheese flying onto Rico's lap. His hands land on Victor's chest, and then his fists close around Victor's jacket.

"That behavior is not acceptable!" Jerry yells, shaking Victor back and forth. "That is not how we act around other people. That is not how we treat other people."

Victor brings his arms up underneath Jerry's, breaking his hold. Jerry staggers back, and Santi finds himself lunging in between them.

"Enough," he says, one hand on Jerry's chest and the other on Victor's. He can feel their hearts thrashing, their lungs expanding, struggling in the thin air. "That's enough."

12

The county-owned Econoline van shuddered to a stop in the Bear Canyon Wilderness Therapy Program headquarters parking lot. Santi was its only passenger, and he hesitated before stepping out onto the cracked asphalt. It wasn't even noon yet, but heat came at him from all angles, the full power of the sun bouncing off the concrete path, the double-wide trailer in front of him.

Santi slung a plastic garbage bag of clothes over his shoulder, and the driver escorted him up the wooden ramp and knocked on the screen door. A heavily bearded man appeared instantly on the other side of the wire mesh. The black hair on his face was thick and curly and, set against the smooth pink of the man's cheekbones, made Santi think of a half-clipped sheep.

The counselor introduced himself as Jerry and extended his hand, which Santi shook as firmly as he could.

"Warm outside, isn't it?" Jerry said, wincing as he pulled his hand away. Santi allowed himself a tiny smile. "Warmer inside, unfortunately, but there's supposed to be a front coming in later this week. Should cool everything down for a bit."

Santi dropped his clothes on the floor next to the wall as Jerry pointed to a brunette organizing food supplies in the next room. She looked younger than Jerry and struck Santi as vaguely nervous when she lifted her head and waved. "That's Amelia. She'll be co-leading."

"This is co-ed?" Santi's unit in juvie had been boys only.

"There are rules, of course." Jerry motioned to a small room opposite Amelia. "We do a little pre-trip interview, if you want to get it over with."

Santi hung back, watching Amelia cut a block of cheese in two pieces. She consulted a list on the table and then put each of the blocks in its own plastic bag. She tucked her hair behind her ear and shook her head, removing one of the blocks and halving it as well. Santi followed Jerry into the interrogation room.

"Figured we should just cut to the chase," Jerry said once they'd both sat down. A green folder rested on the wooden table in front of him. "Why is this going to be different?"

"Different? I don't really—"

"What are you hoping to accomplish here that you wouldn't be able to do in the facility?"

There were a number of things Santi could have gone with, all of them true. He could have talked about his dad, how the mountains had been a haven for them. He could have said that camping food couldn't possibly be as bad as the food in juvie. He could have said that he wanted to avoid going to the Juvenile Justice Center again at any cost. Instead, he stared at the folder.

"Do you want me to tell you what I see?" Jerry said.

It *was* hot. Santi scratched the back of his neck and wiped a trickle of sweat from his hairline. "Not really?"

"I see someone who can't—or *won't*—stand up for himself, won't take command of his own future. I see someone who has the conviction not to divulge the name of his accomplice, the driver, but who couldn't resist getting in the car in the first place. What do *you* see?"

"I'm no snitch," Santi said. "Now everybody knows it."

"You should never have been in that position, Santi. You and I both know that. This whole business here," he said, tapping the file with his index finger. "You're never going to get out of this if you don't take charge once in a while. Learn to be a leader, Santi, that's what I'm saying."

Jerry smiled at him like it was as simple as that. Learn to be a leader. Learn to be confident. Learn to be a different person entirely.

"Let me tell you this," Jerry said. "We're surrounded all the time by the pressure to act a certain way, to live our lives a certain way. Television and Internet and phones and friends. All of that distracts us from ever looking to who we really are."

He pushed the thick file to the side and leaned forward, resting both elbows on the table. "But the mountains have a way of forcing you to listen to yourself, sometimes in a way that you never would have imagined."

There was a squeak, followed by a slam, as the screen door in the other room opened and shut. Amelia's tentative voice wafted into the interrogation room. "Welcome to Bear Canyon. What's your name?"

"Victor," said a male voice, gruff and cocky. "Victor West."

"Are we done here?" Santi said.

"Done here?" Jerry smiled again and picked up the file. "We haven't even gotten started."

13

Santi squats at the edge of the ravine and dips his water bottle into the flow. In the hour since they arrived at the campsite, Fall Creek has swollen from its former trickle to an actual stream, two feet across now, almost worthy of being called a creek again.

Once he deposits the requisite purification tablets into the murky water, he pushes himself to his feet and heads uphill to his backpack. He pulls the torn garbage bag taut around his pack and hoists it next to Victor's, fifteen feet in the air. Normally, everyone's packs would all hang together, but the tents are too spread out for that, so he and Victor are on their own. Besides, there's nothing normal about tonight.

After the fireworks at dinner, after Victor had stormed away, Jerry had pulled himself together just enough to apologize for losing his temper before telling them all to get some rest before the long day tomorrow.

Victor is already inside the tent by the time Santi unzips the rain fly, but he doesn't acknowledge Santi's arrival. With his feet still in the vestibule, Santi inflates his air mattress, lays out his sleeping bag, and dangles his headlamp from the hook at the center of the tent's dome ceiling. He eases out of his boots and peels off his socks with a grimace.

The bandages on his arms come off with the sleeves of his jacket, the adhesive no match for the constant rain, so he crumples them together and tosses the blood-stained wad into the vestibule.

"It's like you played Slip 'N Slide on a cheese grater," Victor says as Santi takes off his jeans, one leg at a time.

Santi makes himself look. His elbows are bruised underneath all the scrapes and soon-to-be scabs. He's got open cuts on his knees he didn't even know about. He'd look even worse without his T-shirt, which covers up the damage from his fall—red streaks like claw marks all over his chest.

Victor inflates his air mattress and nods to Santi's heels. "And that's about the nastiest thing I've ever seen."

After another day of wet hiking, the heels are discs of raw meat the size of silver dollars, way worse than they'd been that morning. "Guess your stepdad didn't take me shopping."

"Oh, come on." Victor tosses his sleeping bag to the floor. "I'm supposed to apologize because it doesn't look like I'm smuggling pepperonis on my heels?"

"I never said you had to apologize."

"Hey, I get it. You're poor. You've had bad luck. Your parents died or whatever."

"Or whatever?"

"My point is that I *know* I've had it easier than you. But I'm not going to wish my life was worse just so you won't feel bad."

"You want to know a secret?" Santi says. "I don't give a shit about your life."

"You're lying."

"And you're a dick."

Victor chuckles. "Good, so we got that out of the way."

The rain picks up again, this time bringing the wind along.

A strong gust shakes the tent like a tremor, and Santi's headlamp jiggles, casting uneven shadows against the thin walls.

Victor shifts gears: "My stepdad threatens me with juvie all the time. Once he even busted out the 'don't bend over for the soap' joke. I guess he figures that if I'm scared enough, I'll straighten up."

"Scared straight doesn't work," Santi says.

"We had some former cocaine addict come talk to us last year at school. He tried so hard."

"But I bet the next weekend half your class went out and smoked weed or drank or did dumb crap anyway, right?"

"*Half* my class?" Victor says with a smirk.

"Dudes who are going to steal shit or get high are going to do it anyway, and anyone weak enough to get spooked by those stories isn't strong enough to resist getting sucked in along the way."

"Is that what you told the judge?"

Santi laughs. "You can have seminars and class meetings until your head explodes, but it's no use. It doesn't matter how much juvie scares you—the other detainees, the guards, the food, whatever. Because in that moment, when you're about to make the decision that puts you inside in the first place, being afraid of getting your ass kicked on unit doesn't even cross your mind."

"I don't think they're going to ask you to give a presentation at my high school."

"You should see these volunteers at the Justice Center," Santi said. "Librarians and tutors and people like that, putting in all this effort just to have some kid disappoint them again. It's like they're cancer doctors. Coming to work every day even though most of their patients are going to die."

"Yeah, but cancer doctors get paid," Victor says. Then, after a pause: "Must be crazy in there."

It's not the first time Santi has noticed the curiosity in Victor's voice. "If you want to know what it's like, all you have to do is ask."

"You're going to make me ask?"

"You're the one who wants to know."

"You really are a douchebag. You know that, right?"

They listen to the rain. It's coming down in curtains against the fly.

It had poured like this the last time Santi went camping with his dad. Just the two of them. Santi, almost ten years old. Rain playing the most epic drum solo on the fabric of their tent. The perfect night.

Two weeks later, a driver in the oncoming lane was grasping for an onion ring from his Sonic extra-value meal. An onion ring on the floorboard, a jerk of the wheel, a swerve, a collision. Their mom's brother, Ray, was the only relative they had left. And that was that. Because of an onion ring.

"What's juvie like?" Victor says.

Santi laughs, and Victor does too. What does that mean, that they're laughing together? Probably nothing. He relaxes into the air mattress.

"There was a guy there," Santi says. "I think his name was Curt, or Curtis. You can ask the librarian to bring you pretty much anything, right? They just want you to read. So this dude Curt had all these books and magazines on birding. And he remembered it all; he could tell you anything you needed to know. Nobody could figure out why birding. There were no trees anywhere near the center."

"Why'd you go the first time?"

"*Only* time. Not first. I'm here with you this time, remember?"

"*Excuse* me. The only time."

"I got caught with some weed when I was fifteen," Santi says. "Nothing big, not even an ounce, but it was enough that they wanted to try me with intent to sell."

This seems funny to Victor. "What were you doing walking around with an ounce of weed?"

Santi shakes his head. His first week in high school, and one of his new friends had asked him for a favor, simple as that. "Wasn't even mine."

"Right."

"It wasn't. I was just a kid who agreed to watch someone else's bag because I didn't know what else to do. Just a stupid kid."

"As opposed to now?" Victor says, but there's a kind of warmth in his insult that hadn't been there before.

"I remember the slippers, mostly," Santi says. "Like shower sandals? Plastic ones with a big wide strap across the top of the foot. Everyone on unit had to wear them all the time. Shuffling around in our socks and slippers."

"Sounds like an old folks home."

"We got to wear real shoes when we played basketball. You had to go to this big pile of black high-tops—I don't even remember if they had a brand—and dig through it for some that would fit. You just had to hope there weren't too many pendejos in there with your shoe size."

"That's what you remember? The footwear?" Victor exhales. "Man, my stepdad was way off."

He could tell Victor what the dude wants to hear, but he's worried that if he opens up even a little bit, it will all come out. The truth. The way he felt that first night. Walking into the facility with everyone else staring at him. That smell. The unit was almost full when Santi got there, and he took the last bed. Everyone else already knew each other, had already formed whatever alliances were going to get them through. And there he was, scrawny Santi.

He remembers lying in his bunk, listening to the sounds of the place, with no idea how things worked in there. The buzzing of doors, always followed by the slamming. The whispers. He remembers thinking of Marisol, wondering what she was doing at home without him. He swore that he would never go back there. When his month was up, he was going to do whatever it took not to go back there. And now look at him.

"What was up with you going all crazy with the Beard?" He turns to Victor, eager to change the subject. "'You have no idea why I'm here'? What was that supposed to mean?"

"Nothing," Victor says. "Forget about it. I was just pissed at him is all."

"Where did you go today? Really."

Victor shakes his head. "Just needed a break."

Before Santi can press the issue, Victor laces his hands behind his head and says, "My dad always used to tell me—my real dad, not my stepdad—that the world doesn't care about you, and if you don't look out for yourself, you're fucked. He used to drill that into me, almost every day."

"He wasn't wrong," Santi says.

Victor exhales a long sigh. "No. No, I'm pretty sure he wasn't."

"What happened to him?"

"He decided to take his own advice." Victor laughs now. A genuine laugh. "He looked out for himself, and four years later the new guy was moving in."

Santi closes his eyes and listens to the rain. That sound, plus the laughter in the tent, is almost enough to make Santi forget where they are, who they are, why they're here.

"Do you hear that?" Victor says. He sits up quickly and turns off both of the headlamps.

"What—"

"Shh. Listen," Victor whispers.

Santi sits up and closes his eyes, but he only hears the rain. And his breathing. Then, the snap of a twig? Tree branches bending and whipping back?

Fear always shocks him, how it sneaks up on him, how it changes him. He should be used to it by now, but he isn't—the way it starts in his gut, spreads to his chest, reaches out from there. The way shame is always just a step behind.

"Is that a bear?" Santi whispers, squeezing his fists tight to keep them from trembling. Whatever's out there, it's getting closer.

14

The sun was still low in the sky. A golden beam pierced the windows of Ray's living room as Marisol sat with her homework at a small table in the corner. Santi lounged on the couch, watching a reality show featuring contestants who ate things for money. His adjudication was the next day, and he was desperate to find something that would take his mind off it.

They had the place to themselves that night. As they did most nights. Over the six years since they'd moved in, Ray's position on raising them hadn't changed: he didn't intend to do any such thing. Ray and their mom hadn't been close—when she died right after Mari was born, Ray had "forgotten" to send a card—and their dad was a goddamn hippie, no offense. Besides, Ray had never asked for any of this.

"Raw snake eggs wrapped in pig uterus," Santi said over his shoulder. Marisol said nothing. "Would you eat that?"

"For how much?" she said. "And is there a time limit? Do I have to eat it whole, or do I get a knife? Is the uterus raw or cooked?"

"Like any of that makes a difference? Órale, Mari, it's a *pig uterus*."

She tapped the end of her pen against the workbook. "I'm just trying to get a sense of the ground rules here. You need all the data if you want to make an informed decision—"

"Blah, blah, blah," Santi said. "Dumb genius."

Marisol laughed. "You'd probably eat it for free."

"Shut up and do your homew—"

Tires screeched outside, and Santi instinctively shot to his feet. A car squealing to a stop sounded different than one peeling out. This was a stop. The dogs next door started barking.

Santi looked out the window just in time to see three vatos in ski masks jumping off the back of an old pickup. Running toward the house.

The dogs went crazy.

"Come on." Santi grabbed Marisol's hand and pulled her down the hall.

"What—"

His heart smacked against his ribcage. "Just, shh."

They were in the hall closet by the time he realized that he was still holding the remote control. He'd left the TV on.

Santi opened the door a crack and pressed the remote, praying that there was a clear enough line of sight, and just as the TV turned off, the front door flew open and slammed against the wall, the wooden doorjamb splintering.

Marisol trembled as he pulled her close. He felt like a coward, hiding in the closet, but what other option was there?

"Do you know who it is?" she whispered.

Santi put his finger to his lips. "It's going to be okay."

There were crashes on the other side of the door. Dishes falling from the kitchen cabinets, maybe, or Ray's jar of pennies in the living room. Santi squeezed her shoulder tighter. How was this their life? What had happened? What were they supposed to do?

Footsteps, just outside the closet.

Marisol flinched, and Santi grabbed the doorknob with both hands, propping his foot against the wall. If he held on tight enough, maybe he could make it seem locked.

He wanted to believe that it was just another home invasion, that Ray's place was no different from any of the other houses in the neighborhood that had been hit, but he recognized the truck. He'd seen it before, out with Eric one night. Eric's cousin's friend, or something like that.

This was a message.

This was Eric's way of reminding Santi not to waffle at the adjudication tomorrow. Or maybe Eric had nothing to do with it. Maybe Eric's boys had just taken things into their own hands, looking out for him, covering the bases. Either way, the message was the same.

Eventually, the noises got farther and farther from the hall closet. The front door clattered against the broken doorjamb. A different screech of tires.

"I'm going to get us out of this house," Santi said. "We're going to be okay. We'll move."

But they didn't move. They couldn't, not for an hour after, at least. Santi and his sister stayed in the closet and sat on the floor and cried.

15

The whipping of another branch, this one closer than the last. Santi forces himself to breathe, to think. Their food is up the hill, dangling from the trees. They haven't eaten in the tent. There's no reason for a bear to attack them.

Santi opens his eyes and notices a bobbing light through the tent fabric. He taps Victor on the shoulder and points toward it.

"You guys?" A whisper. Rico. "You guys awake?"

Just like that, Santi's fear vanishes, leaving only shame, which fills the tent like smog. How could he have thought Rico was a bear? What an idiot. Santi turns the headlamps back on.

"Go away, Rico," Victor says.

"I heard what you were talking about," Rico says. "Dude, Victor, what happened to your real dad? Did he die too? Like Santi's?"

"Stop eavesdropping. Go away."

"Don't be a dick," Santi says to Victor. "Rico, what do you want?"

Rico's light shines just on the other side of the tent wall. "Come on, guys, it's raining out here."

Santi says, "Why aren't you in your tent?"

"That dude snores, man. It's like his big-ass beard catches in his throat or something. I can't handle it."

Victor stifles a laugh. "You're still not supposed to be out of your tent."

"I'll just say I was taking a leak or something. Come on. I have candy."

"You brought candy?" Santi says.

"What kind of candy?" says Victor at the same time.

"Almond Joy. And Rolos."

"I already brushed my teeth," Santi says.

Victor unzips the tent and vestibule. "Take your jacket off first. I don't need you bringing the rain in."

Santi looks at him, incredulous. "I thought you were a Boy Scout."

"Eagle Scout," Victor says.

"Didn't they ever tell you not to eat in the tent? What happens if a bear—"

"If a bear happens to smell the delicious combination of coconut and chocolate that is Almond Joy, then we're screwed," Victor says. "But I'm willing to take that chance."

Rico is whimpering now. "So can I come inside, or what?"

"Jerry told us to stay in our tents," Santi says.

Victor waves Rico inside. "No offense, Santi, but you're not exactly the first person I'd turn to for a reminder of the rules."

"Come on, it's just some chocolate," Rico says. He ditches his jacket in the vestibule and pushes his ass backward into the tent so he can untie his boots. "Make some room?"

Santi keeps his voice low, even though it probably can't carry through the rain. "Can't we just get through this week and go on with our lives?"

"Jerry said this was going to be a transformative experience." Rico scoots all the way into the tent and pulls out two Almond Joy bars and a pack of Rolos. "That's what he called it."

"I don't want a transformative experience."

"Don't be a pussy," Victor says.

Rico laughs. "Yeah, don't be such a pus—"

"You shut up," Santi says. He snatches the Rolos, takes a couple, and tosses the pack to Victor.

There's a welcome peace as the three of them dig into the chocolate, the only sounds the unpeeling of wrappers and the rain on the tent.

"My dad's not dead or anything," Rico says after a while. "But he's not around much."

Victor shoots Santi a glance that seems to say: The kid brought us candy. Might as well eat it while he talks.

"We bounced around a lot 'cause he builds oil rigs," Rico says, leaning to the side and propping himself up on one elbow. His face twitches when he blinks. "Not the offshore stuff, but the ones on land in the middle of nowhere. Have you ever been to west Texas? Man, there's nothing there. You can see why my mom went a little nuts."

When Rico takes a deep breath, Santi figures it's probably his turn to say something. He clears a chunk of caramel from his teeth with his fingernail. "What does 'a little nuts' mean?"

"Not nuts, really. She's my mom and all. But she has this deal where she gets super excited about one thing at a time. For a while, it was a tiny house for the family, like one room to fit everyone. She begged my dad to build it, but then she got all into motor homes. RVs and stuff. She told my dad that as long as we were moving everywhere, we might as well just buy a house with wheels on it."

Rico unwraps an Almond Joy and nibbles off the almond with a crunch. "They don't get along so well."

"So what the hell are you doing here?" Santi says. "I assume we'll find out soon anyway, but—"

"Drugs," Victor says. "I bet it's drugs—"

"I burned a house down," Rico says. Not bragging, just stating a fact. "Not a real house. A shed. There was nobody in it. I don't even feel bad."

Santi laughs in disbelief. "You burned a shed down? On purpose?"

"Have you ever seen one of those movies where someone spills gasoline all over a house and then lights it with a Zippo? I always wanted to do that. So I did. There was this kid I knew who had a storage shed with tools and old boxes and stuff, and there was a can of kerosene. I figured, what the hell? It was sweet the way the fire followed the little trail of gas until it hit the walls. And the fire was so hot."

Santi says, "That's the funny thing about fire."

"No, I mean it was really hot. From far away, across the yard, I felt like I was still right next to the fire. I couldn't believe how hot it was."

"Congratulations," Victor says. "Never met a pyro before."

"Good thing Jerry's carrying the camping fuel," Santi says.

Rico gives an embarrassed shrug, then another full-face blink. "It's not like that. I just wanted to see what it would look like."

"So you're a sociopath," Victor says. "Not a pyromaniac."

Santi says, "I'm glad we cleared that up."

Victor tosses the last of the Rolos into his mouth and smiles with it tucked in his cheek. "Well, it's about that time, don't you think?"

Rico looks crestfallen. "What?"

"Unless there's more candy somewhere, I figure we're done here."

Santi can only chuckle. "That's harsh."

"I don't want to sleep next to that guy," Rico says.

"Well, you're not sleeping next to this guy." Victor points both thumbs at himself.

Rico slides his feet into his boots and shakes out his rain jacket in the vestibule. He's about to put the jacket on when he stops and turns back, as if he's just remembered something.

"What do you think of Amelia?" he says. "Do you think she'd ever, you know?"

Santi laughs. "Órale, you said you already had a hot girlfriend."

"I'm not sure Amelia's your type," Victor says.

But he says it too quickly. Too quickly for there to be nothing behind it. There's the hint of a challenge in Victor's voice. The first bark of a guard dog.

Rico pounds his chest with a closed fist. "I'm every girl's type."

"She's the assistant leader, dumbass." This time Victor's tone is more measured and distant, but still with a healthy dose of contempt. "I'm pretty sure the 'no amorous conduct' rule doesn't just apply to us. Besides, she's a rich college girl. She's fancy, man. What do you have to offer?"

A quick glance at Victor, and Santi decides to have a little fun. "You should try to hit it, Rico. She's hot, ese. But I'm pretty sure she's into me."

"What do they put in the water in New Mexico?" Victor says. "I knew that place was a shithole, but you two are delusional."

Santi shakes his head. "For real. You saw the way she was rubbing on my feet this morning, right? And at lunch, too. She put some real care into it. Some good squeezing. That's a connection. I mean, people don't just do that to other people's feet for no reason, no matter how torn up they might be."

"That's awesome," Rico says.

"Hell yeah. I think she was giving me a foot massage without wanting to admit that she was giving me a foot massage. Like it was a secret. Like the promise of something more."

"Yeah," Rico says, getting into it. "I could teach her a thing or two, if you know what I mean."

"Wow, Rico," Victor says. "Have you ever even touched a pussy?"

"Shut the fuck up, Victor," Rico says, suddenly quiet. He looks away.

"Come on, man," Santi says. "Jerry's going to wake up and then we're all busted."

Victor waves both hands as if surrendering. "You're right. I'm done."

Rico says nothing. He jams his arm through one sleeve of his raincoat, but the other sleeve is twisted, and he can't get his arm in. Santi thinks about helping him, but the kid is so clearly on the edge that he doesn't want to risk a reaction punch. Rico finally gets the other arm through the sleeve, but the jacket's twisted across the back, so now all that's covered are the poor dude's arms.

As Rico scoots forward to leave, Santi notices a glint in Victor's eye, and he knows something is coming. He should try to stop it. He should run interference until Rico is in the clear. That would be the right thing to do.

But he doesn't.

Even Victor himself seems to know it's a bad idea. He covers his mouth and laughs through his nose, but he can't help himself. "I'm sorry, Rico, I really am. What I meant was, have you ever even touched a pussy that wasn't your mom's?"

Rico whirls around and launches himself at Victor. The tent shakes with his windmill punches. Rico is crying now, yelling unintelligibly, his ferocious swings having no effect. Victor crouches into the fetal position, covering his face like a boxer, taking the punches but laughing a little too.

"Oooh, that's it," Victor says, making his voice high like a woman's. "Oooh, Rico, baby, you know where I like it."

16

Slips of paper drawn from Jerry's baseball cap determined the tent pairings: evens with evens, odds with odds. Amelia and Celeste, being the only girls on the trip, did not participate. Santi chose first, sliding his hand into the hat and shifting the papers around a bit before his fingertips finally decided. He peeked at the paper: *3.*

Rico was next, followed by Victor, who had spent most of the short time they'd been together talking about how great he was at building fires and orienteering and being an outdoorsman. Jerry picked the last number and put his hat back on.

"You're lucky," Victor said when Santi showed him the number on his scrap. "I'm an Eagle Scout."

With the pairings out of the way, the six of them sat on the ground outside the Bear Canyon trailer and divided up the food and communal gear.

"Your pack's going to be way too heavy," Jerry said when Santi kept volunteering. "It shouldn't be more than a third of your body weight."

Santi gave him a smile as he tucked a block of cheese next to the bagels. "I can handle it."

Jerry shrugged and went back inside the office for the keys to the Bear Canyon van. When the front door closed, Celeste turned to Santi and said, "Just because this trip is co-ed, don't assume I'm going to get with you."

"What?"

"Don't pretend you weren't thinking about it." Santi hesitated, and she poked her finger at him with a triumphant look on her face. "Aha!"

"It's not like that," he said.

She wrinkled her brows at him. "Oh, so you think I'm ugly?"

"No. What? No."

"Make up your mind. Jesus." Celeste looked over her shoulder and leaned in with a whisper. "I brought some mushrooms for later. Tripping in the woods is next-level. You in?"

"Are you serious right now?"

"Maybe I am," she said with a shrug. "Maybe I'm not. Maybe you'll find out."

"Maybe," Santi said.

Victor grunted and stood up. After hefting his pack onto his shoulder, he walked around to the other side of the trailer.

Santi pushed his feet into the hiking boots Jerry had given him. The treads were almost completely worn, and the fit was a little loose, especially in the toes, but they were better than nothing. He pulled his socks a little higher and tightened the laces.

Rico went inside to take a leak. Celeste twirled her hair and stared off into nothing. Amelia was looking at Celeste.

Amelia finally cleared her throat and said, all cautious, "Where's the name Celeste from?"

Celeste turned, and her eyes narrowed. No more hair twirling. Her hands fell to her sides. "Where's the name Amelia from?"

"Family name. But my friends call me Miels," she said with a smile that obviously took some effort.

"I'm not your friend," Celeste said.

"I—No, I just thought that we mi—"

"And I'm not going to be your friend."

Santi pretended to rearrange the things in his pack but he kept his full attention on the girls. It was like watching one of those nature shows on TV where the alligator explodes out of the water and snatches an unsuspecting bird right out of the air.

"I'm not trying to be your friend, Celeste."

"Well." The girl fixed Amelia with a sarcastic smile. "This must be my lucky day."

Amelia was flustered. She swallowed and looked to Santi for help, but he quickly turned back to his pack. "I meant I'm not *trying* to be anything."

Santi let the awkwardness linger until he couldn't take it anymore, and then he stood up and announced, "I'm going to take these bad boys for a spin."

He made a big show of stepping from one foot to the other as he walked away from the girls and around to the back of the trailer. Victor had his back to Santi, but Santi noticed him tuck something quickly into the top compartment of his pack.

"It's cool," Santi said. "I'm not going to tell."

Victor didn't look up. Instead, he feigned like he was checking the straps around the climbing rope on one side. "What are you talking about?"

"I won't say anything, you bringing booze or a piece or whatever. If that's what you're worried about. I'm pretty good at keeping secrets, as it turns out."

Victor turned around. "You think I brought booze?"

"Or whatever."

"What's in my pack is my business. Got it?"

"Your business," Santi said. He didn't want to start things off on the wrong foot, but this guy wasn't making it easy.

"And anyway, booze is too heavy. If I wanted to medicate, I'd have borrowed some of my mom's Vicodin instead."

"What's the rope for?"

"Be prepared."

"And yet you didn't bring any booze," Santi smirked.

"Are we going to have beef?" Victor said. He hoisted his backpack onto one shoulder and stalked toward the other side of the trailer.

Santi laughed out loud even though he figured he might regret it later. "Have beef?" he called out after Victor. "Who talks like that?"

17

A low rumble, like thunder, but this time, the thunder doesn't stop. It builds upon itself, growing in depth and volume until it sounds like a jet engine coming toward them.

Santi sits up in the tent and reaches for the headlamp. "What is that?"

"Turn the light off," Victor says.

"Listen." Santi's cheap-ass watch has no backlight, so he has to check it under the beam: one in the morning.

The growl intensifies, and the ground begins to shake.

Victor sits up too. "Is there such a thing as an earthquake in the mount—"

Then they're moving. Moving! The tent pitches over, and Victor careens on top of Santi, landing a direct shot into Santi's stomach with his knee. They begin to roll, but slowly. The tent goes dark as it turns upside down, and ten seconds later it's right-side up again, and the light returns. The dangling headlamp sways like a ceiling fan, scattering shadows across the inside.

A broken tree branch pierces the tent, inches away from Santi's head. They roll over again.

It's loud, so loud. Santi knows he's screaming, but he can't hear himself. He can't hear the rain. Just the rumble so powerful that he feels it in his chest.

He tries to push up, but he and Victor jumble together, his legs trapped by the sleeping bag. Darkness again. Another rotation.

And suddenly it's over.

No movement. The only sound, once again, is the rain on the tent, but after what they've just been through, even that sounds like silence. Santi feels wetness on his cheek. Is it rainwater? Blood?

He tries to hoist himself up, but he has no idea where up is. Pressure comes from all sides. He pushes with his arms.

"Victor!" he says. "Are you alive?"

"That's my face," Victor screams. "I can't breathe."

Santi rolls over. The mound he's wrestling with is Victor, covered by both of their sleeping bags. Santi scrambles for the headlamp, finds it. He wipes his face and checks his fingertips, relieved to see that the moisture was just rain.

The tent is in tatters, the aluminum poles bent and twisted, and the dome that had once protected them is crushed. A tree limb pokes all the way through, the smaller branches torn off, creating jagged points like an uneven saw blade.

Victor fights out from underneath the sleeping bags. Blood streams from cuts over his right eye and a gash on his right shoulder, the fabric of his new jacket torn completely through. "What the hell just happened?"

Santi reaches both hands into the slit above him and tears a hole large enough to stand through. He shines the light through the sheets of rain around him and yelps in shock.

"What?" Victor says.

It's as though the mountainside has been bombed, leaving a collection of mud, boulders, and snapped trees. Not even the slope looks familiar. They could be a hundred yards away from where they started, for all Santi knows.

"Hello?" Santi yells. "Jerry? Anybody!"

Calling for the others is no use, not in this rain, so Santi crouches back down and searches for his pants and jacket.

"What happened?" says Victor, more stunned than panicked.

"Everything's gone." Santi shakes his head. Then he notices Victor's feet. "You already have your boots on?"

"I was going to take a piss. Before the . . ."

Santi finds his jeans and pulls them on. His poncho too. He's only able to find one of his boots. He should have kept them inside the tent, like Victor.

"Everything's gone," he says again. "Just gone."

Clothed but still disoriented, they leave the tent and wander uphill. Santi has no socks, so he limps along, one foot bare against the mud and sticks, the other an open wound rubbing against wet leather. He isn't sure which hurts more.

"Do you know where the cooking tarp was?" Santi yells.

They take turns screaming for help, but it's no use. The more Santi yells, the more the reality of the situation sinks in, and the more a sense of dread overtakes the shock of it all.

"Jesus Christ!" Victor says, betraying a panic of his own.

Even with the headlamps, the rain limits their visibility to no more than twenty feet. Santi stumbles repeatedly, crashing to the ground, mud smearing all over his face and chest, but now that the panic has taken over, he feels none of it. The rain doesn't even seem to be hitting him.

"Over there!" Santi says, pointing.

But the movement is their backpacks, swaying in the rain as though nothing had happened. The terrain is getting more predictable, though, with less debris to scramble over. In their search for the others, they must have gotten turned around and walked the opposite direction.

"Thank God." Victor sprints to the twine tied around the tree and pulls on it as though testing its strength. Then he sits down against the tree trunk with the bags dangling overhead.

"What are you doing?"

"Don't add yourself to the victim list," Victor says. "That's the first rule of rescue. We don't know what the terrain is like."

"What about the others? We can't just leave them."

Santi shines the light in Victor's face, and he's surprised not to see a look of panic or stress. Victor's eyes are closed, and he's breathing deeply.

"Victor! What the hell?"

"Okay, let's go," Victor says. Blood from his forehead mixes with the rainwater and trickles down the side of his face. He touches his shoulder and winces, but he can still move his arm up and down. "You might want to take a couple deep breaths yourself, Santi. You'll think more clearly."

In spite of everything, the mud against Santi's foot, the pain in his back, the lack of a freaking campsite, he takes Victor's advice and forces himself to breathe.

"Okay," Santi says. His fingers stop trembling. That's something, at least.

Using the location of their backpacks to orient themselves, Santi and Victor head toward the ravine. When they reach it, they'll simply follow it downhill, and that's where the cooking area will be. "If we find the kitchen," Victor says, "we find the others. Good?"

Santi nods. They point their headlamps toward the ravine and walk side by side. Rocks and mud clutter the terrain, then boulders and branches and broken trees, the debris thicker as they move away from the packs. Five minutes in, they have to climb over the fallen trunk of a tree more than three feet in diameter.

"This thing was snapped like it was nothing," Victor says.

"We're almost there. I'm pretty sure."

Only, when they get to where the ravine should be, there is no ravine. There is no kitchen. Just a vast swath of destruction.

"It was right here, wasn't it?" Santi says.

"They're gone. They're dead."

Santi doubles over. The nasty macaroni and cheese comes first, the ham tasting exactly the same as it had going down. Then comes the bile. Santi turns off his headlamp and rests his hands against his knees. When the dry heaves finally come, he knows it's almost over.

Is there something on the wind? A voice? Santi forces himself to be still between heaves. "Shhh."

"There's nobody here." Victor's voice is matter-of-fact, devoid of cruelty. "We need to get back to the tent, try to salvage as much of it as we can, or get under a tree or something. We need to get out of the rain."

"I said shhh!" Santi stands up again. A girl's voice. "She's screaming for help."

"There's nobody here."

Santi takes off down the hill, staggering with a little hop-jog, trying to touch his bare foot to the ground as little as possible. "Hello!" he yells into the wind.

"Santi!" Victor screams after him.

He's about fifty yards downhill when he hears a new rumbling sound and whips his head around, half-expecting to see another mudslide. "Amelia! Celeste!"

A few more steps and he realizes what the rumbling is. The ravine. It moved. The torrent of water created a new path, and boulders are rolling in the freshly formed river.

The voice again. Clearer this time. "Help me!"

Santi cups his hands to his mouth. "Celeste? Amelia?"

"Over here!"

He stumbles gingerly toward the river, and his headlamp passes over the reflective tape of a rain jacket.

It's Amelia, clutching onto the side of a boulder on the other side of the water. Santi's bare foot lands on a broken branch and he screams in pain, but he grits his teeth and keeps moving downhill until he's directly across from her, only fifteen feet away. Somehow, she's fully dressed.

"Are you okay?" he yells. "Are you hurt?"

"I can't cross." Amelia's voice is high-pitched and trembling, and her face is a mask of terror. "It's too fast."

Santi shouts for Victor, then turns back to her. "We're going to get you over here."

"What happened? What happened to the others?"

"We're going to get you over here," Santi says again. He steps to the water's edge and reaches across, but it's too far. They'll have to find another way. "Calm down."

"It's just you? Just you and Victor? What about—"

"Everybody else is going to be fine," he says, even though he doesn't believe it. "Let's concentrate on you."

Amelia opens her mouth to talk, but the rumble grows louder. Santi motions with both hands for her to calm down, but then the rumble becomes a detonation, and a gust of wind slams into him, and a thick black wave sweeps down the mountain.

"Amelia!" Santi screams. His headlamp shoots across the river, but there's nothing. "Amelia!"

She's gone.

VICTOR

18

Victor West squints through the rain at the broken-down cabin across the meadow. Celeste leaning out the window for some reason, the bearded freak sitting on his pack in the middle of the room. Victor himself is hunched over in the rocky mine-shaft, his back starting to go numb, all of his planning now for nothing.

After four months of training—hiking, running, biking—he's in the best shape of his life. But none of that means a damn thing. You can do all the planning in the world, check all the boxes, anticipate every eventuality, but there's always going to be something you can't account for. When a low-pressure system parks itself on top of you, for example, there's nothing you can do.

Three days was all he needed. By the time Jerry and company reached the trailhead, Victor would have been waiting for them. No need for a search party, no reason to get his stepdad involved, no reason to raise suspicions. Three days, and it would have been over.

But now, the rain. The rain means he can't count on anything.

Even worse, the ghost town is a surprise. Victor had marked the route months ago—the annotated topo map on the Bear

Canyon website is what gave him the idea in the first place—and the ghost town isn't on it.

Most of the buildings are rubble, but at least some are still standing. Useful as shelter, potentially, if things get out of hand. But only if he knows exactly where the town is. He reaches for the top of his backpack and then stops himself. Not here. Not now. Wait until later, until after dinner, when Jerry gives everyone thirty minutes of "personal time."

But as the rain keeps falling, he realizes that he might not have time later.

Fifteen minutes since they left him to go eat lunch in the cabin. He's tired of waiting. He unzips the pack's top pocket and removes a folded, waterproof topo map from a black pouch that also holds a small set of lock-picking tools.

The trees are about twenty feet away, so he'd only be out in the open for a few seconds, but one look down convinces him that even a few seconds is too many, at least if he's wearing his new jacket. The red is too bright.

So much for staying dry.

Victor unzips the jacket and wraps the seam-sealed Gore-Tex around his map. One last look to the cabin, and he's gone.

Water assaults him from all angles before he reaches the cover of the trees. Victor stops behind the thickest trunk he can find, unfolding his jacket and rushing to put it back on.

His chest heaves. The air is too thin, even for someone who has spent his entire life in Denver. Up here, almost 11,000 feet above sea level, Victor's six-second sprint brings a stabbing sensation to the back of his throat.

With the trees and the underbrush, he can hardly see any of the ghost town, much less the people inside. The canopy above him offers just enough shelter so that the rain doesn't pelt the map when Victor spreads it out on the uneven ground.

Out of the corner of his eye, he notices damage to a tree on his left: splintered bark, slivers of wood at the base, long, vertical grooves in the trunk. A mountain lion was here, and recently, judging from the sap oozing down the claw grooves. A mountain lion. Yet another thing you can't plan for.

Back to the map.

His index finger traces along the section of the route marked *DAY FOUR*. Up over the pass, and about eight miles from last night's campsite, the trail crosses a point—Fall Creek—where the elevation lines dip sharply and bounce back up in a *V* formation. There's no light blue line at that point, no water, so Fall Creek appears to be more like a ravine.

Tonight's intended campsite is two miles past Fall Creek, but given how much the rain and Santi's swan dive off the cliff slowed them down, Victor figures that the group probably made it four miles before stopping for lunch, no more. That puts the ghost town about halfway between last night's camp and the Fall Creek ravine.

A pointed rock formation juts into the woods uphill from him like the bow of a ship run aground. Maybe fifteen feet to the top. If Victor can scale it, he might be able to catch a glimpse of the ridgeline through the clouds and use it as a point of reference. Ghost town located, mystery solved, contingency planned for. Shelter if he needs it.

It's worth the risk.

A swirl of wind makes the map billow, and Victor swats it back to the ground with an open palm. It's impossible to refold along the original creases afterward, and he ends up with a half-crumpled mess. The map won't fit in his pocket, so Victor puts it between his teeth and bites down hard.

Any handholds in the rocky cliffside not covered by moss are slick with rain and mud. He hurries while trying not to hurry, keeping his eyes trained toward what should be the direction of the ridgeline, just in case the clouds part.

Halfway to the top, a sharp crack of thunder, followed by the terrible sensation of being watched. What if the thunder isn't thunder? What if it's the mountain lion, at the base of the little cliff? The mountain lion, waiting for him. Waiting. Pacing.

Ridiculous.

So ridiculous there's no need to glance back down to make sure.

He grunts with the effort of the last five feet. Almost to the top, but a ferocious gust of wind knocks him into the cliff and rips the map from his teeth. He flails one arm out after it, but his foot slips. He dangles for a horrifying moment as the wind catches the map like a kite. It soars twenty feet above him before another current pushes it back down and away from the cliff. The crumpled sheet roils in the pouring rain until finally it wraps around the trunk of a tree below.

Victor regains his footing and scrambles to the relative safety of the top. For a moment, he considers climbing back down to get the map, but he's already been gone too long. The ridgeline comes first. He'll grab the map on the way back.

He pulls his hood down tight against the driving rain and waits for a break in the clouds. Just a little window is all he needs, but the clouds taunt him, threatening to part a dozen times before—there's the ridgeline! A double spire, like a pair of needles, shooting to the sky. Obvious enough to find on the map.

Victor checks his watch. Twenty-three minutes since he left the mine. He works back toward the edge of the cliff, praying that the map is still wrapped around the trunk below.

"Shit," he says, and then drops to the ground as if he's been sniped. There's no way he saw what he thinks he saw. He covers his mouth to keep any other sound from escaping. Rain pelts the back of his head as he crawls toward the ledge for a peek. Is that movement by the map? A glimpse of a tail?

Victor presses his cheek into the mud. Once again he hears the low growl. Once again he tries to convince himself it's only distant thunder. Do. Not. Panic.

He scoots from the ledge as slowly as possible and huddles in the protective canopy of a pine tree. Five minutes later, he checks again. The map is gone. Wind, probably. It had to be the wind.

But at least the coast seems clear now.

Jerry and Amelia both have maps of the route; Victor will have to steal one tonight. Yet another way the simple plan has become more complicated.

Victor's troop leader once told him that you're just as likely to get attacked by a mountain lion if you run as if you stand your ground and make yourself look big. The only foolproof way not to get attacked is for the animal never to see you in the first place, so Victor takes a wide loop back to the ghost town, using the slope as a rough guide.

But the clouds are too thick for him to get a bearing on the mountain ridge and too low to see the valley below, and the wind is disorienting, swirling the way it is, like the world is spinning him around.

He should stop.

Stop now and reconsider where he's going, but he's sweating, and because he's sweating, he smells, and the mountain lion is still out there, and what if it recognizes his scent from the map?

Victor starts to run.

No, don't run! Stay calm. But it's not that easy. His legs don't work right. He trips on a fallen tree, catches himself, then trips again, tumbling to the ground, slamming his shoulder into the soft earth.

A thunderclap startles him, makes him flinch, and despair rolls over him as the rumble dissipates.

This wasn't supposed to happen this way. He had a plan. He's been gone for an hour, and if Jerry called it in already, they'll end the trip. If—

On the tail end of another thunderclap, he hears his name. And again.

Jerry's voice, straight ahead and slightly uphill. Victor pushes to his feet, feeling stupid and ashamed for panicking the way he did. Next time he'll trust himself, he promises.

Victor counts to sixty.

Looking nonchalant is the right play here, not letting on that anything was ever wrong. He wipes the mud from his elbow and shoulder and follows the sound of Jerry's voice, his hands no longer shaking. It's not just Jerry anymore; they're all yelling his name.

Victor plasters on a smile and wanders into the clearing. He keeps his pace slow and unhurried, and he waves when he sees them.

19

This time, he'd promised to be on his best behavior. He knew exactly what to expect. It had been three years since Victor's dad had left. Three years and four possible replacements, and the first meetings were the same every time. Big smile, but not too big. I'm not here to take your dad's place. I understand your bond with your mother comes first.

"I've heard so much about you," the new guy said before releasing Victor's hand. The man was narrow-shouldered and big-headed, with a forehead that took up half his face and a salt-and-pepper helmet of hair. He'd worn a suit, double-breasted, and a tie with tiny pirate swords on it.

"Me too," Victor said.

They sat on the back porch of Victor's house, the site of every first meeting. The porch overlooked a gentle grassy slope, at the end of which stood a wall of pine trees, and beyond that, the front range of the Rocky Mountains. It was late September. With the breeze came the first hint of winter.

"I'll be right back with some tea," his mom said. Victor had noticed the changes in the months since she met this one, Winslow. The hair. The makeup. The wardrobe. The jewelry. All of it fancier, more aggressive. Not all at once, a little at a time, but enough to notice.

She put her hand on Winslow's pinstriped shoulder and gave it a squeeze as she passed by. Winslow kept his eyes on the spot where her hand had been until the door closed. Then he looked at Victor. He leaned forward, smoothing down his tie as he moved.

"I don't want to be your dad."

Here it came, like clockwork. "Okay."

"You already have one of those," Winslow said. "And I don't want to be your uncle, either. I don't want to be your friend. I'm here because your mother is a wonderful person."

"Okay."

"We can agree on that, can't we? That your mother is a wonderful person?"

"Yeah," Victor said, becoming uneasy. "Yes."

"Do you ever say that to yourself? 'My mother is a wonderful person.' You should." Winslow scraped his teeth over his bottom lip. "Go ahead. Try it now."

Victor knew he was supposed to act tough, this being their first meeting and all, but he was unable to keep his eyes from widening. "You want me—"

"Just once."

"My mother is a wonderful person."

"Good. That's good." Winslow leaned back and his face broke out into a wide smile. "Now how about you fucking treat her that way."

Victor didn't know how long they sat there after that, in silence. It felt like two hours. Mercifully, the screen door creaked as Victor's mom backed through holding a tray of iced tea.

"You need a hand, Lisa?" Winslow said, his eyes still set on Victor's.

Victor pushed himself to his feet and held the door open.

"Thank you, Victor," his mom said, with surprise in her voice.

20

Victor has been waiting for the downpour to subside, even a little, for over an hour. Lying on top of his sleeping bag, his boots laced tight, his jacket zipped, a dormant headlamp strapped to his forehead. Waiting.

Midnight. The hands on his watch still glowing brightly, and of course they are. A gift from his mom. Only the best for her soon-to-be Eagle Scout. One o'clock. He stares at the tent ceiling, but the thick clouds block out any moonlight, and the darkness is total. Waiting.

Or is the rain just an excuse? Once he unzips the tent, there's no going back.

He feels the reassuring outline of the knife in his pocket. He runs the checklist over in his head. First, the packs. Cut Santi's down and take what food he can. Then to Amelia's pack for the map and the radio, so they can't call Search and Rescue.

Five, ten minutes at the most, and then he's gone. Up past where they were supposed to camp tonight, and off the trail before sunrise. From there, it's not long to Winslow's cabin. Maybe a day, just because of the elevation gain. If all goes well, he'll be there by mid-morning the day after tomorrow.

He sits up and reaches for the door's zipper, but a tremendous gust of wind rattles the tent. Just a little while longer, he thinks. And then I'll go.

How easy it would be to take off his boots right now, to wiggle into his sleeping bag, to pretend he was never going to do anything.

But he can't do that. If he bails, then every time he sees his stepdad's face, he'll be reminded of his own cowardice. And even though ol' Winslow will never find out, Victor will know. He has no follow-through. Over and over, every time he sees his stepdad, he'll hear those words. No follow-through.

It will eat at him until it kills him.

There's a rumble in the distance. More thunder.

Next to him, Santi sits bolt upright. Victor instinctively lies back down.

"What is that?" Santi says, turning on the headlamp dangling from the tent ceiling.

Victor's heart jackhammers against his ribs. He rolls the sleeping bag over himself and whips the headlamp off his own head. "Turn the light off."

There is something out there, a rumble, and it's getting louder. And then the tent is moving, the ceiling is the floor, and Santi screams out. And they roll again. And again.

Victor can't breathe and he can't see and he grasps at his face but his arms are caught and his head smashes against the ground and he thinks this is it. The thickness in front of his face, the repeated pounding to his head. His inability to make it stop. His weakness.

And so he gives up. He hears screams through the fog, but he doesn't fight.

Then everything is still.

The pressure disappears, and the sleeping bag comes away from his face. Victor gasps as if breaking through the surface of a swimming pool. Santi shines the headlamp in his eyes, and Victor notices blood dripping onto the sleeping bag, then on his hand when he touches the throbbing above his right eye. And there's water. So much water.

Santi crouches back down and begins to sift through the mess at his feet. "You already have your boots on?"

Victor mumbles something about needing to take a piss before the world fell apart.

"Everything's gone," Santi says finally. "Just gone."

***

A thick, soupy darkness. Victor follows Santi away from the tent, both of them screaming for help, for the others, for something. The destruction, or what Victor can see of it through the beam of his headlamp, is apocalyptic. Three-foot tree trunks snapped at the base like toothpicks. Boulders poking through the mud like so many icebergs, the exposed tops hinting at their massive size below the surface. And the mud. The mud is everywhere. In some places it's like chocolate pudding; in others it's as thick and rocky as damp concrete. They slog through it, fight across it.

Victor turns and scrambles up the hill, away from Santi, away from the debris. His pack has to be there. It has to be.

And it is. Santi's too, stuffed with food, swaying gently in the wind and rain as if nothing had happened.

Victor collapses underneath his pack and leans his head against the tree. He closes his eyes and smiles, thinking what the guy who sold it to him would say if he saw it now. The seam-sealed roll-top closure, the adjustable GridLock shoulder harness, the ultra-durable fusion points. The salesman rattling off a list of features that meant nothing to Victor at the time.

Santi shouts. And again.

"Don't add yourself to the victim list," Victor says, an impulse from somewhere deep in his brain, remembering the wilderness first-responder course he had to take for scouting. But he's already on the victim list, isn't he? He presses two fingers against his injured shoulder and rolls his elbow up and forward, relieved by the absence of pain. He wipes moisture from his forehead and cheek and uses the beam of the headlamp to check the blood on his hand. Watery, like weak cranberry juice. It could have been so much worse.

Victor looks now to Santi. Panicked, soaking. One boot missing. It's time to go. If they find the kitchen, they'll be able to find the others. And if they find the others, they'll find Amelia's map.

Using the packs as a point of reference, they aim their lights downhill and enter the devastation. With the trees mostly gone, with the ground covered in feet of debris, it's nearly impossible to figure out where they are.

"We're almost there," Santi says. "I'm sure of it."

Except they're not. There is no kitchen, no tarp. Even the ravine doesn't seem to be where it had been.

"They're gone, Santi," Victor says.

Santi keeps stumbling forward, but Victor hangs back. A realization spreads through him, a tingling that reaches his fingertips. He's alive. He survived. Maybe, somehow, there's even a silver lining in all of this.

He can ditch Santi here. Right now, in fact. Santi would be on his own, sure, but it's not like he'd die or anything. Someone would find him. With his missing boot, his torn up heels, and his total wilderness ineptitude, he'd have no choice but to stay here until help came. And he wouldn't starve.

Victor will leave some food from Santi's pack. He's not an animal, after all.

Santi leans over and vomits.

"Did you hear that?" Santi says, wiping his eyes and mouth. "She's screaming for help."

Victor has already made his decision. He'll wander around for a little while longer, letting Santi get farther away, and then he'll head back uphill to the packs. Even if he doesn't have a map, he has an opportunity.

Suddenly, Santi takes off down the hill. He does an awkward hop-jump, lurching forward every time his bare foot touches the mud. Three hops later, Santi disappears into the curtain of rain, and Victor spins in the other direction.

Now's his chance.

But what if there's really someone down there? And what if it's Amelia? And what if she has her pack with her?

Damn it.

He follows the sound of Santi's voice downhill, to the edge of a thunderous river.

Santi points his headlamp across the water, the beam flashing off of something—the reflective stripes of a jacket?

Amelia. Clutching the side of a boulder like it's a raft, a dark torrent of water at least fifteen feet across rushing between them and her. Santi's light flickers back and forth across her body. Just like Victor, she's fully clothed. Shoes, jacket, pants, everything. Fully clothed, which means she must have gotten dressed after the mudslide. Which means she still has her stuff. Which means she still has the map.

Victor turns off his headlamp and watches the two of them screaming at each other in the rain.

What comes next looks like it happens in slow motion. A roar from above, and a curtain of black, and then she's gone.

Victor flees uphill, scrambling away from the deafening noise. He trips on a splintered branch and crashes to the ground, slamming into a boulder and bouncing onto his back in the mud. Rain fills his mouth as he struggles to catch his breath, and he coughs and his chest throbs and for the second time tonight, he gives up.

21

"Two peanuts were walking down the street," his mom said, starting with a joke. "One was a salted."

Victor said nothing. Couldn't even make eye contact. Just stared at the bowl of apples in the center of the kitchen table. Plastic apples, because an entire bowl of real apples would rot now with only two mouths to feed.

His mom filled the silence with a nervous laugh, little staccato bursts. "You don't like that one?"

"It was funny when I was six," Victor said.

He knew what was coming. He'd known it was coming for a long time now. His mom had started dropping hints here and there. In the months since his dad had left, Victor had noticed her becoming increasingly worried—paranoid, even—that she wouldn't be able to provide the kind of male guidance he needed. A couple of weeks before, she'd pointed to a bikini model in a beer commercial on television and asked if the model was his type. If he had a type.

"I don't want to be here just as much as you don't," she said.

Victor laughed. His mom did too.

"I guess we should just get right down to it."

"Okay," Victor said.

The pause was excruciating.

"Okay," his mom said.

Victor pulled his eyes away from the apples just long enough to see his mom looking up at the ceiling as she often did before settling on a punishment. As if seeking guidance from a higher parenting power. The instant her head came forward, his eyes returned to the decorative apples.

"Okay," she said again. "Well, here's the thing. When two people love each other, they are ready to start a physical relationship."

Victor could almost feel the heat coming off his face. But he said nothing. He wondered if this would have been any easier coming from his dad.

"And when that happens, when they're ready . . . it's almost like you think of nothing else . . . You still there?"

"Unfortunately," Victor said.

"So, when it comes time to . . . the man puts his penis into the woman's vagi—"

"Mom, I'm eleven years old. I know about—"

"How much do you know?"

"A lot," he said with an uneasy laugh. What kind of a question was that? How much could there be to know?

"And where did you learn it?"

"Friends," Victor said. "And the Internet."

"Oh, good Christ." His mom whistled through her teeth. "Okay then, let's hear it from you."

"Are you serious?"

"Either you're telling me what you already know, or I'm telling you what I think you need to know." She laughed. "And trust me, my version is longer."

"I know about sperms and eggs and then the uterus and

the baby and the umbilical cord and the baby coming out and all of that."

"What about menstruation?"

The bowl of plastic apples was no longer enough. Victor put his arm on the table and lowered his forehead to the crook of his elbow. "I don't want—"

"We can't finish 'The Talk' without covering menst—"

"Stop saying that word," Victor said into the wood.

"You know you can come to me, right? You can talk to me about anything you want."

"Maybe I could just die right here? Would that be okay with you?"

"He should be here," she said. "I'm so sorry. He should be doing this."

Something in her voice made him want to see her face, and so he looked up, and there was his mom. And she had tears in her eyes and she wasn't laughing anymore. "It's not your fault, honey. You have to know that."

22

The night lasts forever. Victor and Santi suffer beneath the uneven canopy of the largest pine tree they can find. Their tent is useless, so they huddle together and wrap their sleeping bags around themselves—first Victor's, then Santi's, which spills insulation from a gash in the toe. They don't sleep. How could they sleep? They say nothing to each other because there's nothing to say.

Dawn reveals a barren stretch of earth at least a hundred feet wide. The forest around them is gone, replaced by boulders and exposed roots and tree after tree snapped in half. The ravine trickles innocently once again, a full thirty feet to the east of where it had been the night before.

And here they are, under a cloudless sky. The air still holds its morning chill, but the sun has peeked over the ridge, offering enough warmth to dry their clothes, which they've spread across the field of debris.

"We have to go back down," Santi says. His voice is raspy, hoarse from an hour spent screaming in vain for the others. "Back the way we came. We know that route. We know how long it's going to take."

Victor shakes his head. Just once, cautiously. He has a welt over his right eye and maybe a broken rib, or at least a bruised one. "There won't be anyone there for us."

"But at least we can figure out the way." Santi sits barefoot on his pack, whipping two socks in the air to make them dry faster. He found his other boot within the wreckage of their tent, but his heels still look like raw hamburger.

The tent itself is beyond repair: poles snapped in half, gashes throughout the fabric. Their food lies in a pile next to the empty packs. A bag of bagels, some cream cheese and peanut butter, a block of cheddar, two sleeves of saltines, dehydrated beef stew to serve four, two packets of instant oatmeal, six granola bars, a baggie of powdered milk, twelve packs of hot cocoa, and a half-filled gallon bag of trail mix.

"Amelia had the radio. She and Jerry had maps," Victor says. "We just have to find their packs—"

"We have our own packs. We have food. We can salvage the sleeping bags and go back the way we came. We don't need a map."

"We do," Victor says. Impatience makes his skin itch. He needs to get moving. His clothes are dry enough, as is his sleeping bag.

"I saw her get washed away, Victor. I watched it happen. We don't know if it's safe to go stumbling around out there."

"Go down, then," Victor says, knowing now for certain that he should have left last night when he had the chance. "If you're going to be a pussy about it."

"How is this me being a pussy about it? We're lost in the fucking woods—"

"We're not lost—"

"*Stranded*, then. You like 'stranded' better? We're stranded in the woods. We have no tent. We have no map."

"You guys?"

The voice comes from behind Victor. A girl's voice.

Amelia. On the other side of a fallen tree, looking like she's crawled out of a fresh grave. Her hair is matted to the side of her head in a giant muddy clump. More mud covers her jacket and jeans. She holds her left arm tight against her stomach.

Still barefoot, Santi leaps awkwardly over toward her. "You're okay! Are you okay?"

"It's just you, isn't it?" She holds up one hand before he can touch her. "Just the two of you."

"And you," Santi says, still with his arms outstretched as if offering a hug that he realizes she's not going to accept. "How are you even alive?"

Amelia looks out over the mudslide. Her eyes go wide, and she starts to breathe faster.

Santi turns back to Victor and gives him a 'What do I do?' look. Victor returns it with a shrug.

"We haven't found the others yet, but we will," Santi says, like a dumbass, full of false hope.

"Come on, man. You spent half the morning screaming for them and got nothing. They're gone."

"If she survived, maybe they did too." Santi calls out, "Celeste, Rico, Jerr—"

"Not Jerry," Amelia says abruptly. She turns to look downhill again. "He invited me to his wedding."

Her shoulders tremble silently up and down, and she begins to wipe her eyes with the muddy heel of her good hand, leaving dark streaks behind.

"You're okay," Santi says, then points to her eyes. "You, um. You have a little . . ."

Amelia rubs her face against her shoulders but doesn't get all of the mud. Santi reaches up and wipes her cheek with his thumb.

"I don't mean to be insensitive or whatever," Victor says, "but do you know where your pack is, Amelia?"

She says nothing.

He tries again. "Where's your backpack?"

Santi glares at him, but what is Victor supposed to do? The clock is ticking.

Finally, Amelia looks down and shakes her head. No pack.

"Victor wants to keep going," Santi says, "but we don't have a map or a radio, and I think we should go back the way we came. It took us three days to get here. We can get back in two if we hurry."

"But like I told you," Victor says, "there's nothing for us at the trailhead. They shuttled the van over to where we were supposed to come out."

"We need to stay on the trail we know, the one we came in on. This place is remote, but not *that* remote. Not like we're in Alaska. It's a trail! There might be other hikers."

"And there might not."

"We could wait here," Amelia says.

"Wait for what?" Victor says.

"Help?"

Victor has to laugh. "Nobody knows we're here. Nobody is looking for us."

"Besides," Santi says, "you're injured. We need to evacuate you back down."

"I'm okay," she says softly.

The seconds feel like minutes. Victor heads toward the food pile and grabs the bag of bagels, the peanut butter, and the cheddar.

"What are you doing?" Santi says.

"Putting food in my pack."

Santi steps to him, and Victor's hand instinctively goes to his back pocket. Santi stops, and Victor sees the recognition in his face.

"Are you going to stab me?" Santi asks him.

"You guys," Amelia says.

Victor can feel the handle through the denim of his pocket, and he's trapped. What the hell was he doing, reaching for the knife? He just wants to grab the food and get on his way, but now he can't back down, thanks to this asshole. "I'm not going to do anything you don't make me do."

"You guys—"

"You don't think we're dealing with enough right n—Ah, damn it!" Santi's trying to be the tough guy, but his bare foot steps on something sharp, and he hops backward.

"I want my share of the food," Victor says. "That's all."

Amelia screams it this time: "You guys!"

"What?"

She points back from where she came. "I think I saw Jerry's pack."

Victor forces himself to wait as Santi pulls on his socks and boots.

Amelia leads them downhill. A hundred feet later, there it is, half-buried, upside down in the mud. The gray waist belt sticks up like a dorsal fin next to the shredded trunk of what used to be a shrub. Victor should have seen it earlier.

Without a word, he and Santi set their fingers into the ground, but the mud is packed so tightly that they might as well be scraping at concrete. Five minutes into it, they've only dug a couple of inches around the pack.

"Screw this," Victor says. He grabs the waist belt and pulls as hard as he can, but it doesn't budge. He props his right foot against a small boulder and tries again; a sharp pain flowers in his chest every time he pulls, but he keeps going. Again. Again. Again.

"Dude, enough," Santi says.

Victor is panting now, the sun directly on him. Sweat trickles down his cheek. Since when did it get this hot so early? "I can get it."

"Enough!"

Amelia taps him on the shoulder. Victor flinches but releases the waist belt and throws his hands into the air.

"We just have to keep digging." The concern in Amelia's voice is tinged with something that sounds a lot like suspicion. Is Victor getting paranoid? "It's going to take some time," she continues.

"What time?" Victor says. "You guys think that someone is magically going to show up and rescue us? What, like in a helicopter? Is that it? All we have to do is wait here, have some cheese and crackers, and everything will be just fine. Well, everything's *not* going to be fine! We're fucked. Everything we planned is fucked."

"Why don't you go sit down," Amelia says.

"I'm not your dog."

"You're going to have a heart attack or something," Santi says. "Take some deep breaths. She and I can handle this."

Victor watches them from atop a massive gray rock, cursing himself for losing control. He should have been patient. He should have waited until the backpack was almost free, should have positioned himself conveniently right next to the top pocket, should have been there to unzip it and reach inside for the map. But he didn't do any of that, and now there's nothing for him to do but wait.

Of course, when the pack does come free, Santi's the one to unzip the top pouch, and of course the map is there, and of course Santi pulls it out and hands it to Amelia. After untying the rope that's still attached to the pack's carry loop, Santi slings his arm under one shoulder strap and leads them back up.

Victor dismounts the rock and follows, cracking his knuckles one by one. Amelia is so close as they walk, barely three feet ahead, uphill of him so that the map in her hand is basically right in front of his face. He could snatch it so easily—what would she and Santi do? Fight him? Broken arm and gimpy feet?

"We need to pool our stuff," Santi says when they reach their scattered clothes. He spreads their tent's shredded rain fly along the uneven ground and begins removing the items from Jerry's pack. "Take stock of what we have, divide it up."

Amelia stares at Santi for a moment before kneeling down and helping him lay out the man's things. She can't do much, so she basically just straightens out the stuff after Santi puts it down. The two of them work silently for a minute, and then Amelia turns to Victor.

"You want to get started?" she asks him.

"We don't need to pool anything," Victor says. "We have our packs, we know what's in them. I just don't see why we have to unpack everything—"

Santi scoffs at him. "If you're embarrassed about the porn you brought, don't worry about it. No judging, right, Amelia?"

"In case you haven't noticed," she says, "I don't have my pack. I don't have anything."

Jerry's pack yields a small first-aid kit and a half-empty fuel bottle but no stove, which must have washed away along with the cooking pots and everything else in the makeshift kitchen. There's almost nothing to add to the food pile: three sleeves of

Ritz crackers, a half-empty bag of trail mix, an unopened pack of Reese's Pieces. There's also an empty water bottle with a half-inch-thick circle of duct tape around it.

"I should have let him carry more food," Santi says with a wry smile.

At the bottom of the pack they find Jerry's clothes. Three T-shirts, two pairs of shorts, a pair of hemp-looking sweatpants, three pairs of boxers, socks, long underwear, a hoodie, and a baseball cap with the logo of two guitars making up a yin yang.

"That's a lot of hemp," Victor says, nodding to the pile.

"Let me borrow your knife," Santi says, holding his palm out.

"What?"

"Your knife. Can I borrow it?"

Still unsettled, Victor looks from Santi's outstretched hand to the stack of Jerry's clothes.

"Whatever," Santi says. He shakes his head and picks up one of Jerry's shirts—light blue with the faded image of a tent beneath the words *Lyons Folk Festival*. He digs his fingers into one of the little holes around the collar and tears the shirt down the middle with a rip which, coming as it does in the middle of nowhere, sounds way louder than it should. Then another rip as he peels a single strip from the rest of the shirt.

"What are you—" Victor starts.

"Saw this in a movie once." Santi turns to Amelia and nods to her arm. "Where does it hurt the most?"

"My wrist and forearm, mostly," she says.

He folds the larger piece into a triangle and lays her arm on the cloth, one corner of the triangle at her elbow, before tying the other two corners around her neck. Then he ties the remaining strip of T-shirt around her body, just above the elbow of her bad arm, immobilizing the sling against her chest.

Amelia winces through a smile. "Look at you, Mr. Wilderness First-Aid Man."

"It's the least I can do. Like, literally, this is the very least I can do." Santi steps back and hands Amelia one of his own white T-shirts. "You can have this if you want. Not the best fit but probably better than Jerry's stuff."

Among the items laid out is the map, held in place by Jerry's water bottle. Victor walks calmly around the rain fly, but Amelia grabs it before he's even halfway there. She holds the map against her side but says nothing.

"We split the food. Evenly." Victor holds out his hand, trying to be as nonchalant as possible. "Let me take a look at the map, and then whatever happens, happens."

"We're not splitting up," Amelia says. "We need to stay together. I'm responsible now—"

"No offense, Amelia, but I don't think the Bear Canyon Wilderness Therapy Program guidelines are at the top of our priority list."

"I'm the assistant leader," Amelia says quietly. She folds the map one last time before putting it in her pocket. Then, as if convincing herself, she says it again, louder. "I'm the assistant leader."

"We're staying together," Santi says.

Victor can't believe he has to deal with this. Why can't the two of them just let him leave? What the hell do they care where he goes? He certainly doesn't care where they go. If his ribs and shoulder didn't hurt so bad, he'd kick Santi's ass, grab some food, and be done with it.

"We go forward, then," he says. If he's going to have to drag them along with him, he'll make sure he drags them in the direction of the cabin. "We don't go back."

Santi shakes his head. "This isn't a negotiation."

"That's *exactly* what this is."

"You guys," Amelia says, sounding as exhausted as she looks. "Your macho bullshit is impressive and everything, but can we not do this right now?"

Santi smiles. "You hear that? She thinks our macho bullshit is impressive."

"Fine, we go forward," Amelia says. "Just as long as we get away from this."

"Then I guess we're staying together," Victor says. It doesn't matter. He'll have plenty of time to slip away later.

23

This is how people die, Victor thought. He imagined the newscast that night, recounting the sad tale: the helicopter pilot, the Denver-area family of three, the first responders commenting on the isolation of the crash site and the magnitude of the wreckage.

They all wore noise-cancelling headphones, massive ear protectors like the guys out on an airport tarmac. Victor was terrified. He did not want to seem terrified. He pressed his hands on top of his thighs to keep them from shaking, looking out the window at the saw-toothed peaks below until he could stand it no longer.

His mom, sitting across from him, gave him two thumbs up. "This is fun!" she yelled over the din of the rotor blades.

This was not fun. At all. He hated his mom for making him come along, and he hated his stepdad even more for suggesting it in the first place. Winslow had wanted to share his pride and joy with them for over a year, and now, after the wedding, what could be a better time?

"The Weminuche Wilderness," his stepdad said, gesturing toward a ridgeline that looked like the back of a stegosaurus. "The most remote stretch in Colorado!"

Thirty minutes after takeoff in Durango, the helicopter began to slow and then to descend. They approached a clearing about half the size of a football field, just below the tree line. Uphill, a scree field led to another serrated ridge.

Rotor wash flattened the wildflowers as the helicopter hovered above the sloping ground. Winslow got out after putting his headphones on the empty copilot seat. His hair whipped about, moving for the first time since Victor had met him. Winslow reached for Victor's mom, then for Victor. Last were the bags: two small pieces of luggage and a small waterproof duffel of food, and then the helicopter lifted up gently and floated away.

"The Weminuche's around us on all sides," Winslow said as the helicopter disappeared over the ridge. "Copter's the only way to get here."

"It's gorgeous," Victor's mom said. "Truly."

"Can't put a price tag on it," Winslow said, looking around. "You wouldn't believe the deals I had to cut with the Forest Service to make sure there was nobody else nearby."

There was a hint of color—purple, yellow, blue—dotting the vast green field of waist-high plants. "Damn. The wildflowers must have bloomed early this year," he said with a frown. "Come on, let me show you inside."

Victor had figured that anything you had to take a helicopter to would be luxurious, even up at almost 12,000 feet, but this place was neither as fancy nor as big as he'd thought.

Winslow's cabin was basically one big room, maybe thirty feet across and definitely smaller than Victor's bedroom at their new home. A huge support post stood in the middle, extending up to the center of the A-frame ceiling. On one side was a kitchen and small table. A full-sized bed took up most of the space on the other side, with dozens of pillows along the back wall so it also worked as a couch. A sliding door covered half of the downhill wall and opened out toward a view that belonged on the cover of a magazine.

"It was just this room when I bought it," Winslow said. "I added a loft and dug out the basement about five years ago. All supplies brought in by helicopter, of course. Go ahead, take a look around."

Victor climbed halfway up a ladder to poke his head into the loft, then wandered down into the basement, which included another twin bed-slash-couch, a small sink, and four doors—a ridiculous number for such a small room—none of which even led outside. Door one opened to a cedar closet with stacks of Indian blankets; door two revealed a small storage area stocked mostly with paper towels and toilet paper. A room with lots of pipes and two large water tanks was behind door number three. The last one was locked, which seemed unnecessary given how far they were from civilization.

Winslow and his mom had taken off their shoes by the time he came upstairs. Winslow filled a glass with water from the tap.

"You have running water here?" Victor said.

"Sure, running water, electricity, the whole nine yards. In fact, this cabin had power even before a lot of the towns in the area. With all the mining, you had to have electricity."

"Mining for what?" Victor said.

"Lots of things, really," Winslow said. "Zinc, lead, silver, copper." He picked a small vial from the mantel and handed it to Victor. Sitting at the bottom of the vial was a dark yellow cluster about the size of a pea.

Winslow smiled. "But mostly gold."

119

24

Misery is supposed to love company, but Victor's company only makes him more miserable. He should be alone, with his own food and his own pack and his own schedule and his own plan, instead of being the third wheel in some lame spoof of a disaster movie.

With all their injuries, the progress is slow. Santi's feet. Victor's ribs and shoulder. Amelia's arm seems better, at least. The Advil from Jerry's first-aid kit probably helps, but she's recovered so fast that Victor begins to wonder whether she was milking the injury for sympathy, the way he used to in order to get out of running wind sprints at the end of soccer practice.

They make camp in a small, relatively flat clearing in the middle of an aspen grove. A rocky crag juts out from the ridgeline about a quarter mile to the west. It's the most distinctive feature around them, even recognizable on the map. They may be stranded, but at least they're not lost.

As the sun moves past the horizon, the temperature starts to plummet. And beneath the white ribbon of the Milky Way overhead, the cloudless night sky has trapped none of the day's heat.

A fire pit would have taken effort they can't make. Instead, they pile some logs in the center of the clearing. Doused with camping fuel, a match tossed on top. Smoky at first, but soon the wood dries and the roaring fire provides all the warmth they need.

Without a stove or pots to boil water, they eat the squares of ramen like sandwiches.

"Mmmm," Santi says through the crunch of the dry noodles. He offers Victor what's left of his spice packet. "The chicken flavor is tremendous. First class."

All day, they've rationed what's left of their water—a sip here, a sip there, but never enough to quench the thirst—so Victor accepts the packet no matter how disgusting the taste. At least the sodium triggers his saliva.

Crunching his teeth against the noodles, he can't keep himself from thinking of the scat they'd found after breaking for lunch: another tube of oversized cat crap with clumps of hair and bits of shattered bones sticking out. Either they're following the mountain lion or it's following them. He isn't sure which would be worse.

"You guys want to take turns stoking the fire in the middle of the night?" Amelia says, warming her palms by the flames.

"You can have my sleeping bag, if you want," Santi says. "What's left of it."

Amelia snorts in mock offense. "I'll be fine."

"You should take it."

"You don't think I can handle the cold?"

"Handle it if you want, but I still have my sweater, and you're just rocking Jerry's hemp hoodie."

It looks like the two of them share a little moment—does she wink at Santi? does he raise his eyebrows at her?—before Amelia shrugs in acceptance.

"Now I feel like the asshole for not offering first," Victor says with a grunt.

Santi laughs. "I'm not the one who said it."

"Did you guys hear that?" Victor whirls his head around. "Wha—"

"Shh." He holds his hand out and stands, head cocked. Another sound comes with the wind. Is it the mountain lion? Do mountain lions even roar? Like lions at the zoo?

But it's just the wind. It has to be. The wind in the trees.

"Victor," Amelia says. "You okay?"

He turns back to them and forces a laugh. "I'm not the one with the broken arm."

"What if I told you," Amelia says after a moment, "that Jerry left us a little present?"

"I would ask what it is," Santi says.

She leans forward as if to stand up but then sits back down and shakes her head. "Nothing. Never mind."

Santi smiles at her again, like they've known each other forever. "You can't do that."

And now she hits him across the shoulder with the back of her good hand. "I can do whatever I want—"

"That's right," Victor says, "you're the leader now."

"Don't be a dick, Victor."

The fire's orange glow dances in the faces across from him. Maybe he'll leave tonight. Just as he should have done the day before—grabbed some food, made them try to stop him.

"Screw it," Amelia says. She slaps her hand on her knee and goes over to Jerry's pack, coming back with a silver flask.

Santi and Victor share a glance.

"Jerry brought a flask?" Santi says.

Amelia unscrews the top and peers inside, puts her nose to the opening, and takes a tentative sip. Not two seconds later, she starts coughing.

"Wrong pipe?" Santi says, reaching to pat her on the back.

"Just wish we had some salt and lime," Amelia says after she recovers. She offers the flask to Santi, who takes a whiff. "Tequila."

"I didn't know about it until this morning, when I found it in his pack. It's against regulations, right? But it's not like anything matters anymore."

"Jerry smuggled tequila." Santi shakes his head. He grunts with laughter and takes a pull before passing it along.

Victor holds the flask up to the fire: the silver scratched from regular use, with an owl engraved into a large wooden panel on the front. It's almost full, and larger than Victor expected. "This bad boy is serious. It must hold at least ten ounces."

"Twelve," Amelia says. "Probably twelve, I guess."

They sit in silence for a long time, passing the tequila around the fire, coughing a little, wincing through the burn. It's not the smoothest Victor's ever had, but right now, under the stars, after the day they've had, it gets the job done.

"Look at you," Victor says finally as he gives it to Amelia. "Breaking the rules. I have to say that I'm more than a little impressed."

"I'm not doing it to impress you."

"That's not what I—" Victor stops, exhales. "I just meant that . . . we don't know anything about each other is all. You know, surprises and whatnot."

"Okay . . ." Santi angles the flask in front of Victor as if watching the flames against the silver back. "Since we're probably not going to get to sharing circle for you guys, let's have it. One thing. One little nugget about yourself."

Victor laughs. "You first."

"Nah, I already had my turn. Officially, too, and for over an hour."

"I'll go," Amelia says, her eyes still locked on the fire. "I've lived in seven different states and three different countries, never one place for more than three years."

"I thought you were born in Houston?" Victor says.

"I only say I'm from Houston because I've lived there the longest."

"See?" Santi leans back and nods. "That's some high-quality sharing. Was it your dad's job?"

Amelia shakes her head. "Mom's. Oil and gas."

"More surprises!"

Victor takes a long pull, holding the tequila in his mouth for a bit longer this time, enjoying the burn. "This is the type of group activity I could get behind."

"Órale," Santi says. "Enough of the trust talks and the staying on your side of the net and all that—no offense, Amelia."

"None taken."

"Just pass around a beverage and let everyone chill together." Santi smiles. "What do you think, Victor? Different time, different place?"

"Us?" Victor says. "Nah. You think I'm some rich asshole."

"Aren't you?"

"I guess. And don't you have a stick up your ass?"

Santi laughs and reaches for the bottle. "I guess."

"What do you think it was like for them?" Amelia says, as if she's just remembered an errand she was supposed to handle.

"What do you mean?" Santi says.

"On the rock last night, I didn't know what to do. I just sat there and waited. Waited for something to happen. And then I heard your voice and I thought you were going to help me.

But then the slide came again, and I was gone. I was sure I was dead." She shakes her head and stares at the fire, and for a second, she looks just as dazed as she did when she found them this morning. "I should be dead."

"It's not our fault that we're alive," Victor says.

"You don't even think about it?" she says.

"What good does it do? Am I going to switch places with them?"

She's crying again. Santi sits next to her and lets her lean into his shoulder. "They didn't deserve to die."

"Some people do," Victor says to himself.

Santi glares at him. "Jesus, Victor."

"I'm just saying. Hitler, right? For example."

"That's the problem with people like you," Santi says. "It's all theoretical. Death, pain, whatever. Nothing really bad ever happens, so you get to play make-believe—"

"*Theoretical* is a big word for people like you," Victor says with a smile.

The tequila goes down easier every time. First the pain in Victor's ribs goes away, then the feeling in his shoulder. Then basically everything. He leans back against the soft tufts of grass and looks up at the clear night sky, the Milky Way sprinkled directly overhead. Smoke blocks his view whenever the wind shifts, but he doesn't mind. In fact, it's better that way. Billions of stars drilling light through the haze.

Why couldn't it have been this beautiful last night? Why couldn't the storm have come a day earlier? Or a day later?

"I'm not supposed to be here," Victor says to himself.

Santi laughs at him. "Says everyone in juvie."

"My stepdad has a cabin." Somewhere in the back of his mind is a voice telling him to shut up, but that voice is too distant. Victor can't hear it clearly, and besides, the time for keeping it to himself is long gone. "We're close."

"Bullshit. Ese, you must be hammered."

Victor sits—a little too quickly—and has to brace himself against the dirt for a moment to keep himself from collapsing. "Show me the map."

Santi and Amelia look at each other. Not leaving them at the mudslide was the dumbest thing Victor's ever done, and now he knows it.

"Show me the fucking map. I'm not going to steal it from you." He turns on his headlamp and wobbles around the fire. It takes him longer than it should. The ground doesn't seem to be where his feet want it to be.

"Easy there," Amelia says. "We don't have enough water to put you out."

"Ha, ha, ha," he says. "Shut up, I'm fine."

With Santi's help, Amelia spreads the map on the ground. Victor kneels in front of it, pointing to various spots along the highlighted trail. "Here—this X—that's where we were supposed to camp last night. And here was the mudslide, right? We're at least twenty miles from the end of the trail, but here—"

His finger lands about an inch away from the X, on a small clearing just below the thick elevation line marking 12,000 feet.

"See that right there? That bowl. The cabin is just below tree line. There's a satellite phone up there," Victor hears himself say. "Seriously. None of this walking down to the trail bullshit. We could get a helicopter to come pick us up—"

"A helicopter?" Amelia says.

Santi laughs. "Now I *know* you're hammered."

"Why do you think I chose this stupid trip in the first place? Because it was close. Because I knew I could get in there

126

and fuck up his shit. His pride and joy."

Amelia slides the map from beneath his finger and folds it slowly, finding the creases first. There is doubt on her face. Or is it concern? Or fear?

"I thought you said your stepdad was awesome," Amelia says.

"I never said that. I said he was the most badass attorney in Colorado. I said he would sue the shit out of Jerry. I never said he was awesome."

Santi says, "So he's not awesome?"

Victor squeezes his eyes closed, and suddenly he's thirteen years old again, and he's waiting in the living room. Waiting up because his mom is on her first date since his dad left, and he's still awake even though she told him to remember his bedtime.

She's not even mad when she opens the door and sees him. She doesn't even say anything at all. She just laughs. She just tosses her purse onto the chair by the door and walks through the living room and into the kitchen, where she opens the freezer and takes out a pint of cookie dough ice cream and grabs a pair of spoons on her way back to him.

"Wow," she says as she plops down on the couch next to Victor.

He smiles and accepts one of the spoons. "How was it?"

"If I ever try to marry a stockbroker, please shoot me right in the forehead." She spoons out a tremendous lump of ice cream and licks it like the scoop on a cone.

"Stockbroker doesn't sound too bad," Victor says. "I bet he was rich at least."

"Oh, honey, he was fantastic. Rich, smart, good looking." She glances at Victor with a twinkle in her eye. "Just ask him. He'll be the first one to tell you."

And they laugh together and they talk, and when the ice

cream is finally gone, Victor leans his head on her lap and lets her scratch his head until he drifts off to sleep.

Victor opens his eyes now and shakes away the memory. He grabs the bottle from Santi and takes a mouthful. He doesn't even taste the liquid this time. Goes down like water. The clearest, cleanest water he's ever had, just like the tap water from the cabin. He stumbles back but catches himself, no problem.

"I'm fine," Victor says, waving them away. "I said I'm fine."

He screws the little metal top back on the flask and crawls back over to his spot. He's not going to puke. He knows that much. Maybe some spins when he lies down, but he's not going to puke.

Oh, God, the spins. He's on his back, and he closes his eyes, and the spins come, slowly at first, and when he opens his eyes again, he's not sure how much time has passed. The fire looks the same size, but they could have put another log on.

"Gold got too expensive to mine," Victor says. "Price of gold goes down, easy gold is already ripped from the mountain. Simple economics. The miners all left. Supply and demand."

It's Amelia who says, "What are you talking about?"

"Supply and demand," Victor says again. He closes his eyes and buries them in the crook of his elbow, but that makes the spinning worse. At least his chest doesn't hurt anymore.

There's no such thing as drifting off to sleep when you're wasted. You fight the spins as long as you can and then you're gone.

25

His mom's face had lost its expressiveness in the years since her remarriage—the wrinkle-free forehead, the smoothness where the crow's feet had once been—but the eyes gave her away. No amount of Botox could have hidden the fear.

"Tell me it wasn't drugs," she said.

Victor pressed a cold pack against the reddened left side of his face. The bruising would start soon. He'd never had a black eye before, and he wondered if he'd look like a badass—if he was going to get kicked out of the scout troop for fighting, the least he could do was go out as a badass.

More than anything, he hoped that Davis Higley would end up looking worse than he did.

"It wasn't drugs—"

"Drinking, then? Because I can't think of any other reason. If you had been thinking clearly, you never would have—"

She was almost hopeful. Drinking or drugs would be an explanation in itself, but without alcohol to blame, she'd have to consider that he, alone, with no chemical alteration, was capable of this.

"Mom, I—" Victor sat on the edge of his bed and looked around his room. It was spotless. Everything filed away in cubbies and drawers. His old action figures posed on the top of the bookshelf like they were in some sort of museum. "I don't know what happened, Mom. I'm sorry."

"What do you think Winslow is going to say?"

"We don't have to tell him."

"He's your stepfather. He's my husband."

"We could say I quit. We could say I didn't want to jump through all the stupid hoops just so I could call myself an Eagle Scout."

"Your face, Victor—"

"We could say that I fell. We don't have to tell him."

But of course they had to, and they did, with Victor sandwiched between Winslow and his mom on the couch. Victor confessed but kept it simple. A quick disclosure of the facts of the case. There had been an altercation. Punches had been thrown. Blame had been placed. Consequences had been suffered.

Winslow said nothing.

Victor had nothing more to say.

Mom got up. She kissed Winslow on the cheek and said to her husband, "I'll be in the kitchen, honey."

Maybe it was over? Victor was halfway to the door when Winslow's voice stopped him. "Where do you think you're going?"

"To bed—"

"Sit down."

"But—"

"I said sit your disrespectful ass down. Right now."

Victor froze at the cool menace in the man's voice. The living room was dead quiet but for the sound of water in the pipes. Probably his mom in the kitchen. There were dishes to be done, after all. Marble counters to be wiped. Victor sat his disrespectful ass back down on the couch.

"When I was your age—" Winslow stopped. "Your mother and I. We're trying, but you've got to help us."

Victor winced at the word *us*, but still he kept his mouth shut.

"What do you expect us to do?" That word again. Another pause as Winslow clenched and unclenched the fists resting on his knees. He said, simply, "Eagle Scout."

Victor stared at his feet.

"You're going to make this right, Victor. You're going to make this right, for me, for your mom, for yourself."

Victor's mouth opened.

He knew he shouldn't say anything. Just let the man rage at him until he got tired of it. Even though Victor's silence sometimes made Winslow angrier in the moment, it was always better in the long term. You don't put another log on the fire unless you want to keep it burning.

But he couldn't help himself. Victor focused on the cuff poking out from the sleeve of the man's pinstriped suit. Circular golden cufflinks embossed with the image a hawk or an eagle or something. Winslow's stupid initials monogrammed on the sleeve of his tailored dress shirt.

"What kind of an asshole wears cufflinks without a tuxedo?"

Victor braced himself, but Winslow surprised him. There was no fury. Just a low, flat, devastatingly soft statement of fact.

"The second you graduate from high school, you're out of here, do you understand me? No money, no house, nothing. Not from me. I promised myself that I would get you that far. That I'd stick with you, no matter how hard you make it for me. I owe your mother that much."

A week later, Victor knocked on the door of Winslow's home office and entered without waiting for an answer. His stepdad was on the phone. Victor ignored the hand-waving and marched straight to the desk.

"I'm sorry. You were right." He forced himself to say the words, and Winslow put the phone to his chest and smiled a victory smile that made Victor hate the man even more. "I'll try to do better," he continued, swallowing his anger, faking remorse. He placed a completed enrollment form for the Bear Canyon Wilderness Therapy Program on his stepfather's desk. "I think I could learn from this."

26

Victor's tongue sits in his mouth like a filthy sock. His head throbs with every step. At some point in the middle of the night, thank God, he puked the tequila out, but what little Advil they still have is going toward Amelia's arm, so there's no relief for him there. He's desperate to collapse in the shade, chug one of their two remaining water bottles, and put his head between his knees. He can't, though, and only partly because they're still rationing the water.

It's already early afternoon, and they have to keep moving.

He's dehydrated and hungover; his shoulder and ribs still hurt from the mudslide; but most of all he's pissed off. Pissed off and ashamed.

The feeling of stupidity, all-consuming: the tightening of the chest, the sinking of the stomach, the heat at his temples. The same feeling that would paralyze him in school as early as kindergarten. I'm so stupid, I'm so stupid, over and over.

He had told them about the cabin.

Nobody was supposed to know. Nobody. That was the whole point. And now this. Now they know. The secret is out, and it's his fault because he's the stupid one who can't keep his goddamned mouth shut, who can't execute a plan after all, who has no business being out here.

Farther uphill, Amelia and Santi are almost out of eyesight, side by side, Amelia holding the compass and Santi gesturing to the map as if he has any idea what he's pointing at.

The forest thins out with every foot of elevation gain. Fallen trees almost outnumber the living ones, victims of avalanches or beetle infestations of years past. Ahead, two ridges meet at a peak in the center, creating a bowl above them, treeless and scree-filled. Deep red tailings from some abandoned mine ooze down the barren rocks like blood from a stab wound, the red widening downhill. He's close enough now that the terrain is starting to look familiar. Maybe he knows that basin? Maybe he's seen those tailings before?

At least the sky is relatively clear. At least his clothes are relatively dry.

Maybe he can convince the others to leave him alone, to go downhill without him. Santi and Amelia don't even need the map, not really, not if they head straight down. Eventually they'll run into a stream or valley they'll be able to follow to a road.

"Let's go, Eagle Scout!" Santi calls back to him. "We don't have all day here!"

Victor finally catches up to them next to a fallen tree. Years of rot have eaten away at the inside of the splintered trunk, and he half-considers tucking himself into it. Amelia looks okay now, but was she faking the injury or is she faking the recovery?

Santi taps Victor's chest with a light backhand. "Tequila not your beverage of choice?"

"Not all of us are born Mexican."

"There he is!" Santi says. "Our little racist is back. We were worried about you."

He'd meant to lean against the trunk for support, but a wave of nausea hits him, and he sits instead on the rotting wood and hunches forward, staring at a moss-covered rock between his feet. The weight of the backpack pushes his elbows into the meat of his thighs. "You guys must not have gotten as drunk as I did."

"We didn't have much of a chance," Amelia says, her tone thick with judgment. "Not the way you took it down."

He can't shake the fog from his brain no matter how hard he tries. What, exactly, did he tell them? Maybe they'd played him for the fool he is—maybe they were just pretending to drink last night, taking little sips and letting him drink himself into oblivion so they could get a little privacy for some back-woods action.

Stupid. So stupid.

"I think we're pretty close," Amelia says. "You want to take a look?"

Victor leans farther forward, centering his weight above his legs, before he stands up with a groan. Deep breath. Eyes closed. Another breath. He stares at the map, but for some reason, none of it makes sense, like it's a piece of modern art, all lines and shapes and colors. He looks up and around, trying to orient himself, searching for some hint from the land. "Where are we?"

Santi smirks. "They don't teach map reading in Boy Scouts?"

"It's called orienteering, and shut the hell up."

Amelia points to a small space above the thick 12,000-foot line. "Here's where you said the cabin is." Her finger travels down below the 11,000-foot line, just east of what looks like a ridgeline: a Florida-shaped peninsula, topo lines nestled closely to show drastic elevation gain. "And here's where we are."

"That ridge right there," Victor says, pointing to the formation above them. Rock spires rise from the top like the edge of a bowie knife. "You can see the other side of it from the cabin."

"You sure?" Santi says.

"I'm either sure or I'm not. No going back now."

"What's the deal with this cabin?" Amelia says. It's an innocent enough thing to say, given their situation, but something about the way she says it—the tilt of her head? the squint of her eyes?—makes him uneasy.

"It's nothing," Victor says, dismissing her with a flick of his hand.

"A cabin at 12,000 feet doesn't sound like nothing. Especially one with a satellite phone."

Satellite phone? This fog in his head. Too thick. What did he tell them last night?

Victor steps forward as if to continue the hike, but Santi and Amelia are in the way, and it would be too aggressive to go around them. Like he's avoiding them, like he has something to hide.

"Of course it has a satellite phone," Victor says. "You think the phone company's running wires all the way up here?"

"How are you going to drop a bomb on us like that and then just pass out?" Santi says.

"I didn't pass out on you. I went to sleep."

"But you think the phone is going to work?" Amelia says.

Before Victor can even respond, Santi has to chime in: "It makes sense now what you said to me the other day about choosing to be here. You wanted to break into your own family's cabin, right? That's why?"

"He's not my family."

"'Mess up his pride and joy.' That's what you said last night."

This catches Victor off-guard. *Pride and joy*—that's his stepdad's phrase. Did he really say that? Why would he have told them that?

"Let's say you do." Santi gives him a smug laugh. "He's going to know it's you, right? He has to."

They're needling him, that's what they're doing. Taunting him. They know he feels shitty and his head hurts and they know he can't think straight. "He didn't even read past the title of the brochure. All he cares about is that I'm gone."

"Yeah, but come on," Amelia says. "Do you actually think he won't make the connection?"

Victor shakes his head, which is a terrible mistake. Sharp stabs to the temple replace the dull throbbing.

"Like he wasn't going to notice?"

"Shut up!" Victor says. He takes a step back to regain his balance, but there's a rock where his foot needs to go and he twists his goddamn ankle and it's over before he can do anything about it.

He grabs his leg with both hands. So much pain, a burning just beneath his anklebone, and then he's on his back like an upside-down turtle. Pathetic and hungover and screaming and stranded in the fucking wilderness with a thug and a debutante.

"Stay away from me," he yells when they bend down toward him.

He unclips the belt and chest buckles of his pack and slithers out of the shoulder straps, wrenching himself up onto his hands and knees.

"Victor," Amelia says, the gentleness in her voice cutting through the pain. "Victor."

He hears the unclipping of buckles and then packs hitting the ground. A zipper. An open bottle of water appears in front of him.

"Here," Santi says.

Victor wipes his eyes against his sleeves and rolls over to sit. He takes the water without looking at Santi. He drinks more than he should, but he doesn't care. The cotton in his mouth is finally gone. He swishes some water in his mouth and spits it onto the ground at his side.

"He told me I was out of the house after high school. He told me once I graduated, I wasn't his problem anymore. He told me so many things."

Amelia squats down next to him. She reaches her good arm out to touch him, but stops.

A deep growl of distant thunder causes all three of them to whip their heads up, and although what Victor sees of the sky is mostly cloudless, he knows that relief from the rain is only temporary. There's a chill in the air.

"We should get going," Santi says.

Amelia offers her hand to Victor. "Can you stand?"

The throbbing in his ankle is still there, but he's surprised by how little it hurts now. More of an inconvenience than an injury. He got lucky. Even so, he makes a show of testing it out, limping more than he needs to. Cringing with every step.

Santi reaches for his backpack, but Victor swats his arm away. "I can get it."

"Let me at least—"

"I said I can get it." Acknowledging their kindness would be too much; Victor's ashamed enough already. Pack back on, he shrugs into its weight and adjusts the buckles. "Let's go."

"Your ankle's okay?" she says.

He nods, but once again he steps with an unnecessary wince. It feels important that they see him as injured. He'll be less threatening that way.

"Let's just get around that ridge," Victor says.

Without another word, Santi helps Amelia into her pack, threading her broken arm through the shoulder strap and refastening the sling. Victor tries to ignore the way they look at each other. Once they're all geared up, Santi navigates a path up through the forest. Slowly, apparently out of concern for Victor's injured ankle.

Victor swears not to say another word about the cabin. And no more drinking, even if the others want to dip into Winslow's supply. No more loss of focus. It's all going to be fine, as long as he can regain control. But how to regain control of a situation that—he has to accept—he never had control of in the first place?

The closer they get to the cabin, the more the panic builds inside him. What's worse, the other two seem to feel his anxiety. They share glances when they don't think he's looking. They whisper to each other when he can't keep up with them. What are they saying? What are they planning to do when they get to the cabin? And just how much did he tell them last night?

He can still salvage it, though. He's sure. At least he didn't tell them about the gold. There's no way he would have told them about that. No way. Even he isn't stupid enough. No matter how much he drank last night, there had to have been a part of him that knew not to.

But if he didn't, then why are they whispering to each other like that? Whispering, glancing back, whispering.

It's too much now. The panic comes at him in waves. How did he get here? Hiking through the goddamn wilderness, hungover and milking a rolled ankle, and with people dead behind him, dead and buried under tons of mud.

If he's honest with himself, he knows that it's Winslow's fault, all of it. Without Winslow, he's not here. Without Winslow, he doesn't leave the group at lunchtime, get lost, get stalked by that mountain lion, make everyone late. Without Winslow, the group sets up camp at the planned site. Jerry, Celeste, Rico. Without Winslow, they live. Without Winslow, everyone lives.

27

Elena got an Orange Julius because she always got an Orange Julius. They sat on the second bench in the little sliver of park lining Cherry Creek by the mall because that's where they always sat.

They'd been together for almost a year before she met his mom and Winslow. A year of dates and texts and calls and—ultimately, thrillingly—sex, Victor's first. He had no intention of jeopardizing any of it by letting his family into the picture. But Elena didn't want to be shielded from them. She wanted to be with Victor, she said, and that meant all of him.

It only took three weeks after that first meeting—a dinner that included casual references to immigration policy and repeated comments about how Denver couldn't possibly have enough to offer a young person who was truly curious about the world—for Winslow's poison to seep its way into their relationship. Victor and Elena had tried to hold on, had tried to fight it, but there was nothing they could do.

And the thing was, she wasn't even mad at him. Or maybe she had moved from mad to disappointed, and that made Victor feel even worse.

"So, what, that's it?" she said. "Because he tells you that's it? Because your mom—"

"Don't."

"You're saying she's not part of this?"

His mom would never have been part of this if not for Winslow. Victor knew that to be the truth. Elena would have loved the woman his mom used to be, and his mom would have loved Elena. They would have laughed so much together, probably at Victor's expense most of the time, and none of this would be happening.

"I'm telling you that it has nothing to do with either of them." He was lying, and poorly, and they both knew it. Victor waited for Elena to call him out on it, but she didn't even seem up for that. "I just can't be in a relationship right now. That's all."

"After almost a year. Now you just can't be in a relationship."

He was supposed to get out of Denver, to see the world, to change it! But how could he do that if he got involved with someone? How could he do that if he got her pregnant?

The situation was simple: if he couldn't get his mom and stepdad behind this now, if this relationship was such an issue before she even went to college, before he even finished his junior year, what chance did they actually have?

And who said he even wanted a future with her? He was only a junior!

"You'll be in college next year," he said.

"In Denver—"

"Doesn't matter. We were never going to get through that anyway, so why not just break it off now, before anyone gets hurt."

"You did not just say that."

"You know what I mean."

"What if you just moved out?" she said.

"I'm still in high school," Victor said. "Where would I go?"

"Come live in our garage apartment. Move in—"

"I love you, Elena. You know that." Victor waited for a little girl on rollerblades and her mom to pass by. "But that's crazy."

"Why is it crazy?"

"People don't just move out. And besides, what about your parents? Are they going to pay my tuition now?"

"You don't need to go to private school."

Victor laughed. He didn't mean to, but the laugh was out there whether he'd meant to or not. Elena laughed too. She bit at the end of her straw and looked away. She slurped on her Orange Julius even though there was nothing left.

Finally, she said, "You should go to your dad's."

"I don't even know where he is."

"Find him. Show up."

"I'm just supposed to leave my family—"

She slurped again. "That's not a family, Victor."

28

They hike by moonlight to save the batteries on the headlamps, and an eerie glow removes all color from the landscape, casting ghostly shadows through the trees, over the rocks, making the mountainside feel like another planet entirely. But around midnight, the rain returns, clouds obscuring the moon. The dark is so thick now, a living, breathing thing.

They're nearing the cabin, Victor assures them, a half-mile away, so they strap the headlamps on and power through without stopping to put on rain gear. They'll be dry soon enough.

His fake ankle sprain has gotten fake worse along the way. He's trying to buy himself time, but the more time he buys himself, the darker it gets, the colder it gets, the more miserable they all get. And what is he buying time for?

He wonders if mountain lions are nocturnal.

Victor feels it coming. The loss of control. He can feel himself panicking again, so he makes himself stop. Forces a deep breath, like hitting "reset" on himself.

It'll be uphill, past a boulder the size of a Suburban. So familiar. Victor knows exactly where they are. This was his rock. His place. How many times had he sat here over the last five years, with his .22, waiting for rabbits or marmots or anything stupid enough to come across his path? He'd never been one for meditation, but it didn't take him long to realize that if he was absolutely still, the wilderness would come alive. Mule deer would saunter by in front of him, birds would land right next to him, and those stupid, stupid marmots would poke their fat little heads right up.

He knows this place. He knows the game trail that cuts across the scree. He knows the cluster of tall pine trees encircling the cabin. He's the only one who knows this place.

The temptation, in this moment, to run away and hide. To turn off his headlamp and disappear. To find the cabin by himself. The map is borderline useless in the dark; without the ridgeline to look at, the topo contours mean nothing. The others wouldn't stand a chance. Not until morning, at least.

"You coming?" Santi says.

"Huh? Yeah, sorry. Just resting."

Santi and Amelia trudge back, their headlamps on Victor like the lights of an oncoming truck. He has to turn away to keep his eyes from watering.

"You sure we're close?" she says.

Victor nods. He's tired. So tired.

His clothes are plastered to his skin beneath the backpack, the thighs of his jeans stuck to him as though painted on. They should have put on their rain gear.

They should have done a lot of things.

"Want some peanuts and raisins?" Santi says, holding out a plastic baggie with what's left of the trail mix. "I ate all the M&M's. Sorry."

"What if the phone doesn't work?" Amelia fishes the Advil container from her pocket and hands it to Santi, who shakes it a couple of times.

"One left," he says as he opens it and hands it back to her.

"The phone'll work," Victor says.

Amelia tilts her head back and gulps and washes the pill down with the last of their water. "I'm just saying, what if? I mean, we could have been halfway down the mountain by now. Maybe we would have run into other people. Maybe we could have made better time if we were on the trail. If we weren't headed straight uphill—"

"It's going to work," Victor says again.

Santi whirls on him. "Don't yell at her."

Was he really yelling? He didn't feel like he was yelling. "What else am I supposed to say? It's going to work or it's not going to work. Either way, we're standing out here in the middle of the goddamn rain in the middle of the goddamn night—"

"Have some peanuts," Santi says, tossing the baggie to him.

Victor lets the bag hit him in the chest. "I'm not hungry."

"My ass." Santi shakes his head, and the headlamp beam shifts like a searchlight. "Just so long as you stop yelling at her."

"I don't need a bodyguard," Amelia says.

Victor chuckles. "You guys make a good couple."

"And you make a crappy Boy Scout," she says.

Santi bends down to pick up the plastic baggie. "He's right, though. It doesn't make much sense to worry about it until we get there. If the phone doesn't work, then we use the cabin as a base. There's water, there's food. We get some rest and go downhill. By the time that happens, we'll officially be lost. They'll officially be looking for us."

People like Victor are not supposed to be jealous of people like Santi, yet here they are. Santi is the one Amelia looks at without pity. And Victor is . . . what is he, exactly? If Jerry had lived, maybe they would have been able to figure out the answer to that question in Victor's group session. He chuckles.

"What's so funny?" Amelia says.

Victor stares past their headlamps and wipes away the water dripping down the side of his face. He walks between them, leading the way again, remembering to limp. "What isn't?"

And soon they're wading across the helicopter's landing zone through waist-deep wildflowers. Down the trail made wider every year by runoff from the snowmelt. The cabin hidden until they're almost right on top of it.

The motion detector sets off a floodlight, crisscrossing tree shadows along the cabin's horizontal siding, revealing thick wooden shingles instead of an aluminum roof because Winslow likes the rustic look.

"I'd almost convinced myself that you were making this up," Amelia says.

Victor ignores her. The spare key hangs on a hook underneath the old picnic table by the fire pit outside. In the winter, the table disappears under six, seven, eight feet of snow. It can't have many seasons left in it.

The key does not slide in easily, and Victor turns it upside down to try again, but this is even worse. A sense of alarm begins to creep over him. He leans down, shining his headlamp on the lock at an angle, and turns the key over again. It's like he's stabbing at the lock.

"You want me to give it a try?" Santi says because he's so helpful and caring and kind and nothing bad that ever happened to him has ever been his fault.

But the key slides into the lock, the deadbolt settling flush against the side of the door with a gratifying click. Gratifying because Santi can go to hell. The door is thick, a new addition, installed a year ago after endless discussions with the custom door guy from Durango. Probably carved from a thousand-year-old tree.

Victor leans into it and it opens and he stands in the doorway.

He pauses for a moment before flipping the light switch, passing his headlamp across the room like a TV detective investigating a crime scene. The beam hits the bed-slash-couch in the corner, authentic Indian blankets piled high against the pillows, then lingers on the coffee table by the fireplace. Above the stove, pots and pans dangle from the wrought iron pole stretching from the wall to the center post. The oven's digital clock reads 1:23 AM.

It strikes him that he's never been here alone.

Winslow's rustic wooden shingles muffle the sound of the rain against the roof, which is now only a harmless patter. Victor turns on the light and steps inside, shrugging off his backpack and leaning it against the table near the door.

The others enter behind him, and Victor watches them take the place in. It is impressive, he has to admit. Not so much the size or what's inside, but the fact that it exists at all. Up here, in the middle of nowhere. Electricity and water and a refrigerator.

After Santi helps Amelia out of her pack, she wanders over toward the large sliding glass doors. "I bet the view is amazing."

"Can't put a price tag on it."

"We should start a fire," Santi says, digging through his open backpack and pulling out dry clothes.

"Mi casa es su casa." Victor hears himself speak, and it's as though he's in a dream.

So strange, being here with them, after everything that has happened. So strange being indoors again, where the rain can't get to them. So strange. A small red basket hangs from the center pole, filled with bags of dried fruit. Dates, apricots, cherries, raisins, figs.

"They're past their expiration date," Victor says as he opens a bag of Mission figs. "But that doesn't matter. It's so dry up here, things last forever."

"I kind of thought it would be bigger," Santi says, pulling on a dry white T-shirt.

Victor laughs. "Next time we're stranded in the wilderness, I'll be sure to find a bigger place."

Now Santi's the one laughing. "I meant that as a compliment."

"Can we fill up our water bottles?" Amelia says.

"Cleanest, clearest, coldest water you're ever going to taste." Victor goes to the sink and plays with the faucet; nothing comes out. "I'm going to have to open up the valve downstairs."

"You should get dry first," she says.

"Are you thirsty or not?"

"Ease up," Santi says. "We're here. We made it. You can be happy."

I'll be happy when you're gone, is the first thing that pops into Victor's mind. "We're not supposed to be here."

Amelia tilts her head and gives him a little squint. "He'll understand."

But Winslow won't understand.

It's different now that Victor has made it this far. Now that he's inside the cabin. He thought he'd feel great—triumphant, even—but instead, he's as afraid as he's always been. He feels the way he's always felt in this place: like an intruder.

He feels Winslow's glare burning into him, as if it's radiating out from every item in the house. How can Victor still be scared of a man who isn't even here?

"He doesn't like it when people mess with his things."

"We were stranded. He'll und—"

"Can I go turn on the water now? Are we done with this conversation?"

"Yes, Victor," Amelia says flatly. "I'm thirsty."

"Good." He spins away from them and says over his shoulder, "Just don't touch anything."

He leans hard on the railing as he steps slowly downstairs. Once he's out of view, he puts his full weight on his ankle for the first time all day. The initial steps are tender, as though faking the injury tricked his body into believing it was real, but soon he's able to walk without a limp at all.

Emerging into the basement room, he sees the two single beds. Four closed doors. A small Navajo rug takes up much of the floor. The beds are stripped and unmade, pillows on top of sheets folded at the foot of each. It's all he can do to keep himself from collapsing onto one of them.

The footsteps upstairs change from loud thumping to muted shuffles; those two have taken their shoes off. He checks the doors. As he'd expected, all are unlocked except the one.

He opens the door to the water pump and flips on the light. The room is about six feet wide by twelve feet deep, with two fifty-gallon tanks at the far end taking up most of the space. It's loud in here: water from the underground spring uphill rushing through a diverted pipe, bypassing the house, and flowing back into the small creek below. The pipes freeze in the winter, so they have to drain the whole house before leaving. It's quite the production.

He finds the valve below the green tank and turns it all the way to the right.

A warm shower would feel so good right now, but he decides

against filling the hot water tank. No need to make the place any more comfortable for the others.

Somehow, he'll get rid of them.

And when they leave, he'll do what he came to do, and then he'll take some supplies and he'll go down the mountain, and when he's back home, he'll look Winslow dead in the eyes.

Winslow won't have any idea, not for a while at least. And even then he won't be able to prove anything. But Victor will know. Every dinner table conversation, every family meeting, every single time he looks at the man's face, Victor will know.

The tank has to fill before Victor can turn the pump on and send water up through the house, and that won't happen for a few minutes, so he leans back against the wall and lets his body slide to the ground. So tired.

The footsteps above him have stopped. They must be on the couch. Maybe snuggling together, dry and snuggling as he sits down here with his wet clothes and his ribs throbbing again and now another headache, a dehydration headache made worse by the altitude. He needs water. He needs rest. He needs everything.

Santi and Amelia. He has to get them out of here, and soon. He should call for help tonight, on the satellite phone.

Satellite phone.

Victor laughs in spite of everything. Because that's the funny thing about a lie. In order to make it work, you have to devote yourself to it. If you're less than one hundred percent committed, you're going to slip up, let the truth come out, blow the whole thing apart.

Only now, with them all safely inside, with the water coursing through the wall behind his head, with Santi and Amelia upstairs—in his stepdad's cabin!—doing who-knows-what, does Victor let himself acknowledge that Winslow always takes the satellite phone home with him.

He knew it was a lie when he said it, but what were his other choices? Santi and Amelia had been threatening to go down, and he'd had to think fast, to say something. This was the only way he could convince them. He didn't start out believing it.

He'd only come to believe it because he'd wanted it to be true.

His ankle throbs against the leather of his boot. Maybe the ankle really is hurt. He'll take the boot off in a little while. Right now, he just wants to close his eyes. Everything will sort itself out. He knows this place. He has the advantage. He just needs some rest.

***

A woman's voice says his name. *Victor*. Gentle, kind. And again: *Victor*. He's back home and none of this has happened and his mom is waking him up.

"Victor?"

He opens his eyes to see Amelia squatting down inside the water room doorway. Her feet are bare, and she's wearing dry clothes: Jerry's hemp shorts and a loose white T-shirt. She's reaching out to Victor with her good arm, her bad arm still held close against her stomach, and he sees down her shirt, and she's not wearing a bra because her bra must be wet, and is she coming on to him right now? That doesn't make sense, not at all, what with Santi upstairs and everything—

"We found another first-aid kit. We should take a look at your ankle."

"Huh?" Victor says.

She seems to recognize where he's looking, so she sits back. "What are you doing down here?"

He presses his palms into his face. "Just waiting for the tank to fill up."

"Are you okay?"

"Yeah, sure," he says, pushing himself to his feet and limping over to the green tank, which is full and has been for who knows how long. "Of course. We're good now. Should be good."

"Santi made some cheese and bagels. You should come upstairs."

Victor flips a switch on the wall between the two tanks, and the whir of the small pump fills the room, drowning out the other sounds. "We'll have water soon."

The downstairs sink sputters, spitting out air like a car with a faulty muffler, then finally comes to life. There's water coursing through the house now, so they'll have to close all the faucets. It's on the checklist.

"Where's the phone?" she says. "We should make the call now so they can come get us first thing tomorrow morning."

"In a minute," Victor says. "In a minute."

The tank is cold against his palm, full of water that would otherwise be flowing beneath the house. How lucky they are! Does he have any idea, Winslow always says, how much value the underground spring adds to the property? Not that they'll ever sell it, of course. The cabin is priceless.

Victor stands there long enough, says nothing for long enough, that Amelia goes back upstairs. He's bought himself some time, maybe five minutes, but even he knows that there's no more stalling to be done.

29

By the time Victor was sixteen, he had gotten used to the helicopter. The slight forward lean as it gathered speed, the rollercoaster-like tilt from side to side when it banked a turn, the uneasy wobble when it hovered above the landing zone.

They'd spent more time at the cabin that summer than ever before, because that's what you do when you're a family. You take a helicopter into the middle of nowhere, dragging your stepson away from his friends.

There was no television, no cell service. There was nothing at all to do, which was the whole point, wasn't it? Victor would just have to figure out how to entertain himself.

It was only after he ran out of books to read and hikes to take that he discovered Winslow's old Remington .22. A lever action rifle with a walnut stock, it was leaning on the corner of the mantelpiece—had in fact been there all along—and one morning Victor asked if it was real.

Winslow smiled as he pulled it down. "My father gave it to me." A click sounded as he pulled the lever forward and snapped it back into place. "Have you ever shot one of these?"

"We don't believe in guns," his mom said, but it was as though she didn't mean it. An instinct, a reflex, and then a trace of regret in her eyes.

Winslow smiled. "It's a kid's gun, Lisa."

"Yeah, Mom. If I can't even handle a .22, what good am I?"

A quick tutorial, a box of bullets, a warning not to shoot himself in the foot, and Victor was off. He hiked uphill and set up a row of empty cans. The first time he actually shot the gun, he was surprised at how fake it sounded. The pop was high-pitched, almost like a cap gun, nothing like the low brashness of the guns in the movies.

He sucked at first. Little tufts of dirt exploded behind the cans. Then he realized that, like a dumbass, he was closing his eyes a split-second before pulling the trigger. It was a good thing Winslow hadn't been there.

After that, though, Victor only got better. He taught himself to control his breath, to settle his hands, to keep his eye on the target throughout the whole process. Starting with cans, then wildflowers, and then birds sitting on branches. The first time he shot a marmot, his cry of victory echoed throughout the valley. Sometimes it felt like the only time Winslow wasn't sneering at him was when Victor asked him to buy more ammo.

One afternoon, chased inside by a sudden thunderstorm, Victor walked into the cabin to the sound of his mother and Winslow yelling at each other.

"This place used to be about getting *away* from business," she said. "You said so yourself."

"I'm talking real wealth, Lisa. Long-term, generational wealth."

"Why do you need *more*?"

Victor almost didn't believe his ears. As what seemed like a matter of policy, his mom and Winslow never so much as raised their voices at each other around him, to say nothing of actually *fighting* in front of him.

He drifted toward the top of the stairs even though he knew he shouldn't have.

"And what about Victor?" his mom said. "This is your time with him. Up here, you promised."

Victor could only imagine the look on Winslow's face; his mom might as well have suggested that Winslow spend more time drinking his own piss.

He darted away at the sound of approaching footsteps, and by the time Winslow emerged from downstairs, Victor managed to fake having just come into the living room, his rifle slung over his shoulder.

"I got a chipmunk," Victor said. "Really tiny one too."

Winslow brushed past him, grabbing his raincoat from a hook by the front door. "I'm going for a walk."

"It's pouring outside," Mom said, but the door had already closed.

She plastered on a smile and sat on the makeshift couch with a stack of magazines. Not having any idea what to do, but certain that he didn't want to linger awkwardly in the same room as his mom, Victor took his rifle downstairs.

The door—the one Winslow always locked—was cracked open. Victor pushed slowly against the wood, slid through the opening, and . . . How boring. An office with a desk.

He didn't know what he'd been expecting, but a simple office didn't seem worth all the lock-and-key business. Lying open on the desk was a briefcase with a phone inside, like some sort of mobile command unit. The big liar. All this time, Victor had been told that there was no way to contact the outside world.

Still, a secret satellite phone didn't seem worth the locked door either.

Next to the phone was an oblong golden paperweight about the size of a tennis ball. Dented and bulging, it looked like a clump of dried play-dough. Victor moved around the desk and looked up at the walls, which were papered with maps.

Old maps, new ones. Some with topo lines, some that looked hand drawn. Aerial-view photographs tacked on top in places. Each map with a distinctive stamp in the bottom right corner. San Juan Mining Company. Gold Cloud Mining Company. Elias Bristlecone Mining Company. Felton Mining Incorporated. Rectangles on the maps, highlighted in blue and yellow and orange, isolated here, overlapping there.

Victor looked from the maps to the gold paperweight on the desk and then to the maps again. He stepped closer to the wall, squinted at a series of circles that must have been drawn in red marker.

"You shouldn't be in here."

He jumped at the sound of his mom's voice. She stood in the doorway, wringing her hands together. "What is all this stuff?" he said.

"He wouldn't want you to be in here."

"You're not afraid of him, are you?" She said nothing. Victor stepped back around the desk toward the door. "Are you?"

"He doesn't like it when people . . . you know."

Any questions Victor had about the mining maps were pushed aside by the way his mom kept glancing over her shoulder.

"Mom, you married him."

"Come upstairs. Let me get you some hot chocolate. You must be chilly."

She ushered him out and closed the door. They stepped wordlessly up the stairs, and by the time Winslow had returned from his walk, she had a cup of hot chocolate waiting for him too.

30

Victor pauses just below the top of the stairs, tries to listen to them talking, but he can't make out any words. They sound oddly happy, though. Occasional laughter punctuates the muffled conversation.

He's trapped. So many times over the last two days he could have avoided this. Could have left Santi during the storm. Even after they found Amelia, he could simply have refused to go anywhere with them.

No, he thinks, that's not entirely true. He'd needed the map. Once the mountain lion came into the picture, once he'd lost his own map, he'd had no choice. It wasn't his fault—he couldn't have anticipated those things.

But now he doesn't have any choice. They're here, and they need to be gone.

He takes a couple of tentative steps with his ankle, getting the limp right, and then turns the corner into the living space. They stop talking—of course they stop; they must have been talking about him—and watch as he opens the cabinet, pulls out a glass, and fills it at the kitchen sink.

He has to give Winslow credit. It *is* the clearest, cleanest, coldest water Victor has ever put to his lips, and he takes the glass down in one pull. Fills another, then another. The others still haven't said anything.

"Do you want to play cards?" he says, setting the glass in the sink. "I'm pretty sure we have a couple of decks up here."

The look Santi gives him is priceless. Open-mouthed. Eyes blinking. Head shaking slightly in disbelief.

He moves over to the table, careful to remember the limp, careful not to overdo it.

"Maybe we can play cards after we call for help?" Amelia says, her arm in the sling again. He notices she's wearing a black bra now, can see it through the thin fabric of her T-shirt. Jerry's shorts come down past her knees. She looks ridiculous.

"In a minute. I'm starving." The bagels and cheese feel dry in his mouth, so he limps back to the sink and fills up another glass of water. He can sense their impatience in the air. How is he supposed to get them out of here?

"I wonder what they thought, you know? What went through their heads when the mudslide came. Or if they even thought of anything. If they were so tired that it just took them before they even woke up." Victor finally turns to them and leans back against the counter. "Amelia, what did you think?"

Santi finally speaks. "Come on, Victor—"

"I'm not jumping over the net, am I? Notice how I'm asking about her feelings? Notice how respectful I'm being?"

"I don't want to talk about it," she says, keeping her gaze on his.

"You survived. Why not talk about it? I'd be celebrating." Little crumbs of bagel tumble from Victor's mouth, landing on the counter next to the sink. Mice will come if he doesn't clean them up. Winslow hates mice.

His mouth has never been so dry. It reminds Victor of the

time Davis Higley challenged him to eat ten saltines and whistle. They were eight years old, and they giggled like little girls as Victor blew cracker powder all over his friend.

"Victor?" Amelia says.

"You guys need to leave." He doesn't look up when he says it. Doesn't want to see the reactions because he doesn't know what to say after that.

But he imagines the looks on their faces. Santi probably all angry, sneering, or the opposite, a disbelieving laugh, like *Good one, Victor.* Amelia probably with the same vacant expression as when she'd stumbled upon them after the mudslide. Eyes seeing but not believing.

Then Amelia says, "What?"

And Santi says, "We need to use that phone, is what we need to do."

"There is no phone," Victor says.

"You said there was a phone."

"I can't find it." Victor keeps his voice calm, trying to lay out the basic facts of the situation. "It's not here. We shouldn't be here either. You need to go."

Where they should go when they leave doesn't really occur to him, only that they need to leave. And frankly, he doesn't care. They can take their food and the map and hike straight downhill and they'll run into the trail eventually.

It's not even his fault that they're here. He told them to go down, and then he told them not to follow him. His hands are clean on this one.

"Bullshit," Santi says. "You want to tear up your stepdaddy's crib, go right ahead. The hell do I care? But you better let us use the phone."

Victor plants both feet firmly on Winslow's reclaimed

hardwood floors—from an old pickle factory in Pennsylvania!—and says again, "There is no phone."

Santi steps toward Victor, who tenses his fists, ready. "If there's no phone, why are we even here? It doesn't make any sense."

"You should have gone down when you could." It takes everything Victor has to keep his voice measured and even. He's never been very good at that part. "I told you to go down without me."

"Where are we supposed to go now?" Amelia says.

"Why are you even on this trip?" he says to her, contempt trickling into his voice. "What are you doing here?"

"Where's the phone, Victor?" Santi says.

"What part of 'There's no phone' do you not—"

Before Victor finishes, Santi runs over to the bookshelf to the left of the fireplace and starts pulling down books. It happens so fast—Victor trying so hard to remain calm—that he doesn't react until at least a dozen volumes, including his mom's dog-eared *Southern Colorado Birder's Anthology* and two of the leather-bound guest books—oh God, not those—have already been tossed across the room.

"Santi!" Amelia says.

Victor leaps across the small room, but Santi has already cleared the shelf. Books litter the floor like dead pigeons. Spines cracked, pages bent, covers splayed open. "Where's the phone? It doesn't make any sense."

Santi keeps the coffee table in between them. He feints right, then darts left, and he's past Victor and to the stairs before Victor can react.

Amelia jumps up between Victor and the staircase. "You guys—"

She yelps in pain as Victor pushes her aside. He's got his full weight on both ankles now, doesn't care anymore about pretending he's hurt.

Doors downstairs open and close and then Victor catches up to Santi just as he's slamming the door to the storage closet.

"Stop," Victor says, and he's trying to be strong but his voice comes out pleading. "Let's talk about this."

Santi runs to the office door. Victor is bigger, and he should be able to stop him, but Victor can't make himself react. He can't match Santi's rage or energy. The best he can do is yell, "Stay away from there!"

Santi stops with one hand on the doorknob. Looks at Victor. Cocks his head as if he understands.

Amelia appears at the bottom of the stairs.

"I don't have the key," Victor makes himself say. "He never lets anyone in there."

Santi jiggles the knob a little, but of course it's locked like it always is, and the slight pause in the action is enough. Enough for Victor to step forward, to break out of his trance. He dives at Santi, tackles him around the waist, and their momentum rips Santi's hand off the knob. They stagger away from the door.

Santi knees him once in the stomach, and Victor loses his breath for a second and lets go of Santi's waist and steps back to recover. He gasps for air, but now the adrenaline has come. He's going to kick Santi's ass like he should have a long time ago, and he hardly feels anything. Adrenaline coursing through his body, making him strong again.

Victor swings wildly and misses and loses his balance, but he manages to pull Santi down to the hardwood with him, and now they're not even really punching each other anymore, just rolling on the ground, clawing, pushing at each other's faces.

Then an elbow to Victor's cheekbone, a lucky elbow, and his eyes start to water and he can't see. It doesn't hurt, not really, but he can't see, and he feels another hand on him, on his leg, pulling him back, and he squints through the tears and sees Santi escaping ahead of him.

He kicks the other hand away, hears a high-pitched yelp from Amelia. Then two loud thuds. He pulls himself up to his feet just as the sound of splintering wood fills the room.

The door is open. Santi is inside.

Victor takes a step toward the office, but his legs don't want to work, and he stumbles to his knees. His fingers tremble uncontrollably until he makes fists, shakes his hands out, makes fists again. His heart crashes against his damaged ribs. He wipes tears away with the back of his wrist.

Santi runs back past him, enraged, and disappears upstairs yelling words Victor doesn't understand, leaving Victor there on the basement floor. Amelia stands at the foot of the staircase, glowering at him. Victor wishes she would say something. Then a clattering comes from above and she follows Santi upstairs without a word.

Still breathing heavily, Victor turns back to Winslow's office and pushes himself to his feet. The doorjamb is shattered. Shards of wood, some as big as his arm, litter the floor inside. The maps that had papered the walls lie crumpled and shredded around the small room. The desk lies on its side, drawers half open, contents scattered about: stapler, pens, note cards, paperclips, hundreds of sheets of paper.

He lifts the desk right-side up, and the drawers rattle as he shoves it against the wall. He kicks aside the torn maps on the floor, the office supplies. He checks the drawers and checks them again and then pulls them all out and turns them over just to be sure. He drops to his hands and knees, his cheek flush against the hardwood.

It has to be here.

Victor had managed to get inside the room only once more after his first look—Winslow, on a hike with Victor's mom, had uncharacteristically left the door unlocked—but once more was enough. The maps. That argument with Victor's mom about wealth. The chunk of gold just lying on the desk as if it were nothing.

Winslow had reopened the dormant mines.

When Victor got home, a little research told him that the nugget on Winslow's desk could be worth over $100,000, and that's when the plan began to take shape.

He would figure out a way to get up there by himself somehow. He would learn how to pick a lock—that turned out to be the easy part; lock-pick set delivered to his home, how-to videos abundant online—and he'd break into this room without a trace, and he'd take the paperweight with him.

And if he did it right, Winslow would never be able to prove a thing. The man's suspicions would make it even sweeter. Now Winslow would know what it was like to live with someone who had stolen what he valued most. Now Winslow would be angry and hurt and unable do anything about it.

Only now, the door is cracked and the doorjamb is destroyed. Only now, on his hands and knees, shuffling among the mangled maps, Victor can't find the paperweight.

Only now, the cabin is a mess and the gold is nowhere to be found and there is going to be hell to pay.

31

Victor and Davis Higley had grown up together. Played together. Gone to school together. Friends at first because their mothers were friends, then something closer to family after Victor's dad left, sharing the holiday kids' table. Mother's Days, Thanksgivings, Easters.

It got old by the time they were twelve. Year after year of dinners together, and every time, Davis's mother telling Victor's mother how well Davis was doing in school, how Davis was the captain of the soccer team, how Davis and Rachel Fisher were so happy together. And every time, Davis's dad taking it upon himself to provide Victor with the fatherly advice he was no longer getting at home.

By the time Winslow joined the fun, it was so far past old that Victor rarely said a word.

"That guy seems to have it all together," Winslow told Victor more than once. "You should pick his brain some. See if he has any tips for you."

What kind of a name was Davis anyway? Who could trust a guy with a last name as a first name? Might as well have been Wellington. Wellington Davis the Third.

They'd been Webelos together. Graduated from Cub Scouts to Boy Scouts together. And only a month before the end of their junior year, the two soon-to-be Eagle Scouts stood in the park together.

It was a bluebird Sunday afternoon. Victor and Davis in full uniform behind a folding picnic table covered with stacks of scouting literature. *Troop 99* emblazoned on their shoulders. The yellow bandanas around their necks. Hiking boots and wool socks pulled halfway up their calves because their scoutmaster thought it best they "look the part."

Torture. Every second he had to spend with Davis was a reminder of what he would never be. While Davis flagged people down, selling himself, selling scouting, Victor decided he wouldn't talk unless he was answering a direct question.

"How's your project coming?" Davis said during a lull in the traffic.

Victor's Eagle Scout service project—a neighborhood lending library—was not going well. He was only halfway through building the shelf, and he hadn't even started to collect books to fill it. He knew better than to ask about Davis's project, though. Some crap about renewable energy education or recycling or reducing carbon footprints. The asshole had already been on the local news twice.

"It's good," Victor said.

"I'm sure it will be awesome."

"Fuck off, Davis," Victor said.

It was the first time he had ever actually told Davis to fuck off, and now that he'd done it, he wondered why he had waited so long. The satisfaction of that one puzzle piece finally clicking into place. It just felt so right.

"What did you say?"

"You heard me."

"Okay," Davis laughed. "Might as well get it out in the open."

"Get what out in the open?"

"Come on, Victor, I've been dragging your ass along with me for the last three years. My mom took pity on you, what with your dad leaving and everything, and she told me to make sure you made it to Eagle."

"What the hell are you talking about, took pity on me?"

"I get it," Davis said. "Your dad left and your stepdad is kind of an ass. But damn, dude, you have to stop feeling sorry for yourself."

Then suddenly Victor had done it.

The first punch was to wipe the shit-eating grin from Davis's face. He threw the second punch because the first punch felt so good.

Davis hit back, but Victor didn't even feel it—the pain of it, at least. Felt pressure on the side of his body, on his chest, but not the pain. Like when he got a cavity filled at the dentist, he could feel the dentist working around in there, but not the pain. It was miraculous.

Davis pushed him away and staggered backward, stunned. Victor recognized the look on his face. Betrayal, surprise. Life wasn't supposed to work this way. His eyes were watering.

Victor lowered his shoulder into the other boy's chest and the two of them crashed into the picnic table. Brochures went flying as a table leg buckled. Victor was on top of Davis now. He ripped the stupid yellow scarf from around his neck and threw it to the side.

To say that Victor had snapped wouldn't be exactly right. That would imply that he had been whole and then became broken, but that's not what it felt like. In fact, it was the opposite.

He was made whole. Everything he hated was right there in front of him, and he could *do something* about it! Davis with the house. Davis with the family. Davis with the father.

Victor felt hands on his shoulders, trying to pull him away, but at that point it didn't matter, because Davis was getting hit and getting hit and getting hit and Victor was the one doing the hitting.

32

Victor stops in the doorway because of how closely they're huddled next to each other. Because of how quiet the living room is. They shouldn't be this quiet after the fight downstairs. They don't see him.

Amelia rests her good hand on Santi's shoulder. They both look down at something in Santi's hand. She whispers into his ear, and Santi shakes his head. She whispers again, this time with more urgency but Victor still can't hear, and Santi shakes his head again.

But then Amelia shifts her weight and a space opens up between her body and Santi's, and Victor catches a glimpse of the object in Santi's hand.

Victor steps into the room now, next to the fireplace now, but they don't even seem to notice.

And what had been in Santi's hand is now in his pocket.

And what's in Victor's hand is the Remington.

And Victor is halfway downstairs again before he even wonders if they saw him grab the thing off the mantelpiece.

With the office door shattered, Victor's original plan will never work, but he can figure out another way. Until then, Victor will fix the maps, put the books on the shelves, drain the house so the pipes won't freeze. Winslow will forgive him if he explains everything, if he explains how Santi tried to rob the place and how Victor stopped it from happening. He can blame everything on Santi, but first he needs Santi to give back the paperweight.

Santi won't just hand it over, so Victor needs the rifle. He'll point it at them, wave it around a bit, and get the gold back. But if Santi calls his bluff, he'll have to do something, right? Like a warning shot, to prove he's not messing around. He has to load it. Just in case.

The ammo is exactly where it should be, on the second shelf to the right of the door in the storeroom. The little box refilled just as he'd left it. A hundred bullets in the clear plastic case, a ten-by-ten grid, each bullet rattling against the edges of its own little slot as Victor snatches the box off the shelf.

He kneels on the hardwood floor, lays the butt of the rifle between his knees, and lets the barrel rest against his shoulder. He unscrews the loading rod from below the barrel and pulls it out and his fingers are shaking as he pushes the ammo through the little bullet-shaped hole.

A little scrape as each bullet slides down the magazine and a click when it reaches the bottom. One, two, three bullets, and then one leaps from his fingers and clanks on the floor. Victor holds his breath. Like a marble on the hardwood, the sound echoes, seems too loud for its size.

The bullet stops against the feet of an old coat rack. Victor lets himself exhale, tries to hear any part of the conversation upstairs, but they must still be whispering.

Back to the Remington. Another bullet loaded, then another, and another, and now he's lost count. Why does he need to load the full fifteen rounds, anyway? So he stops. He guides the loading rod back into the magazine. It takes both hands. Victor turns it the wrong way at first, and it doesn't catch, but once he tries clockwise, the rifle is loaded. He'll put the ammo box back later.

His kneecaps twitch when he stands, but his legs work well enough to get him back upstairs.

He turns the corner into the living room and sees Santi wearing a raincoat, hunched over the top of an open backpack, stuffing things inside. Amelia stands just behind him, a red poncho in the hand of her good arm.

Santi freezes the moment Victor steps into the room. Amelia yelps and hops backward, and the poncho opens like a parachute as it flies out of her hand.

Victor holds the gun across his chest. He doesn't point it at them, can't bring himself to actually point it at them yet. Now that he's here, in the room, holding the gun across his chest—not pointing it at them—the idea of bluffing Santi into handing over the gold seems ludicrous.

"Give it back," he says to Santi anyway.

"Those were mining maps in there," Amelia says, blinking through her realization. "You came up here to steal—"

"Nobody was supposed to come with me. I told you to stay. I tried to get you to stay."

Still hunched over the open backpack, Santi says, "You're not going to kill me."

"I'll let you take as much food as you want," Victor says. "I'll give you the map, and you can go down to the bottom of the trail and flag a car. You can say that there was a mudslide and you don't know where I am, and that's how you get out of this. All you have to do is give back what you stole from me. What you stole from him."

"Victor," Amelia says. Too slowly, too gently. "This isn't you. You're not thinking clearly."

171

"How do you know who I am? You're just some debutante from Houston who's never had shit go wrong."

She's coming at him with her good hand up, toward him like she's not afraid of what he's going to do, like she has no idea what he's capable of. "I know you don't want to be doing this."

"You don't know anything about me! Why do you think I'm even on this trip? You think I'm an Eagle Scout? I put my best friend in the hospital!"

Santi still hasn't moved, not even an inch, and Amelia finally seems to notice this. "Santi?"

Victor wants to scream, but he's not going to. That will only make things worse. "You think I don't see you working against me already? You think I don't know what happened last night after I went to sleep?"

"Nothing happened," Amelia says.

"You think I'm stupid!"

He doesn't mean to point it at them. He really doesn't. And besides, it's more of a wave anyway, kind of a swipe across the room, but Amelia shrieks, a mix of fear and pain as she covers her eyes with her forearm. Santi snaps up, hands in front of him, and he finally looks scared.

Amelia's going to cry soon. Victor can hear it in her voice even though he can't see her face.

"I don't think you're stupid, Victor."

"Holy shit," Santi says. "This is crazy."

"This was supposed to be mine! I had a plan! You should have left when you could. I told you to leave."

"Let's think about this, okay?" Amelia says. "We can fix it. What do you want to do?"

The idea comes to him fully formed. He sees himself in brief glimpses—snapshots—packing food, lacing his boots with a double knot. Setting the fire. Running. Escaping.

"Burn it," he says. "I'll burn it all down. He'll never know."

Santi is moving now, gradually placing himself between Amelia and the gun like he thinks he's some hero. He's staring at Victor the whole time. Side step, side step, but Amelia is crying now, crying for real, and Victor can't concentrate. If she would just shut up, he would be able to think.

"Stop crying!"

"It's in the middle of a forest," she says, trying to stifle her tears. "You can't do that."

"Don't tell me what I—"

Santi snakes his hand out toward the kitchen counter and all of the sudden he's holding a knife, pointing a chef's knife at Victor—that's why he was moving across the room.

"Santi!" Amelia says.

Victor almost laughs. "Are you out of your fucking mind?"

Santi sidesteps back across the room, knife out the whole time, and he slides one of his arms through the strap of the backpack. He kicks the poncho over to Amelia, and it lands at her feet. She seems to resist looking at it.

"Santi," she whispers.

But Santi won't stop staring at Victor, won't stop pointing the knife at him, won't stop moving toward the door.

"Stop." Victor raises the rifle and points it directly at Santi. His throat is suddenly dry. "Please stop."

The barrel trembles and becomes blurry and Victor feels a thin strip of metal pressing into the skin of his index finger.

Someone is stealing from his stepdad, and Victor is going to be blamed for it. And it makes no sense at all, but he has never pointed a gun at another person before and none of this makes sense.

AMELIA

33

Amelia Timmons looks at the shadowy outline of Celeste next to her. Celeste curled into a ball, the sleeping bag covering her head as it has every night. Sleeping like a stone, or a log, or a baby. Sleep being her escape from the day.

This was a mistake, this whole thing is a mistake. Everything about it.

Screw it, Amelia thinks. If she can't reverse the mistake, at least she has a way to take the sting out of it.

The patter of rain on the tent masks the rustling sound of her sleeping bag's nylon cover as Amelia sits on top of it, sliding her legs into her jeans. She eases her arms into her rain jacket, opens the tent's door flap, just wide enough to crawl through. Zip. Zip. Zip. She can hear the zipper's teeth opening individually, like the starting clicks of a roller coaster.

Amelia crouches in the tiny space of the vestibule and puts her feet into her still-wet hiking boots. The fabric of the rainfly presses against her back. There's a headlamp in the pocket of her raincoat, but she doesn't dare turn it on—not yet.

More zipping. The roller coaster rises as she closes the tent, opens the vestibule, closes it again.

Screw it, she thinks again as she sloshes uphill toward her backpack. This is all too much. Too much sharing and responsibility and too much leadership and too much of basically everything.

The pretending is the hardest part. Pretending that she's in some sort of control, pretending that she has any idea what she's doing. One week of orientation with Jerry and the rest of the Bear Canyon staff was not enough. One week of role playing—not enough to prepare her for Celeste. When Celeste cries in the tent, in the anonymity of the dark, crying that she doesn't know what to do, has fucked up her life so bad, has ruined everything. When Celeste asks Amelia what to do now, what does Amelia say? What is she supposed to say?

She knows what she wants to say.

She wants to say that they're not so different, she and Celeste.

She wants to say, *No shit, life sucks. Let's go get high.*

But she can't. She's supposed to listen. She's supposed to share the experiences Jerry assumes are hers, the decisions he assumes she's made, to try to show Celeste and the others that there is another way. That a person can make good choices. She's supposed to say all of this from her side of the net, not offering feedback, just telling her own stories and letting the others make the connections for themselves. It's more impactful that way—that's what the research says.

Now under the canopy of some sort of pine tree, Amelia kneels to tie her wet laces. The drops coming through the branches are less frequent but much larger; when even one of them hits her hood or shoulder, it sounds like the crack of a distant rifle.

Mud squishes underneath her boots as she passes Jerry's tent. Jerry and Rico. Poor little Rico. She probably has more in common with him than with any of them. The need for approval, the awkwardness, the cluelessness, the lack of self-confidence, the—

See, this is her problem. Too much thinking. Too much self-exploration.

She wants *not* to think. She wants not to self-explore. She wants to get out of her own head.

On with the headlamp now. She's far enough from the tents that the light would be out of view even if someone happened to wake up. Her pack dangles from a branch, and she unties the rope, easing the pack to the ground. She unfastens the two clips and flips over the top pouch. One final glance over her shoulder, even though only an idiot would be out here in the rain.

She unwraps the garbage bag lining the main compartment and reaches into the bottom for her last clean pair of wool socks—the pair she was never planning on wearing. Inside is a Ziploc inside of another Ziploc. Double-bagging it, just in case.

After re-twisting the garbage bag and re-latching the top pouch, she leans the pack against the tree trunk and brings the little package into the light of her headlamp. A silver flask; a beautiful, engraved panel of stained teak wood on the front. An owl. A gift from her ex-boyfriend. It was custom, he'd said. One of a kind, he'd said. Just like her, he'd said.

She'd filled it to the top, but she doesn't need all of it, really, just a little something to take the edge off. A little something to steer her mind away from this place and these people.

Along with the flask, the baggie holds a pack of gum and a tiny sample bottle of perfume: extra protection for afterwards. Better to smell like perfume than tequila, and if they notice the scent of lavender tomorrow, it'll just reinforce what everyone thinks of her. Yep, just little ol' Amelia from Houston, Texas. Bringing perfume into the wilderness.

Playing the role.

It's not like she's going to get hammered. Besides, given all the pressure she's under, it barely even counts. She crosses the little creek, which seems not to be as little as it was during the day, and walks for a minute or two longer. Just to be safe.

That first sip. That bite always so surprising, the bitter warmth, that burn down the back of her throat. She closes her eyes as she swallows.

The rain around her seems to intensify, but it could just be the tingling from the tequila. She sees herself doing all of this, watching herself as she might have watched the others. Judging as she might have judged the others.

These last few days, she'd convinced herself that she wasn't going to drink it. That the trip would be like a window cleaning, that it was going to wipe away the grime that had built up over the last few years.

But she didn't even make it a week.

She laughs to herself a bit. I should be on the trip, she thinks, not leading it.

It's been maybe twenty minutes since she left her tent, and now the rain starts to come sideways, and while her jacket is holding up well enough, soon she's soaked from the waist down. It doesn't matter; she's been soaked the whole week. And her pants are quick-drying, so she can just tie them to the side of her pack tomorrow. If it's not still raining, because then it wouldn't matter anyway.

Besides, she's not cold. Not now.

Reaching into her pocket, she opens the two baggies with one hand and maneuvers the flask back inside. It's the strangest thing: every time she touches the engraving, she thinks, *Tyler Stafford gave this to me.* Even though she hasn't seen him in months. His full name still on the tip of her tongue.

It's hard to remember now. With how it ended, those last weeks. The fighting and yelling and—worse than anything— the late-night phone calls, silence for minutes at a time, neither of them able to say anything, neither of them able to hang up. It's hard to remember what they were trying to save.

But she should try, shouldn't she? She should try to remember how Tyler felt like home after a life spent moving from country to country, from city to city. Should try to remember the lightness of her breath when his hand reached around her back, that index finger tracing the skin just under her belt. She should remember, because otherwise, what was the point of it all?

Something's wrong.

Another sound joins the patter of rain on her hood, that second sound growing louder. She's never heard anything like it, but it's wrong, so clearly wrong, even though she doesn't know why.

The earth seems to rumble, but not from thunder. And now she can't even hear the rain.

Camp. She has to get back there, has to get back in her tent and lie down and crawl into her sleeping bag and let the Cuervo ease her to sleep. Running now, but the ground is slippery and rocky and wet and there's no oxygen up here. The headlamp is pulled tight over the hood of her raincoat, so she can't see much from side to side, either. The beam hits rocks, trees, little tufts of grass.

The sound is growing louder. Constant now. The source of it getting closer with every unstable step she takes.

She trips, because of course she does, and the headlamp flies off her head and into the muck, and it's gone. She screams into the ground because it's the only thing she can think of doing.

She looks straight ahead, but with the clouds, the rain, the night, she can barely make out the terrain. Pushing herself up on her hands and knees, she uses the sleeve of her raincoat to wipe the mud from her face, from her mouth.

Her coat is soaked through.

Amelia staggers blindly ahead. She has to be close to camp. That deafening noise more like rumbling thunder now. But the thunder isn't coming from above; it's coming from straight ahead.

A river. She's not *that* drunk, is she? After a couple of sips? She would have remembered a river.

A light appears uphill, across the creek which is no longer a creek, and she slips, climbs again, and now she's standing on top of a boulder.

"Help me!" she screams, and the light starts bobbing toward her.

Guilt floods through her, nearly choking her. The others are out in the rain, searching for her. Celeste probably woke up and saw that Amelia wasn't there and got worried when Amelia didn't come back. The darkness, the rain, and Amelia's out of the tent, not safe, and the others are looking for her, risking their lives for her, and because she was drinking to get out of her own head.

"Help me!" she screams again. She clambers down off the rock, toward the current, but there's no way she can cross. It's too strong, too fast. So loud.

The light bounces toward her, and it's Santi, and he's kind of hopping. "Are you hurt?" he yells. He's only wearing one boot. As he adjusts his headlamp, the beam sweeps down across his face, only for a moment, and Amelia can see that he's terrified.

She opens her mouth, but all of the sudden, the constant rumble grows louder, and there's a tremendous gust of wind coming from uphill.

She doesn't know what makes her climb back on the boulder. Instinct, maybe, but probably luck. She pulls herself onto the rock and looks up to see a wall of black coming toward her. When she jumps backward, the boulder jumps right after her, knocking into Amelia while her feet are off the ground. Like a bus. The impact spins her around and throws her ten, fifteen feet backward, and she's flying.

She's flying.

The sound is deafening, and Santi is gone, everything is gone, and she lands and feels her arm snap, and so much pain that she's going to vomit, but before that happens, the darkness gets even darker and now there's nothing.

***

It's dawn when she opens her eyes again. Dawn when she tastes the earth in her mouth. Dawn when her left arm throbs. She gasps from the pain, pushes the grit from her mouth with her tongue, but she does not move. She doesn't even know if she can move. But her eyes are open, and as long as she can see, she's alive.

As long as there's pain, she's alive.

Her clothes are soaked through, even beneath her raincoat. She has no idea where she is. Shivering. Her entire body aches, but her arm hurts the most, more than anything she's ever felt.

A push up with her right arm, settling back onto her haunches as a wave of queasiness overtakes her. Then one foot on the ground, another foot. Standing up through the nausea.

A thick brown expanse coats the mountainside, mud as far as she can see, with boulders, branches, and snapped tree trunks strewn among the ooze. It's like an enormous melted scoop of Rocky Road ice cream. She starts climbing up through it.

The others.

They're probably still out looking for her, hours later. She'll need a story. Santi and Victor will have told Jerry about seeing her, and he'll want to know why she was out of her tent.

She notices a wool sock lying on the mud behind a snapped-off pine branch. Gray wool with a bright orange heel, which means it belongs to Jerry. Amelia decides to grab it for him; maybe he won't be as mad if she comes back with his lost sock.

Except that as she gets closer, she sees that the sock still covers a foot. Heel facing the sky, toes pointing downhill. Body under the surface.

She drops to her knees and tries to dig him free with the arm that isn't killing her, but the mud has hardened like cement, and after a minute of frantic scratching, she hasn't even cleared away an inch.

The sock has a tiny hole in the heel, she notices. Of course it does. She tries not to picture his body underneath, but she can't help it. Jerry is dead.

She should be dead too, she thinks, and the sensation spreading through her is not relief. It's shame, regret. Guilt.

Tears overwhelm her until there are no more of them left. And when she's done, she lies on the mud beside him.

34

The fire crackled through the silence. They sat in a circle, evenly spaced, the second night of the trip, their faces illuminated by the flickering embers, with Jerry leading Santi's group sharing exercise and Amelia trying to learn. It was important that she learn.

"We moved to Albuquerque after that," Santi said as his heel carved a rut in the dirt in front of him. "Living with my mom's brother, Ray."

Santi was still a mystery to her. Technically, he deserved to be here. He was, after all, the only one sent by an actual judge. But so much about him didn't seem to fit. The way he walked, for one, all gangly, like bad computer animation. How does a guy who walks like a newborn giraffe end up in juvie for stealing a car? Or the way he occasionally stopped in the middle of the trail to look around, to take in the scenery while the others powered forward, heads down like they were on a busy city sidewalk.

"None of this matters," Santi said. "You have to know that, don't you?"

Jerry let the question linger in the embers of the fire. "None of what matters?"

"You can be as careful as you want. You can wear your

helmet and put on your seat belt and look both ways before crossing the street. You can stay out of trouble and hang with the right crew and finish your homework and eat your vegetables and none of it matters." Santi took a deep breath and kept his eyes focused on the fire. "This place, this trip. It's fucking pointless."

"It's not pointless," Jerry said.

"Life is life," Santi said. "We can't do nothing about it."

Amelia shuddered, but not from the cold. Jerry glanced at her, concern flashing across his face, before turning his eyes back to Santi. She didn't know how he could do this, how Jerry could maintain his serenity, his patience, his optimism week after week, trip after trip. Up against such anger and self-doubt every time.

Her mom's voice popped into her head: *Jerry will be a marvelous reference someday.*

"I just wish everything could go back to the way it was," Santi was saying now. "Me and my dad and my sister. No onion ring, no Tahoe, no broken family."

Victor snorted. Everyone looked at him.

"Sorry," Victor said. "It's just . . . 'broken family'?"

"Don't be such a dick," Santi said.

Before Victor could respond, Jerry gave both Victor and Santi the stop-sign hands and said, "Let's try that again, Santi. Okay?"

"Wait, *me*?" Santi said. "Let's try that again, *Santi*?"

Amelia noticed Victor smiling. She noticed Santi notice it too. Jerry waited. Victor waited. Finally, Santi forced himself to say, "Don't be so inconsiderate."

"Remember not to cross the net," Jerry said. "Stay on your side. How can you rephrase that? Try an *I feel* statement."

This was, Amelia had learned, one of the linchpins of the Bear Canyon method. Personal growth made possible through the effective give and take of feedback. The effective give and take of feedback made possible through *I feel* statements.

The fire popped. Santi took a deep breath and then said to Victor, "I feel that you're being inconsiderate."

Rico laughed. Jerry shot him a quick look and said, "Try again, Santi."

"When you say those things," Santi said, slowly, pausing to chew at the inside of his cheek, "I feel ignored and rejected."

"Good!" Jerry said with a clap. Bless his heart, Amelia thought. "That's good! Can you see that keeps Victor from being defensive? If you say, 'Victor, you're being inconsiderate,' his immediate response is bound to be something like, 'No, I'm not.' Am I right, Victor?"

Victor shrugged.

I feel that the Bear Canyon method is total bullshit, Amelia thought. No, that wasn't right. That was an *I think* statement disguised as an *I feel*. Try again. Okay, *I feel* anxious about the fact that the Bear Canyon method is total bullshit.

35

"Look at you," Victor says, taking the flask from her. "All breaking the rules."

Amelia shakes her head at his surprise. Being a good girl is like having a superpower, like being invisible from suspicion and blame. People want to see her that way. Everyone wants to see her that way. Her parents need to see her that way. She's the easy one, after all.

It's like a drug, that invisibility, and the more you take it, the harder the withdrawal will be when it's gone. It's one thing for everyone to assume you're a screw-up. At least then, if you do screw up, it's expected. And if by chance you do well, if you prove them wrong, it's like you just cured cancer. But what happens when everyone thinks you're perfect? What happens if you prove them wrong then?

Maybe that's one reason she signed up. She was feeling less and less like the girl other people saw. If she did this—wilderness therapy, at-risk youth, choose your buzzword—maybe she could convince herself that she was, in fact, good. If she did this, she would look like an angel compared to the delinquents and head cases she'd be leading through the wilderness.

But everyone has secrets, don't they?

"I should be dead," she says.

It's the truth, and it scares her. Every breath she has taken since the mudslide last night—the first breath, really, since she shouldn't even have made it to the second—every breath has been stolen.

Does this mean she has to believe in God now?

No, she can't believe in God, not after this. Definitely not after this. Because if there is a God—a God responsible for keeping her alive—there has to be a reason for it, and that's too much pressure. She doesn't want to go through life with that kind of pressure, always wondering if she's honoring these stolen breaths.

Victor is hitting the tequila hard. He offers her the flask, but she waves it off. He offers it to Santi, who waves it off as well.

It's strange, she thinks, as she watches Victor point at the map, talking almost incoherently about a cabin in the middle of the woods, a cabin that just happens to be within hiking distance from their trail, a cabin that just happens to have a satellite phone. It's strange how unprepared she is for the moment she's living in. The night, the fire, the alcohol, the pain in her arm. All of it.

Victor stares at her and grunts. He grabs the flask and staggers back to his side of the fire, bending over, patting the ground as if to reassure himself that it's still there. He slumps on his side and pulls his knees to his chest.

"Supply and demand," Victor says. She can barely hear him.

"Victor?"

Victor doesn't react at all. A log in the fire pops like a gunshot, and Amelia flinches and yelps in pain from the flinch.

Santi walks around the fire and eases the flask from Victor's grip, and still Victor doesn't move.

"I think he's gone." Santi comes back around and settles down next to Amelia, offering another pull. "How's the arm?"

She takes the flask with her good arm but doesn't drink. "Better with this."

"Do you know what that was all about? The gold? Mining?"

Amelia shrugs and instantly regrets it. "You think his step-dad really has a cabin up here?"

Santi laughs. "At this point, I'd be surprised if he didn't."

"Where do you think he went yesterday? When he said he was lost, where do you think he went?"

He shrugs. They watch the fire together for a long time, the flames burning down to coals. The wind is gone now, so the smoke billows straight up. Amelia follows it, leaning back to look up at the sky, so clear and full of stars tonight that it looks fake.

"I'm usually the smoke magnet," Santi says with a sad kind of laugh. "Now we're so lost, I can't even get the smoke to find me."

"We're not lost," she reminds him. And herself.

Santi pushes himself to his feet and walks over to one of the nearby trees, where the branches low to the ground are dead and dry. Two loud cracks, and Santi returns with two thick branches, laying them crosswise on top of the fire. Victor doesn't move.

"We could leave him," Santi says like he's offering up an option for dinner. We could have pizza. We could have sushi.

Amelia shakes her head.

"We have the map," he says. "We can leave some food behind. He's wasted. Even if he wakes up, there's no way he finds us."

"We can't leave him," she says.

"He'd leave us."

"Maybe." Even as she says it, she knows Santi's right. Victor has wanted to leave them ever since this morning. "But *I* can't leave him. Besides, if he's right about the phone, we can get help faster. It makes more sense."

"You don't owe him anything."

It's not him that she owes, she thinks, and for some reason, she remembers the moment she met Victor, when she noticed his eyes drop to her chest, when she made the decision to tell him that she had a boyfriend.

A lie like that is easy at first. The words just roll off the tongue, and it's done. It's the maintenance of the lie that's the hard part. New details here and there to establish the lie in three realistic dimensions. So much effort.

"I don't have a boyfriend," she says tentatively, dipping her toe in the pool, checking the temperature. Something like hope flashes in Santi's eyes, and Amelia quickly waves it away. "That's not what I meant. I don't know what I meant. I don't know why I said that—"

"Kind of a strange place for you to hit on me—"

"Stop," she says.

"It's not like the world is coming to an end or anything."

The laughter comes unexpectedly. She hits him with the back of her good hand.

Santi shrugs and looks away, but she keeps her eyes on him, on the shaggy hair covering his forehead, the fire reflected in his eyes. He may be caked in mud—they all are—but he looks comfortable out here, no matter how dirty he is, no matter what he's been through. Another day, another time? she wonders.

"Why did you get in the car that night? With your friend?"

He laughs. "I'm not really ready for sharing circle tonight."

"You knew you were going to get caught, right? I mean, you had to know—"

"I had an idea," he says. "Yeah, I had an idea."

"So, why? Why do we do stuff like that?"

He grunts, dismissive. "We?"

"I should have been in my tent last night," she says, "with Celeste. Should have been buried and mangled, just like Jerry and Rico. Just like Celeste. I should have died."

"You were lucky."

"I was out."

This is enough to pull his eyes away from the fire. "You were out?"

Maybe it's the way he's looking at her. She's seen it so many times: disbelief morphing into impatience, as if she's insulting him by even suggesting that she could behave contrary to the assumptions he's already made. Maybe that's what makes her decide to jump right in the deep end.

"The owl represents strength. Wisdom. Magnificence." She holds up the flask and shakes what little's left inside. "This is mine."

Santi smiles, then sighs. "They never suspect the white girl, do they?"

"Something like that."

Santi tilts the bottle over his open mouth, waiting for the final two drops—three—before he lays the flask at her feet. A sudden gust of wind blows the smoke straight at him, so he stands and puts his hands in his pockets, turning his back to the fire. "What am I going to do about my sister?"

"Probably not get thrown in juvie again is one strategy," she says.

He laughs so loudly, so suddenly, that she glances over at Victor to make sure he's still asleep. "Damn, that was cold."

"Sorry."

191

"No you're not. I deserve it, anyway." Santi's face is still covered in shadows, still turned away from the fire. "He kept telling me that the choices I've made don't have to define me. Jerry. What does that even mean?"

Amelia finds herself regurgitating a line from the training manual. "We don't have to keep making the same decisions. That's what he thinks it means."

"But the 'define' part. What else is going to define us?"

Santi takes his seat again. He holds a live pine bough over the fire, and the green needles begin to crackle as they burn.

"Lots of things, maybe," Amelia says. "Do you believe in God? That God has a plan for us?"

Hundreds of tiny embers flicker and glow as Santi waves the bough gently above the fire. "Why?" he says. "Do you *want* God to have a plan for—"

"No, no. I don't want *anybody* to have a plan for me. I can hardly make it through the day dealing with my parents' plan."

"So what do you want?"

Such a simple question, but it takes her by surprise. Has she ever really considered what she wants? What she really *wants*? Her whole routine in high school was built around just getting to another day, but that had nothing to do with what she wanted. Survival is a need, not a want.

36

It never got online, at least. That's what she kept telling herself. That her mistake wouldn't follow her around for the rest of her life.

Wishful thinking. She didn't need the Internet for it to follow her around. She would remember everything.

She knew who he was before he ever spoke to her, of course. Everyone knew who he was. But his name sounded different coming from his mouth, the upperclassman talking to the new girl, the freshman only a month removed from a midyear transfer, and she remembered thinking: Benny? That's a dog's name!

Later, she would wonder why she hadn't seen it coming. She would think that maybe she'd been disarmed by the name. A fluffy, cuddly, harmless little dog's name.

She would remember looking in the mirror before leaving her house. Brushing her hair over and over again. That euphoric giggle. Maybe it's nothing, she would remember thinking. Maybe he's just being nice. Maybe he invites lots of freshmen to his parties.

She would remember the conversation with her parents as she left. *Be safe! You know I will. We love you! I love you, too.*

She would remember arriving at the party with her new

friends, other freshmen just like her, and she would remember wondering where her new friends had disappeared to so quickly after they'd arrived.

She would remember that first taste of punch. She would remember climbing the stairs. The pulsating bass from the living room speakers. So dark in that house for some reason, light coming from outside, from the kitchen, from any room but the one she was in.

She would remember being the one to lead him upstairs as the giddy elation exploded in her chest, his hands on her waist as they climbed. He steered her down the hallway to his room. She was in his room. There was a bed.

She would remember that he smelled of mouthwash.

And she would remember that it was the smell of mouthwash that cut through the effects of that punch. Making her look around as if for the first time, making her wonder why she was here. What she was doing in this boy's bedroom.

She would remember feeling like she shouldn't be doing this.

She would remember also feeling like she *should*. After a lifetime filled with moving, and new schools, and more moving, a whole life of never feeling like she belonged, she was here, in his room, just one month into her newest school. She was older now, and fifteen, and she was pretty, and she was going to make such great friends this year, and here was the proof. This time, she was going to belong.

She would remember making the decision—this was the new Amelia. She had the power to decide for herself, so she did. Yes, she decided. Yes, she would. Yes, of course she would.

And she would never forget the door opening. The cluster of faces in the doorway. Those smiling faces in the doorway. The laughing.

She was on her knees, and the door was open, and she looked up at Benny, and he didn't run over to close the door, and he didn't tell them to close the door, either. He laughed.

And she froze.

And he told her to get back to it.

Later that year, when her mom got transferred again, Amelia collapsed in tears.

"I'm so sorry, sweetheart. I know you're upset. I thought this was going to be our forever home, too. I know Houston isn't California, but we'll make it up to you. This is our last time, I promise."

Her mom held her close, and the rush of relief was so strong that Amelia couldn't fight it. She let herself melt. It didn't even matter that her mom didn't know what her tears meant.

37

"What the hell were you thinking?" She's whispering because talking in a normal voice after what just happened would be insane, because there's nothing normal about any of this.

They huddle shoulder to shoulder in the main room of this ridiculous cabin in the middle of nowhere, looking down at the piece of what has to be gold in Santi's hands. A gnarled chunk the size of a plum, bulges all over like it's an enormous wad of used chewing gum.

"I don't know," he says. "I was pissed. I just grabbed it."

"You have to put it back." She can feel the dampness of her ponytail swinging against her shirt. Still damp, after all this time.

She had thought everything was going to be okay. In fact, she'd counted on it. As long as they made it to the cabin, they'd be okay. They'd dry off, they'd rest, they'd find water. They'd use the satellite phone to call for help. Everything would be okay. Everything would be okay. The only thought that kept her going.

But everything is not okay. Somehow, everything is worse than it was. There's been a fight. There's no phone.

"Before he comes up here," she says, "you have to go put it back."

She and Santi turn at the sound of footsteps behind them, just in time to catch a glimpse of Victor running downstairs.

"Do you think he saw anything?" she says, but Santi isn't next to her anymore. He's reaching for his raincoat and there's nothing in his hands.

"Come on." He snatches his coat off the hook on the center post and jams his arms through it, zips it up.

"What do you mean, 'Come on'? Where's the gold?"

"We have to get out of here," he says in a whisper that sounds nothing like a whisper.

"What are you talking about? Did you put it in your pocket?" Things are happening so fast that she can't seem to catch up. The present moment is always just out of reach.

Santi winces as he jams his feet into his boots. "You saw him. He's lost it. There's no phone up here. He's been lying to us this whole time."

"We need to stay—"

"For what? There's nothing for us here—"

"We'll get dry. You can apologize. We'll get out of this."

"Look, we need to go. Now." Santi comes over with her boots and motions for her to put her feet in.

"My arm hurts," she says, and though she doesn't want to sound like she's whining, it's the truth. "I don't think I—"

"Why did he bring us up here if there was no phone? What was he planning to do? Who do you trust? Him or me?"

Neither of you, she wants to say. But instead she lets him slide her feet into her still-damp socks and then her still-damp boots, and now he's tying the laces for her. "I don't know where my jacket is."

He stands up and hands her a red poncho. "Here, you can wear this."

Leaning against the side of the small table is Jerry's backpack. Santi lifts it onto the chair and begins stuffing the food inside. Food they'd taken out on purpose because they were supposed to be here in the cabin for a while.

Victor steps into the room. Holding a rifle across his chest. Amelia yelps. The poncho flies out of her hand, a fresh pang of agony in her arm.

"Nobody was supposed to come with me," he says. "I told you to stay at the campsite. I tried to get you to stay."

"Victor," she says, "this isn't you."

She feels like an idiot saying it. What the hell does she know about who he is? She steps toward him anyway, and strangely enough, the look of panic in his eyes doesn't make her afraid. She sees him, sees that he doesn't want to be doing this.

It's clear to her now. So clear. Victor doesn't know what he wants.

Everything is still going to be okay. Santi will give the gold back, and Victor will put the gun away, and they'll sleep tonight and regroup, and then they'll go down tomorrow. They've been through a lot. All Santi has to do is to give back the gold.

But the panic in Victor's eyes spreads, takes over his body. He waves the gun at them, back and forth, as if he's playing with a sparkler. She flinches each time the gun passes by her; each time, the pain in her arm builds on itself. The fear builds on itself, until finally she can't hold it in.

"Stop crying!" he says.

Amelia presses the heel of her good hand against her eye sockets in a futile attempt to stop the tears, and when the room comes back into focus, she sees that Santi is now standing between her and Victor.

And he's holding a knife.

She's going to have to choose. She doesn't want to choose. She just wants to be dry again, to have no pain in her arm, to sleep.

"Stop," Victor says in barely more than a whisper.

But Santi doesn't stop. He keeps shuffling his feet, shrugging to bring the backpack higher onto his shoulder, closer and closer to the door.

Victor raises the rifle and points it directly at Santi. "Please stop."

They just need to breathe, Amelia thinks. This is so far past normal that none of them have any idea what to do next, how to get out of it. Breathing is the first step. Breathe, lower the gun, put down the knife. If they can just get that process started.

But a high-pitched pop fills the room. The mirror behind Santi explodes. Fragments clatter to the ground, but she can hardly hear them through the sudden ringing in her ears.

Santi leaps toward the door, covering his head as if anticipating another shot, but there is no other shot. The rifle rests loosely in Victor's hands, aimed at nothing. Victor stares at the shattered mirror, terror in his wide eyes as if he's just seen a ghost.

Amelia snatches the red poncho from the ground and takes two huge steps to the doorway. Santi's still on his hands and knees, so she half-kicks, half-pushes him off the floor. She yanks open the door, and they burst through the mud room and her shoulder crashes against the heavy outside door and now they're into the rain and the darkness.

It's too dark, and the ground is too uneven for running, but enough light from the cabin's living room streams downhill that Amelia can pick out a path without falling, at least for the first dozen steps. No time to check a map; all she can think is that they need to hurry.

She doesn't dare stop to put the poncho on. She needs her good arm out for balance, so she can't even hold the poncho over her head as she runs. Puddles splash her bare shins. Within seconds, she's soaking again.

"Santi!" Victor yells into the darkness.

They don't talk. They don't look back. They just keep moving. Downhill, one step at a time. The rocks underfoot are slick from the rain, but soon her eyes adjust well enough to see their outlines on the mountainside.

After what seems like ten minutes, Amelia stops to catch her breath, but when she looks over her shoulder, the cabin is still so close behind them.

"Santi!" Victor yells again. The sound carries even through the rain.

A gunshot. Amelia and Santi hide behind the trees.

Another gunshot, but there's no way he sees them. Who knows if he's even aiming downhill.

She pulls the poncho over her head now. "We have to keep going."

Her arm doesn't even hurt, not like it did before. The pain will come back, she knows—it's probably just the adrenaline. And she's not even afraid. She's moving faster, yes, almost running now that her eyes have adjusted, but it's not fear that's making her move so fast.

It's anger.

She and Santi walk for a long time before Amelia stops again, under the canopy of an enormous tree.

"What do you want to do?" he says, joining her in the relative dryness.

"Not talk to you any more than I have to."

She's angry with Santi, sure, but not just him. Angry with herself for believing him. For almost believing *in* him. Believing that he was as innocent as he claimed to be. That the car wasn't his fault. The drugs weren't his fault. That he was just in the wrong place at the wrong time.

He unshoulders his pack and pulls a headlamp from the top compartment.

"And not get shot," she continues, nodding at the light. "You really think the headlamp's a good idea?"

"He's not following us." Santi zips the compartment closed and pulls the headlamp over the hood of his rain jacket.

"You don't know that."

"We would have seen his light. He doesn't know where we are."

"*We* don't know where we are."

"I'm sorry."

"I missed the part where you being sorry changes any of this."

The tone of her voice surprises her. She's not whining, not apologizing, not doubting. In place of the usual deference is something more focused, something stronger. It's not all there yet, but for the first time in her life, she gets the sense that it could be.

It doesn't look like she's the only one who notices, either. Santi cocks his head slightly to the side before turning away. He can't meet her gaze.

She adjusts the sling underneath her poncho, allowing herself to sit up straighter, holding onto that tone.

"Give me the headlamp."

"Why—"

"Santi."

She holds out her palm. No explanation necessary; she's prepared to wait like this until he hands it over, which he does without further protest. She manages to strap it over the poncho with one hand and turn it on.

"We're going to find a place to sleep now," she says. "And don't fucking tell me you're sorry again."

It's only now, after the excitement of the chase wears off, that Amelia lets herself accept how much trouble they're in. The temperature has dropped to a level they haven't felt yet on the trip. They've only got one backpack between them, and who knows how much food and what gear Santi jammed into it.

She pushes herself to her feet, figuring that if they continue downhill, they'll have to run into a trail or a river eventually. Either way, they'll be able to follow it. If they can get down, they can get out.

Mercifully, the terrain becomes less steep, level enough so that they can walk directly downhill rather than having to zigzag. And even though the rain hasn't let up, the clouds in the distance have thinned, letting a hint of moonlight through.

The slope wants to funnel them to the right; the left is blocked by a long hill about two hundred feet high.

"Wait," Santi says. The first word he's said to her since she took the headlamp from him. "Over there. What's that?"

She turns the light, following his outstretched finger. Visible against the side of the hill about a hundred feet away is a shape that doesn't make sense among the trees and bushes and rocks: a rectangle, darker than the hillside around it.

As they get closer, Amelia recognizes a mine entrance, about four feet tall and three feet wide. Like in the ghost town where Victor ran away, but with more room inside this one. Her light travels at least ten feet into the tunnel before hitting the collapsed wall at the back.

The tunnel smells dank and musty, but it's dry. The rain can't reach them here. She crouches over and yelps a little as she steps inside.

"What?" Santi says quickly, alarmed.

"Just my arm." The brief respite from the pain is over.

"You scared me." Santi laughs as he removes his pack. "I thought something was living in here."

She's surprised to find that the tunnel is warmer than outside, though it's still cool. The inside must be insulated by the earth.

"I can't believe you saw this," she says.

"My eyes must have adjusted better than yours. You know, because I don't have a headlamp."

"I know you didn't just accuse *me* of stealing," she says. "What time is it?"

He extends his wrist so that his watch is in her shaft of light. Three thirty in the morning. They've been walking for almost two hours.

She props her headlamp against the tunnel's back wall, and the beam casts creepy shadows on the way up. Exposed rock covers most of the walls, chipped and uneven, with roots poking through the occasional patches of dirt—dangling from the ceiling, protruding from the side walls. Rocks the size of Amelia's head dot the ground, but once she and Santi pile them at the back of the tunnel, the uneven floor is level enough to sleep on, with a slight incline up toward the entrance.

Amelia pulls her right elbow through the armhole of the poncho and tries to lift the whole thing over her head, but her ponytail catches on the hood. Santi reaches over to help, but she waves him off.

"I'll give him back the gold, if we ever see him again."

"You should just get rid of it," she says. "Leave it here, in the mine, where it belongs."

"He'd never believe that I ditched it." Santi takes out the chunk and turns it around in his hands. The gold sparkles even in the dim light of the headlamp. "I wouldn't believe me either."

Their one inflatable sleeping pad takes up almost the entire width of the tunnel. Santi pulls their only sleeping bag from the pack—an inventory of everything else can wait until tomorrow. They've got no rope to hang the pack with, so they lean it against the slope outside. If a bear comes along, they'll just have to hope it attacks the food in the pack and not them inside the tunnel.

They lie next to each other on the sleeping pad, fully clothed and soaking wet, Santi on Amelia's good side so that he doesn't accidentally knock against her arm in the middle of the night. Her feet graze up against the rocks at the tunnel's end, and there's almost no room between their shoulders and the side walls. Santi covers them both with the unzipped sleeping bag.

BO fills the small space, but Amelia knows she stinks just as much as he does.

Besides, at this point, comfort is a luxury. After pushing herself all day simply to get to the cabin, and then scrambling downhill in the wet darkness, Amelia is just grateful to be horizontal.

Her exhaustion is so intense that she's almost asleep when he starts talking.

"I thought there would be bunk beds in juvie, like the movies. Sharing a cell with someone worse than me. That's what I figured. I had my own space, though. Big enough to hold a bed and a shelf, with a yellow line across the entrance that only I could step over."

She chooses not to respond. She wonders if he knows she's still awake.

"I thought I wouldn't belong there. I was a good kid, right? Not like the other dudes in there, right? But I was full of shit."

The wind picks up outside, gusts that rattle through the trees, the sound louder—finally—than the drone of the rainfall. It's like alternating between the crashing of waves against the beach and a gentle murmur of hushed conversation.

"All I could think about, from the second I stepped over that yellow line, was what it would be like when I got out. What I would be like when I was on the free again. How I would be different." Santi takes a deep breath and pulls the sleeping bag higher onto his chest.

"Jerry was wrong, you know. That my decisions don't define me. I can tell you that for damn sure. Every decision I've ever made has led me right here. Freezing and wet in a dark cave, lost in the middle of nowhere. If he was alive, that's what I'd tell him. That he was wrong."

38

Amelia's sister, Charlene, had cut her hair. What had reached almost to her waist the day she left for college was now clipped on the sides and back, with just enough bangs to cover half her forehead. It was just easier that way, she said, not having to blow-dry it and style it.

Amelia couldn't stop staring.

Charlene sat across the Thanksgiving dinner table, home from the University of Virginia for the first time, having just arrived that morning. She and her sister hadn't kept in touch as much as they'd promised.

"When you really think about it," Charlene said, munching on the tip of a green bean as though it were a cigar, "you're making the most important decision in your whole life. It's not just four years, you know. It's the rest of your life, really."

Amelia made grooves in her pile of sweet potatoes with the tines of her fork. It was a Timmons family rule that everyone was in charge of at least one dish, and the potatoes were Amelia's. Charlene handled the steamed green beans. Dad took care of the turkey and everything related—stuffing, gravy, cranberry sauce—leaving Mom with dessert, which was an old family recipe at the limits of her cooking ability: lime Jell-O under a thick layer of Cool Whip.

"I mean, think about it, right?" Charlene continued, nodding at their parents. "You guys met in college. Most of your friends are from college. Your first job—"

"I don't want to talk about it right now," Amelia said.

"Have you written your essays yet? You should totally get on that."

"Charlie," their dad said. "I think she's got it under control."

Amelia grunted a laugh. Applications weren't due for over a month, but of course she'd written her essays.

"I can't believe you're not even *applying* to UVA," Charlene said. "You should at least come visit me before you decide."

"Too much of a Greek system," Amelia said.

"You say that like it's a bad thing."

Their mom reached out and patted the table next to Amelia. "She's still working on her list."

Charlene laughed. "Come on, Ellen, are you still—"

"Don't call me Ellen. Only two people in this world get to call me 'Mom,' and you're one of them."

"Okay. *Mom.* Are you still working the Princeton angle?"

"Princeton has something for everybody," Mom said, now turning to Amelia. Her tone was light but firm, as though reminding Amelia it was time for bed. "The social scene—"

Dad cleared his throat. "Ellen, she said she didn't want to talk about it."

They sat in their normal places—the same arrangement, no matter the table, no matter the layout of the house. Kids across from each other. Parents across from each other. But Amelia had gotten used to the table without Charlene, and the four of them had become three, and now her normal seat didn't feel so normal anymore.

Charlene said, "Stacy Neff said you haven't been out at all this whole year. What the fuck is—"

Mom's eyes went wide with shock. "Charlie!"

"Sorry." Then back to Amelia. "What the heck is up with that?"

"I've been busy," Amelia said.

"I mean, you only get one chance at senior year. At least you had an excuse when you were with Tyler."

"She's doing cotillion," her dad said, trying to be helpful.

"*Cotillion*." Charlie stabbed her fork into the mashed sweet potatoes and stared at Amelia. "I take it back, then. Look at you."

"It's not for another three months," their dad said, "but you wouldn't believe the planning that goes into it. I should never have joined the parent committee; these moms are *committed*."

Cotillion had once been a kind of extracurricular manners class. Kids from the area private schools would gather at the Junior League to learn about how to set a formal dinner table and which fork to use and how to ask a girl to dance and how to dance with the boy who's just asked. It was innocent and Southern.

Somewhere along the line the focus on manners disappeared, as did the classes at the Junior League, leaving only what amounted to a bonus prom. Corsages and designer dresses, boys covering dinner at an expensive restaurant, followed by a dance that ran on smuggled booze at whatever venue was stupid enough to open itself up to the liability of hundreds of obliterated minors.

"It's not for me," is what she'd said to her dad when he came home from the parent information meeting.

"Okay," he'd said, but it was not okay, and she'd caught the disappointment in his face. This was what her parents had worked so hard for: to give her the opportunities and experiences they never had. This was about making it up to her—all those moves, the schools, the cities—finally providing the kinds of social connections and experiences she deserved.

So she'd changed her mind. And now she, too, was committed.

Amelia placed her knife and fork together on her plate in the four o'clock position and scooted her chair back. "Who's ready for some green Jell-O?"

39

Amelia wakes to the sun, of all things. She doesn't move at first, wanting to enjoy the heat against her face, but other sensations soon intrude: a stiffness in her neck, the familiar throbbing in her arm, a rock wall against her left cheek, and Santi's back pressing against her right shoulder. Santi lies curled on his side; in the night, he managed to drag most of the sleeping bag his way.

She eases the rest of the bag on top of him and uses her right hand to push up into a seated position. The entire left side of her body, from her ankles to her face, is covered in dried mud. She grabs her boots from the end of the tunnel and crawls slowly outside, on her knees and good arm, pushing the boots forward a few inches at a time.

When she can stand, she does so gradually—first kneeling, then rolling up as if she's unfolding herself. She slides her feet into the hiking boots, which unfortunately are just as wet this morning as they were the night before. Her clothes are almost dry, at least. Her ponytail is filthy, caked with so much dirt that it keeps its shape when she tries to shake it out, like it's been dipped in concrete.

Mercifully, no bears ransacked their backpack during the night. But even though Amelia's hungry, she decides not to rummage for the food. She doesn't want to know for sure how little of it there is.

Stepping away from the mine, she's startled by how none of what she's seeing looks familiar. None of the ridges, none of the mountainside, none of it. Even the valley way off in the distance, which—based on where the sun is coming up—must be to the north, is unrecognizable.

They seem to have stopped in an elevated gully. To the west, the mineshaft cuts into a hill rising about two hundred feet, with higher ridges visible behind it. To the east, beneath the sun, is a large scree field, lined with elk or deer tracks. To the south, uphill, is a ridge bigger than the one at the west; it has to be where they came from. If Victor is following them, that's the route he'll take.

Thanks to the elastic waistband of Jerry's shorts, she's able to pull them down one-handed to squat and pee without calling Santi for help.

Now that she's moving, her arm begins to throb. Wearing the sling for the last two days has caused all sorts of compensatory pain: soreness in her upper arm, a twinge in her shoulder, and an ache on the left side of her neck. She could use a massage.

The swish-swish sound of sleeping bag on air mattress reaches her from inside the tunnel. Santi groans, then yelps in surprise. "It's ten thirty?"

He's at her side a minute later. Though the mud has made dreadlocks of his moppy hair, the rest of him is nowhere near as dirty as she is.

"Wakey, wakey, eggs and bakey," she says.

"Did you sleep okay?"

"You hog the covers."

"Yeah," he says with a shrug. "Did I snore, too?"

She should still be furious with him, but she can't summon the same anger she felt last night. Maybe it's the simple fact that what's done is done, or maybe it's because he looks ridiculous: tilting his head up to the sun, basking in its rays like some Rastafarian iguana.

She doesn't mention any of what he talked about the night before, and if he's expecting her to say anything, he doesn't let on.

"We have to get moving," she says. "What do you want to do first? Take inventory or figure out where we are?"

"Have you eaten already? I'm starving."

"Inventory it is, then." She leads him back to their gear, noticing over her shoulder his tentative steps. For a moment she thinks of how huge his blisters must be by now; then her arm reminds her that she still wins the injury competition.

Amelia ducks inside the tunnel and drags the air mattress onto a patch of uneven ground while Santi stuffs a handful of synthetic filling back inside the six-inch gash in the bottom of the sleeping bag and drapes the bag over the branches of a nearby tree.

When he's done with the sleeping bag, he grabs the backpack, kneels down next to Amelia, and removes its contents piece by piece, separate piles for the gear and clothing. There's not enough of either.

"That's it?" she says.

"We were in a hurry."

"Don't *we* me."

In addition to the sleeping bag and pad, the gear pile contains the map, Victor's kitchen knife, an empty fuel bottle, her empty flask, Jerry's water bottle, and the duct tape wrapped around it. They've also got the rest of Jerry's clothes: a baseball cap, sweatpants, a hoodie, long-underwear bottoms, a T-shirt, and the red poncho Amelia wore the night before.

The gear pile, unfortunately, dwarfs the one next to it. Their only food is a sleeve of saltines, a sandwich bag of powdered milk, a chewy Quaker chocolate-chip granola bar, one pouch of dehydrated beef stew, and two packets of cinnamon-and-spice instant oatmeal.

"At least we have the map."

"I should have grabbed my own backpack," Santi says.

They decide to split the granola bar for breakfast, given that they have no water for the milk, stew, or oatmeal, and the saltines would turn their mouths into chalk.

She tries to savor her half of the granola bar, taking tiny bites at first. That just makes her stomach angry, so she gobbles the rest—and regrets it immediately. Santi is focused on his half, nibbling here and there, lost in his own little world, showing all of the restraint she was incapable of. She hates him.

"That bar was only 100 calories," she says, turning the wrapper over in her hands. "And everything we have left, combined, can't even be more than 2,000."

"How would you know that?"

"I spent a lot of time putting all the food together. Plenty of opportunity to stare at nutrition information." She licks the metallic inside of the wrapper, hoping for a smudge of chocolate, but comes up empty.

Santi finishes his half, and they look at each other, and she can tell what he's thinking.

"We're going to starve out here," she says matter-of-factly.

"Who knows, maybe we'll find some mushrooms or berries or something." He slaps his knees as if pulling himself from a trance. "Okay, plenty of time for doom and gloom once we're back at it. First we have to figure out where the hell we are."

They spread the map over the sleeping pad, using the sun to orient themselves and the mine's narrow hill to ballpark their location. They estimate that they're only about two miles from Victor's cabin.

"I thought we came farther last night," he says. "I mean, I know it's not the easiest terrain, but—"

"Straight down is the fastest," she says, pointing at the map. "It's a little over twenty-five miles. We could do it in two days."

"Probably closer to three, with your arm. And the food, too; we won't have a lot of energy. We're not going to be able to jog." He sits back, and a sudden burst of anxiety hits his face. "You know, if Victor is following us, he'll probably figure that's the way we'll go."

"What are you saying?"

"I think we should head here first," he says, dragging his finger across a thick stack of elevation lines, charting a route up and over the ridge to the west. On the other side of the ridge is a tiny blue spot, indicating a lake.

"You want to make this *harder*?"

"I don't *want* to, but if he's coming after us, there's really only one way down from his cabin, right?"

Now he drags his finger from the clearing above Victor's cabin toward the valley. It passes exactly over their current position, and she knows that Santi's right. If they take the most direct route, the terrain will funnel Victor right toward them.

"He wouldn't even need a map," she says.

Santi glances at the food, and the worried look returns to his face. "I don't know, though—we don't have enough food to mess around with extending the trip."

"We probably don't have enough food, period." Amelia forces a laugh. "We're going to have to figure something out one way or the other."

"The hard way it is." Santi stands up with the map and folds it backward, neatly, so that their location is on the visible rectangle for easy access. "You carry this. I'll carry everything else."

"You know that's not as impressive as it was the first day, right?"

"As long as it's still a tiny bit impressive." He tears a strip of duct tape from Jerry's bottle and uses it to patch the gash in their sleeping bag.

"By the way," she says as she watches him stuff everything into the backpack, "since when are you so comfortable reading a topo map?"

He shrugs as he eases the sleeve of saltines down the side of the pack. "If nobody thinks you know how to build a fire, they probably won't ask you to build one."

"You've been sandbagging us?"

"A little?" he says, peeking at her through the inch between his thumb and index finger.

She has to hand it to him: he hasn't built a fire the whole trip. "I can't wait to see what else you've got up your sleeve."

"Come on." He shoulders the pack and nods up toward the ridge to her left. "Let's go find some water."

The dry heat is a welcome change from the humid oven of Houston. She can feel the sun toasting the side of her face, can hear her mother's mantra. *Sunscreen, Miels, sunscreen. You don't want people cutting on you when you're my age.*

Amelia may be out of sunscreen, but she's dry. Dry for the first time in days.

Their new route takes them over the mineshaft, then along a slight dip before a steep rise to the ridgeline. A narrow band of trees covers a section of the slope like a brushstroke, top to bottom, and they keep to it as much as possible, even though it means they have to zigzag every twenty or thirty feet in order to stay covered. It's not just because of the sun, either. The higher they climb, the more visible they become, and if Victor spots them climbing the ridge, this whole evasion plan will have been for nothing.

They stop to rest about a hundred yards from the ridgeline, in the shade of the last tree before their path becomes fully exposed. A hundred yards of rocks and tufts of wild grass. Lunchtime has come and gone with no lunch, and Amelia's been dreaming of a glass of ice water since they started walking three hours ago.

Santi squints in the direction of Victor's cabin while they catch their breath. "I don't see anything," he says finally. "Nothing that looks like a person, at least."

"We should go straight up," she says, pointing to the top. "No zigzag, no rest. Just go."

"You okay?"

"I'll be fine," she says, already knowing how much it's going to hurt to jostle her arm when she runs.

And it does. Agony the whole way—sharp pains when she bounces and a general burning in between. Fifty yards on, she starts to slow down. Every muscle in her body screams for her to stop, and she doesn't know if she's ever going to get enough air into her lungs.

They reach the top and continue for another ten feet down until they're completely hidden from the other side. Santi collapses next to her, gasping for breath.

"Jesus . . . That was . . . I think I'm gonna . . . pass out."

Amelia tries to spit, but there's no moisture in her mouth, so she just ends up moving her tongue all around. She's sweaty and her throat hurts, and her chest feels like it's going to explode, and she wishes the rain would return, if only for a few minutes.

This side of the ridge is magnificent. Tiny patches of dirty snow dot the shaded areas beneath the crags on the north-facing end. Rivulets of water run from the snow into a small lake that is somehow both green and blue at the same time.

"So thirsty," he says with a moan.

She forces a laugh. "I'll be sure to save some for you."

It takes them forever to get down to the water. The slope is steeper on this side, rocky and uneven, with only the occasional tuft of grass for a foothold. Even though Santi has the pack, Amelia lags behind, extra cautious with every step because of her arm, and he reaches the lake before she does.

He immediately drops the pack and pulls out the bottle. He gives it a good rinse before filling it, but just when he's about to put it to his lips, he turns around and waits for her to join him.

"Not thirsty?" she says.

"You're from the South, right?" He offers her the bottle. "It's rude to drink before a lady gets her beverage."

"Such a gentleman." She can't help rolling her eyes, but she accepts the bottle and drinks immediately, not even pausing to inspect the water for little crawlies. The sensation in her throat is like the first touch of aloe gel on a bad sunburn. The water's coolness radiates from there, into her chest, her stomach.

Santi kneels on a small rock at the lake's edge and cups handfuls of water into his mouth over and over.

"Careful not to drink too much too fast," she says, stifling a burp herself. "You'll make yourself sick."

"I don't care," he says with a smile. He scoops a handful onto the back of his neck and then sits up. "I'm going in."

"No you're not," she says.

"Just for a little bit."

"What about Victor?"

He points up to the ridge. "What was the point of doing what we just did?"

"Still. We should get as far away as we can before dark."

"I'm filthy, tired, hungry, thirsty. And now, because the sun decided this was a good time to come out of hiding, I'm sweaty, too."

"The water's barely above freezing." She points to the patches of snow across the way, the tiny streams connecting them to the lake. "Look at that."

"We went on a hike once, my dad and I did. There was a lake with a freaking snow-covered island in the middle—had to be at least 12,000 feet. My dad jumped right in and swam all the way to the island, then he got out and sat on the snow and waved my sorry ass over."

"Did you do it?"

"Hell, no. I thought he was crazy." Santi's laugh is genuine, warm, and completely out of place. He lets it linger for a moment before looking away and shaking his head. "Anyway, I'm getting in this time."

She says nothing as Santi removes his shoes and socks, then lays his shirt and pants out on the wildflowers.

"You're going to have to imagine the rest," he says, now sporting only a pair of blue boxers.

"You're not worried about shrinkage?"

He flips her the bird and picks his way toward a rocky out-cropping that juts out into the lake. He stops at the edge as if summoning the courage to jump.

The blood on his feet shocks her. His blisters have doubled in size—at least—since she last dressed them. They cover his entire heels; it's amazing he's been able to get this far.

"Just try not to squeal," she says.

With a big splash, Santi disappears into the blue-green water. He doesn't whoop, but his eyes are wide with shock as soon as his head comes back up, and she can hear him bring in air through his teeth. A quick rub of the hair, a doggy paddle to the shore, and he's out. The whole process couldn't have taken more than ten seconds.

"I thought you were going to swim to the other side," she says.

Santi hugs himself and shivers as he steps carefully away from the water. "I'm not insane."

"Help me take this off," she says, surprising even herself.

He raises an eyebrow and smiles, but he doesn't say anything as he unties the strip of T-shirt from around her chest and helps her out of the sling.

After kicking off her boots and laying a sock on top of each, she peels off her shorts, only momentarily thinking of her choice of underwear, the quick-drying poly-pro granny panties she stocked up on before the trip. Black, with a black sports bra.

She knows Santi is watching her. She's known it the whole trip, since the moment he came into the trailer while she was packing the food. He's bad at hiding it, like they all are. She knows this, but it doesn't matter. She raises her shoulder, pull-ing her elbow close to her body as gently as possible, and eases her arm backward through the sleeve. By the time she gets her shirt off and lays it next to the rest of her clothes, the sun is already prickling the pale skin of her legs.

"You'll have to imagine the rest," she yells up at him, and then she jumps.

When she hits the water, it's as though her body forgets how to operate. Her lungs stop working, her skin feels nothing, her heart flutters ineffectively.

For a moment, it feels like she has to get out and get out now. But then that moment passes, and she knows that she has to stay in. This here, this is where she is. She has never felt more present in her life. The lake, the water around her, the stinging in her flesh, so cold it feels hot. But here she is.

She looks up at Santi, relaxing in the sun, and she waves, and he waves back.

Amelia feels the damage to her body. Feels it in the cuts on her face, the muscles of her back. And her arm. She realizes that she's still holding it against her stomach, even now, and she lets it go, lets it float. Lets the water surround it.

She turns over on her back, taking note of the cloudless sky before closing her eyes, breathing through her nose, arms at her side, legs bent as if they're dangling off the edge of a bed.

The needles are gone; now she almost doesn't notice the temperature. She could stay like this for hours. Imagine how good it would feel! How quickly she would heal!

That's when the gunshot rings out.

40

The National Shooting Center could have been mistaken for a city park. Dogs on leashes, men and women walking hand in hand. A silver-haired lady with osteoporosis pushed a baby jogger that had been modified to carry three shotguns, barrels pointing down.

Amelia wandered toward the main office, already feeling the humidity, flinching instinctively from the constant crack of gunfire. Tyler Stafford was waiting for her on the bench outside, two shotguns laid across his lap. He hopped up as she approached, rested a gun on each shoulder, and leaned forward for his kiss.

She pecked his cheek, thinking it would be the last time, and looked around again as if in a dream. "I can just show up and shoot? Do I need a license or anything?"

"My uncle owns the place, so we're good," Tyler said. He motioned to a path downhill with the butt of one of his shotguns. "Come on."

Ten stations were arranged in a semicircle, all pointing away from the center, raised platforms with wooden lattice on each side. Spent shells littered the ground—green, yellow, and red—like heaps of broken Christmas lights. Young boys in orange T-shirts pressed buttons to release the clay pigeons and marked scores on sky-blue note cards. It was mini-golf with guns.

"This is the weirdest date I've ever been on."

"And you've lived in Moscow," Tyler said. "I'm honored."

That was the strangest thing about Houston. Sometimes it didn't seem like the redneck haven she'd always thought Texas would be. Sometimes she and her parents went to literary readings or art galleries or *The Nutcracker*. Other times she ended up at a gun range with her dualie-pickup-driving boyfriend.

She'd been in Houston for almost two years, had been dating Tyler for a third of that time. Technically, he was her fourth boyfriend since that night at Benny's, but the other three didn't last long. She'd tried, but as soon as she felt herself opening up, starting to trust, she'd bailed. Every time. She'd had to bail. Had to protect herself. She wanted to trust Tyler, too, but how could she? How could she trust anyone?

When they reached the first station, Tyler showed her how to load the shotgun, a twenty-gauge with one barrel atop the other. He flicked a lever and the barrels hinged forward, exposing two holes the size of his thumbnail. He handed Amelia a yellow shell, slightly larger than a tube of ChapStick, and another.

She'd come out here to break up with him, but she wasn't counting on it being so crowded. It would have to be afterward, when they were finished, alone and away from all the guns.

"Don't be nervous," Tyler said, reading her face. "You're going to do great."

He handed her earmuffs—massive ones, as if they were on an airport tarmac—and when she put them on, it was as if she'd instantly removed herself from the world. The gunfire disappeared almost entirely, replaced by the sound of her escalating pulse.

An orange disc leapt into view from the left. It hovered for a moment, just above the tree line, before gravity took hold. Amelia aimed in the general direction and pulled the trigger. The kick shocked her, engulfed her whole body, tiny vibrations racing from her shoulder down to her toes.

"Aim in front," Tyler yelled.

It didn't seem fair that she couldn't use all her senses. Her movements felt slow and approximate, like she was trying to thread a needle on the moon. The second clay came from the right, at a steeper angle, and disappeared into the brush by the time Amelia convinced herself to squeeze the trigger.

Tyler put his hand on her shoulder and his mouth up to her earmuff. "You'll hit the next one."

They moved through the stations. Tyler shot expertly, but Amelia didn't hit the next one or any of the ones after that. She was too far ahead or behind, not high or low enough. She stopped the gun instead of following through.

At station eight, the old woman selected a pump-action from her baby jogger.

When it was Amelia's turn, Tyler huddled behind as Amelia brought the gun up and cradled it against her cheek. She felt her elbow begin to shake, her breathing become shallow.

People waited behind them, watching.

This time the clay came from a tower overhead, streaking from left to right. Amelia pulled the trigger.

Tyler at her ear again. "Keep your eyes open."

"They *are* open," Amelia yelled back. "Pull!"

The orange disc sprang skyward from deep within the trees; it seemed to hang motionless at the apex of its flight, at least for a fraction of a second.

A fraction of a second was enough. The clay disintegrated.

Amelia broke open the gun, and the spent shells jumped out of the barrel.

She turned and stormed past Tyler, past the father and son waiting in line behind him, past everyone.

Tyler followed. "See how good that feels?"

"I don't know what I'm doing." Amelia ripped off the earmuffs and hurled them at the ground. The crack of gunfire was sharper now. "I don't know what I'm doing!"

"Come here." Tyler grabbed her hand and pulled her into the shade of an oak tree next to a small pond. "Forget the guns."

"I can't do this anymore," she said. "I just can't."

"It's okay. I know."

So this was how it was going to end. With her crying—she promised herself she wouldn't cry—next to a filthy pond while old ladies shot guns all around her. She squinched her eyes closed and counted to three. Eyes open. She was ready.

Before she could say a word, Tyler looked over his shoulder and pulled something from his back pocket. A rectangle the size of a paperback, wrapped inexpertly in yellow paper.

"I like you, Amelia. A lot. You're not like anyone I've ever met before. You're smart and funny and—"

"Tyler—"

"Let me finish, otherwise I'll never get it out," he said with a nervous giggle. "I don't just like you. I love you. And that's okay, you don't need to say it back. Not until you're ready, if you're ever ready. I know it's hard for you to commit—usually it's the guy who has a hard time—"

He cut himself off, lifted one of her arms by the wrist, and placed the gift gently inside her hand, closing her fingers around it.

"Wow," Tyler gave a little sigh of relief and shivered as if a chill had gone through him. "I've never said that to anyone but my parents."

He paused expectantly, nodding an invitation to unwrap it, and she let the yellow paper fall like a leaf to the ground.

The flask was stained teak and polished silver, the owl's wings spread wide as if in flight. She'd promised herself she wouldn't cry, it was true, but now she didn't mind the tears as she looked up at him.

"It's one of a kind," he said. "Just like you."

He leaned in to kiss her, and she met him halfway, and if anyone around them was still shooting guns, she couldn't hear it.

41

Her body is almost too numb to function, and by the time she thrashes her way to the shore, Santi has already collected her things. He helps her out and then hustles back to his clothes and starts getting dressed.

"How close do you think it was?" she says, shivering in the hot sun.

"The other side of the ridge, at least."

Her fingers don't want to bend. She blows hot air on the knuckles of her right hand until she's able to make a fist. "I told you we shouldn't have stopped here."

"Maybe it wasn't him," Santi says, a little too hopeful.

"Who else would be shooting a .22 in the middle of nowhere?"

"You're sure it was a .22?"

She gives him a wry smile. "I live in Texas."

The combination of numbness, wet skin, and broken arm makes it so that Santi's completely dressed before Amelia puts one leg in her shorts.

"I'm going to help," he says, and she nods quickly. There's no time for modesty now. He holds the shorts' elastic waistband open and bends over so she can balance her good arm on his back. "Do you need help with your shirt?"

"I'll manage."

Santi fills their bottle with lake water and stuffs it into the backpack while she struggles into her shirt. When she's ready, he motions for her to sit down on the rock so that he can slide her shoes and socks on for her.

"It seems like just yesterday you were doing this for me," he says.

"That was before you started stealing again."

"Ahh, memories." He pulls the knot tight on her second lace and helps her up. "Now your arm."

She looks up to the ridge, but there's no movement. Even so, they're too exposed where they are. "We should get to the trees first. Get hidden. We can take more time then."

Santi nods and pockets both the sling and the fabric they used to wrap it against her body.

Fighting the urge to look up again, she starts toward the trees, which can't be more than a couple hundred yards down-hill. Slowly at first, but then she finds herself moving faster and faster, starting to panic, imagining Victor cresting the ridge, the glint of the rifle in the sun, the crack of a gunshot.

Running now, but the effort of holding her arm against her chest is more than she thought it would be, and it bounces horribly with each step, shooting spasms of pain through her elbow, her shoulder, her neck.

And suddenly she's throwing up. Only halfway to the trees, still exposed, bent over, resting her right arm on a boulder and emptying what little there was in her stomach: the lake water, bits of undigested granola bar, white-yellow bile. Santi pats her gently on the back while she pukes again. Her arm feels like it's on fire now, but at least the stabbing pain is gone.

After one last dry heave, she wipes her mouth on her

shoulder and stands—just a little unsteady—and forces a smile. "Like I said, don't drink too much water too fast."

Santi glances quickly up at the ridge and then back to her. "Do you need more time?"

"I can make it."

She's more careful now—slower. Santi does a terrible job of masking his impatience, but they're able to make the trees in ten minutes without her puking again.

As soon as the ridge is out of sight, she collapses to the ground and leans against the trunk of a huge pine. Santi drops the backpack next to her and offers the full water bottle.

"I'm good," she says after the tiniest of sips.

"It's your arm, isn't it?"

"I'll be fine."

He pulls out the kitchen knife and points it at her. "Wait here. I'm not interested in 'fine.'"

Now that they're hidden, now that the immediate threat is over, Amelia's fingers begin to tremble. She closes her eyes and forces herself to breathe. In and out. Slowly. Repeat. How strange, to have to remind herself to do something she's done all her life without thinking.

If only Victor hadn't guzzled her tequila. How nice a little bit would feel right now. She chuckles.

"Yeah, this is hilarious."

She opens her eyes to see Santi smiling down at her, offering his hand. She has no idea how long he was gone.

"Can you stand?"

One more deep breath, and she lets him help her up. Under his arm are two branches, each about a foot long and as wide as a quarter. Freshly stripped of bark, they bleed sap from both ends. He steps to her left side so that she doesn't have to extend the arm.

His fingertips tap the redness on her skin. "Looks like the swelling has gone down, at least."

"Freezing mountain lake will do that."

She holds the branches while he digs through the backpack, coming out with Jerry's long underwear and sweatpants. He uses the knife to split the sweats into two pieces, setting one of the legs to the side and cutting inch-thick strips from the other. Amelia can't help but marvel at the difference between the Santi in front of her now and the one from the first three days.

"You didn't need my help with your blisters, did you?"

Santi freezes, knife in midair, and a mischievous smile spreads across his face. "Flirting has never been a strength of mine."

"Yeah, tending to the open wounds on your feet was actually very sexy."

"I'll have to remember that. You know, for when we get out of here." He winks and then lays four strips of sweatpant over the top of the backpack. Next, he wraps one of his branches evenly with the pant leg he didn't slice to ribbons and uses the long underwear to wrap the other branch.

"Aww," she says, "I was going to wear those."

"Hold this right here," he says, carefully positioning the sweatpants-padded branch behind her forearm. She holds it in place while he covers the front of her arm with the other branch. The sweatpant ribbons are so long that by the time he's wrapped all four around the splint, it looks like Amelia has a fabric cast from her elbow to her hand.

"Is that too tight?" he says, pinching her fingertips one by one. "Can you feel this?"

"I don't even know what to say, Santi. That's incredible."

"My dad and I used to go up into the mountains. Just the two of us at first, camping for weeks at a time, even when I was little, and then Marisol would tag along. That's what I remember most: him up there, sipping coffee in the morning, sitting by the fire, wearing a bandana over his head like a pirate. So happy. 'Who needs church, Santiago,' he'd say on Sundays, 'when God's already in the mountains.'"

Santi turns away and picks up the water bottle. "Probably shouldn't have stopped at the lake, I guess, but at least we're clean now."

"I'm sorry about your dad," she says.

"Yeah." He puts the sling back over her head and helps her nestle the elbow into place. "Me too."

With her arm properly splinted and tied against her body, Amelia feels infinitely more secure. "Thanks for this."

"I should have done it earlier." Santi pulls out the saltines and the sandwich baggie of powdered milk from the backpack. "Quick snack, before we go?"

"Not even that hungry," she says, grabbing three crackers. "I had half a granola bar a few hours ago."

They each munch a handful of powdered milk—it tastes like a combination of chalk, butter, and crushed aspirin—and take a few sips from the bottle.

"You think this water's going to make us sick?" Amelia says. "There's a lot of wildlife out here. Elk, deer, mountain lions."

"That's the last of my worries," Santi says. "Although if I'm going to get sick and die out here, at least it's with you."

"I don't know whether to be flattered or depressed."

"I'm serious. I can't imagine doing this with any of the others. Victor? Rico? *Celeste?*"

"Celeste wasn't so bad," Amelia says. "She was just in over her head. Just like the rest of us."

Santi nods to himself before standing and packing the water bottle. "We should get moving."

***

The next morning, weak from hunger and rationing the remains of the lake water, they're still eighteen miles from the nearest service road. And even if they get that far, it's another twelve road miles to the edge of the wilderness area.

The topo lines indicate that they've crossed below the 10,000-foot threshold, but all that extra oxygen doesn't make breathing any easier. At least the terrain has changed. The slope's become more gradual, grassier, with the occasional aspen cluster shimmering among the firs and pines. They've seen more wildlife too. Rabbits and big, furry marmots, and the occasional mule deer.

Dinner the night before was a scoop of powdered milk and the pack of dehydrated beef stew, both eaten dry to conserve what little water they had. The beef stew in particular was nearly impossible to get down. Crunchy, and saltier than she could have imagined. It was as if all the sodium instantly sucked up whatever moisture she had left in her mouth.

Breakfast is a packet of oatmeal for each of them, which means they're down to a half a bag of powdered milk and a half-sleeve of saltines. While Santi eats his oatmeal dry, Amelia tears off the top of her packet and pours a little water inside, hoping the oats will absorb at least some of it. After ten minutes, however, she gives up and just empties it into her mouth.

Santi looks at her expectantly.

"Better hot," she says. "If you can believe it."

"Too bad we don't have a pot."

"Or water."

"Or matches."

"Victor would see the fire anyw—"

"Shh," Santi says, holding his hand out like a traffic cop. He whispers without moving his mouth. "Don't move."

Amelia's stomach drops. Based on the scat they've seen throughout the trip, she knows there are mountain lions around. Bears, too, even though they haven't seen any tracks or scat.

Very slowly, Santi leans down and picks up a rock the size of a baseball.

No, no, no. If there's a predator behind her, the last thing they want to do is piss it off. Amelia can feel her pulse in the swollen flesh of her arm. Throbbing. She tries to make eye contact with Santi, but he is too focused on whatever he's looking at.

"Santi, no—"

With a burst of movement, Santi steps forward and hurls the rock as hard as he can. She hears it clatter against other rocks, and her instinct is to shut her eyes and brace for an attack. When no attack comes, she turns around in time to see a rabbit scurrying away up the hill.

"Damn." He rubs his shoulder. "I think I threw my arm out."

Amelia jumps to her feet and punches him in the chest. "You scared me to death! I thought there was a mountain lion behind us."

"If there's ever a mountain lion behind us, I won't have to tell you," Santi laughs. "You'll be able to see by the puddle in my pants."

"How far did you miss by?" she says, willing her heart back under control.

"Too far. I wasn't even—"

"Shhh."

Santi laughs. "Okay, maybe I was a little dramati—"

"No, listen," she says, cocking her ear to the sky. A buzzing. Faint, but it's there. "Do you hear that?"

The two of them freeze in place, listening, and sure enough, the buzz becomes louder. Something mechanical, inorganic, which is probably why her brain registered the sound so early. Coming closer.

"We need a mirror," she says. "Get the knife!"

Awareness flashes across Santi's face, and he runs to the backpack. Then the buzz is upon them—a small airplane with a single propeller, appearing over the ridge from the west. Santi pulls the knife from the side of the backpack and tries to angle it toward the sun, but the trees are too thick, so he starts uphill, toward the small clearing they passed the night before.

The plane isn't directly overhead, but it's close. She guesses that they have maybe twenty or thirty more seconds before it's out of view again. The hope is unbearable. Hope that the knife is shiny enough. Hope that Santi can get a good reflection.

Hope makes her feel helpless. Alone in the shade, her arm throbbing, while someone else does *something* to try to get them out of here. But hope is all she has left.

So she has to hope.

And wait.

She waits as the plane flies overhead. Waits as it continues on without changing course. As the buzzing fades into the distance. Now she waits alone in the shade for Santi to return, and when he does, the disappointment on his face scares the hope out of her.

He sits on the rock across from her, laying the knife in his lap, and shakes his head. "We're going to die out here."

"Stop saying that. They'll come." She tries to color her voice with optimism she doesn't feel. "That was just one plane, okay? Without the mudslide, we'd only be getting off the trail today, so we're technically not even missing at this point."

"You really think someone will come looking?"

"Of course," she says, maybe a little too quickly. "Hey, we're not dead yet. We just have to stay alive until then. What if we tried to trap a rabbit?"

"With what? We already ate the stew. And I don't know what kind of berries *we* can eat, much less the kind that will bait a rabbit."

"What about the rhyme your dad taught you?"

"White and yellow, kill a fellow," Santi says. "Purple and blue, good for you. Red ones are probably okay if they're not growing in clusters. That last part didn't even rhyme, so I don't know how useful it is."

Amelia notices a young aspen tree in the cluster behind Santi. About ten feet tall, with a trunk about two inches thick where it reaches the ground. The tree's absolute straightness is what catches her eye, the way it grows perpendicular to the ground, no curve to it at all.

"Let me see the knife," she says.

The handle is wooden: two separate pieces affixed somehow—glue, maybe—on either side of a single shaft of metal. If they can cut down the tree and strip its branches, they might be able to split one end and slide the knife handle inside.

When she suggests it, he shakes his head. "A spear would take too long. We should get moving again."

"We stick with the plan," she says, pleasantly surprised at the conviction in her voice. "We follow the map and try to get out. But we have no food, Santi. If we come across an animal on the way—another rabbit, maybe, or even a deer—maybe you can get close enough with the spear."

The knife isn't serrated, so sawing the tree is out of the question, but Santi cuts little wedges into the trunk, going around in a circle like a beaver, until they're able to bend it down and slice through the remaining wood. After he cuts the top of the tree and trims off the remaining branches, they're left with a straight shaft about seven feet long.

Splitting the thick end proves to be the most difficult step, and the most dangerous. Amelia holds it vertical while Santi forces the knife down; if it slips, her arm is a ribbon. But eventually he's able to get a fissure started. He wedges the blade inside, torques it from side to side to open more space, then repeats the process until the fissure is the length of the knife handle.

After Santi harvests two more ribbons from the leftover leg of Jerry's sweatpants, they're done with the knife. Amelia lays it on top of a nearby boulder, and Santi picks up a rock the size of a football.

"You're sure about this?" He pauses with the rock above his head. "If it doesn't work, we've just ruined our only tool."

"I don't think we're going to have the energy for hand-to-hand combat with a marmot," she says. "Just be careful the blade doesn't bounce up and stab you."

Santi shrugs. "Good point." A smile creases his face for the first time in hours. "Good point. Get it? 'Cause it's a knife?"

"I'm laughing on the inside."

He slams the rock down. One of the handle's sides snaps off, pinwheeling out to the left of Amelia's head. The other side of the handle is intact but shows a slight crack along the edge. Two more strikes and they're left with a single scratched piece of metal.

Santi pries the end of the aspen shaft apart and holds it open while Amelia wedges the knife handle inside. Next, Santi tears a narrow strip of duct tape from the water bottle and wraps it around the handle to keep the knife in place. Sitting cross-legged on the ground with the business end of the spear in his lap, he coils the strips of sweatpants around the wood as tightly as he can.

As he's tying the first strip, he winces and puts one hand to his waist. "My stomach doesn't feel so good."

"I know. I never really understood the meaning of 'hunger pangs' before now."

"That's not it," he says, looking up at her with concern. "I think it might be the water."

"Do not get sick. That's the last thing we need right now."

"Easy for you to say," he says, shaking off the discomfort. He ties the second strip and adds another layer of duct tape for good measure.

He hands the end product to Amelia, and she holds it like a staff, with the tip of the blade two feet above her head. She can only imagine what she must look like now: her arm in a splint, scratches and scabs on her face, leaning on a homemade spear. "You know nobody is going to believe this, don't you?"

"I don't even believe it." Santi rolls over onto his hands before slowly pushing himself to his feet. "I should have chosen to go back to juvie instead."

Yeah, Amelia thinks. This isn't what she signed up for either.

42

Bayou Banks Country Club belonged in a documentary about the lost glory of the South. The guardhouse, the fountain, the rows of blooming azaleas, the plantation-inspired architecture of the main building. White pillars, an enormous American flag beside an even more enormous Texas flag. Her mom was a member now, a privilege open to her after the promotion to Vice President of Pacific Exploration. Her mom the member— her dad loved that. Loved being the spouse in the club directory, his name in parentheses after his wife's.

Amelia parked in the shade of an oak tree and wandered through the open pool area to the club's side door, feeling like as much of an imposter as she had every other time she'd been there. They weren't really a country club family now, were they? Had that happened?

They were close, the four of them—now only three, with her sister away at college—because they'd had to be. Socially, they'd never been much in demand; in many of the countries where they'd lived, people were even more skeptical of a stay-at-home dad than they were of a woman as the primary breadwinner. That didn't stop her folks from trying. Every time they'd moved, they embraced the local customs, and this was no different. Oil executives in Texas joined country clubs.

So here Amelia was. Mid-April, and it was already so hot. After three years in Houston, she still hadn't gotten used to the daily sauna. The back of her neck was soaked by the time a blast of air conditioning greeted her inside the doorway, just about freezing the sweat solid.

Ever since the membership had gone through, her mom had made an effort to spend time in the ladies' locker room, which—even though it technically contained lockers—was more like a women-only sanctuary. Plush white carpet with a checkerboard design, a marble countertop along the back wall with two towering vats of cucumber-infused water, and flowers everywhere. So many flowers.

Her mom was at a small table with three other women, playing mahjong. Even though the women didn't discuss quite as much business as the men did in their locker room—which, according to Amelia's father, sported four poker tables and a full bar staffed with two bartenders—it was still important to be seen.

Amelia stopped in the doorway and watched; it was like a zoo exhibit. The rare and exotic species of country club women, all white jeans and sundresses.

Ivory tiles like squat dominoes were spread face down in the center of the table, with each of the four women collecting tiles into some combination or other. Amelia's mom held one of the tiles and tapped it gently on the table in front of her, deciding what to play.

"You're clicking your tiles," one of the women said, shooting Amelia's mom a big smile and the unfriendliest friendly look Amelia had ever seen.

"Hi, Mom," Amelia said, wandering over.

Her mom made the introductions, and though Amelia concentrated, she immediately forgot the names. The one with light gray hair and a boy's haircut looked familiar, at least.

"Aren't you a cute little thing," said the one with a pink sweater slung fashionably over a sporty tank top.

The one with a massive turquoise necklace said, "Your mother was just telling us about your college news! Congratulations! I'm sure Pomona will be just wonderful."

"Even though it's not in Texas," said Pink Sweater with a wink.

"Are you showing your horse this summer?" Boy Haircut said, her tone suggesting that there was only one appropriate response. Amelia finally placed her. Boy Haircut's daughter Carolyn rode at the same barn as Amelia.

Horse shows were boring, and Amelia was a terrible rider, but it's what the right families did. The other girls with hundred-thousand-dollar horses. The jodhpurs, scratchy and sweaty against the inside of her legs. The heat. That Houston heat.

Her mom rescued her. "Amelia is going to be leading—"

"Assistant-leading," Amelia said.

"Assistant-leading a group with the Bear Canyon Wilderness Therapy Program this summer in Colorado. They take kids from the juvenile justice system and teach responsibility and self-worth."

Boy Haircut bared her teeth in a shape close to a smile. "Well, bless your heart."

Pink Sweater arched a manicured eyebrow. "You're not worried about being in the middle of nowhere with those people? They *are* juvenile delinquents, aren't they?"

"They're not bad kids," Amelia said, quoting the recruiter. "They've just made bad choices."

"I'm not sure I'd go that far," said Boy Haircut. "I mean, they're in the system for a reason, aren't they?"

43

The sun pummels them from directly overhead as they stagger downhill. They stay in the shade as much as possible, but the trees can't cover them all the time. It's hotter at lower altitude, and the air is still too thin to offer much UV protection: the worst of both worlds. Amelia never thought she'd wish so much for the rain to come back, but if the alternative is being roasted alive, maybe the rain wasn't so bad.

Amelia's skin, paler than Santi's, has taken the worst of it, but both of them are burned on the cheeks, their lips chapped and split. Her hair, now out of the ponytail, lies across the back of her neck. She's wearing Jerry's hat, while Santi has wrapped what's left of Jerry's sweatpant leg over his head and tied it under his chin so that he looks like a sickly grandmother.

Dinner the night before was the last of the food—two saltines and a couple pinches of powdered milk—and though they've tried to hunt, they haven't come close to success. Marmots are quicker than Amelia gave them credit for, and the rabbits just seem to taunt them.

What's worse, the spear might not even last long enough for Santi's aim to improve. The knife handle is a little wiggly in its slot, and after one particularly bad throw, the blade chipped on a rock. Amelia joked that it looked more dangerous as a serrated blade anyway, but neither of them laughed.

They rest because they have to rest. She finds shade and Santi heads off into the woods to do his business again, the giardia having wreaked havoc on his intestines.

She pulls the map from the side of the backpack and spreads it on her lap, even though she knows there's nothing but bad news. No food and a sick Santi means they haven't covered nearly as much ground as they'd hoped. Yesterday morning they'd woken up eighteen miles from the service road. Twenty-eight hours later, they're still over thirteen miles away.

What's left of the liquid in their bottle looks disturbingly like tea. After running out of water just before dinner last night, they had to scrounge three-day-old rainwater from a melon-sized depression in a huge granite boulder. They strained the water through the fabric of Amelia's T-shirt to get the big stuff out, but it still tastes like piss and moldy bread.

Amelia drinks it anyway, letting the fluid coat the inside of her mouth until there's almost nothing left to swallow.

"How close are we?" Santi says when he returns.

She forces a laugh. "Just over the next ridge."

"You dead yet?"

"Not yet." She offers him the water bottle. "Finish it. Looks like we're going to hit a little stream in about a quarter mile."

"That could take us all day." Santi shakes his head but empties the bottle.

"How's your . . . you know."

"My ass?" he says. "Not good. Leaves and pine needles aren't exactly Charmin on my—"

"Your stomach. I was asking about your stomach."

"Oh." He leans on the spear for support. "Not good either."

Even with a chipped blade, the spear should work. It's heavy enough to offer at least *some* killing power, and the shaft is almost completely straight, so it should fly true. But Santi's awful with it, and Amelia doesn't trust herself with a throw because of her broken arm, so what should be their salvation has turned into the world's most intimidating walking stick.

"My boyfriend used to take me hunting on his ranch. The ranch hands would spread corn all around, and we'd climb up into the deer blind and wait for the deer to come running."

"Sounds boring."

"Well, it was secluded at least," she says with a wink. Santi smiles for the first time all day. "Then the deer would wander over," Amelia continues, "take a little nibble of corn, and . . . boom."

"Did you ever shoot one?"

"No. It always seemed so unfair. Luring the poor little guys like that." She holds the spear while Santi puts on the backpack, which he still insists on carrying, even in his condition.

"I wish we had some corn right about now."

The sound of the river comes to them in less than an hour, the rushing water like a distant freeway. They reach a dense band of underbrush and power through the thick branches as the river becomes louder and louder. The bushes are up to Amelia's chest in places, with green leaves that stretch up- and downriver as far as she can see.

She had thought that reaching the water would be a good thing, but she realizes—once they're through the underbrush and to the rocky bank—that the river is much wider and the current much stronger than she'd imagined. It's about twenty feet across, at least two feet deep, and churning fast enough to create whitecaps.

"Little stream, huh?" Santi says.

"Want to find another way?"

He shoots her a look. It's here or nowhere.

He rolls up his pant legs, and they take off their boots and stuff their socks deep in the toes. Then they tie the laces together, slinging them around their necks. Amelia steps into the current first and plants the spear downstream, careful to angle the knife forward, away from her head. The water is no warmer here than in the snow-fed lake, and in only a few seconds, her leg is numb halfway up her calf.

On Amelia's other side, Santi leans on her shoulder for support and steps in the water. They try to coordinate their steps, but the strength of the current tugs at their feet, and they have to fight not to get their legs tangled. Half the time, when she steps down, her foot slips off one rock and into the side of another, pinching her foot between the two.

And while she's using the spear for balance, Santi uses her, which means that each step he takes pulls her down, pressing her feet harder into the rocks. Every inch is a struggle.

When Santi is two feet away from the other side, he dives to the riverbank, sliding his arms out of his pack and rolling onto his back in one stilted, awkward motion. Amelia takes the next two steps carefully, her feet still tender on the rocks, and when she's safely on the other side, she collapses into the bushes beside him.

Crumpled branches poke into her back. She closes her eyes to the sun as it bakes her face. All she hears is the water. She tries to lick the chap from her lips.

"You dead yet?" she whispers.

"Not yet."

She rolls over and crawls to the rushing water, and she dunks her face into the cold for as long as she can hold her breath. Then she does it again, letting her unbound hair fall forward into the river. Afterward, she sits cross-legged in the bushes while her hair drips water down her face, down the back of her neck.

Next to her, Santi dips his makeshift scarf in the water and reties it on his head. Then he fills the bottle and chugs the whole thing and fills it again.

"We should go soon," he says. But when he reaches for Amelia's boots, she waves him off.

"Just a little bit longer." She knows they have to leave, but it's so peaceful here.

Santi works his feet into his boots and pushes himself up, and Amelia watches him stand there: his eyes closed, his hands at his sides, his palms turned out to the sun, the trace of a smile at the corner of his mouth.

He must sense her watching him because he looks down at her, and the smile turns sheepish. Before he can say anything, his eyes go wide at something downriver, and he darts to the ground.

Amelia says, "Wha—"

Shh! he mouths, with a finger to his lips. His eyes are alive, but not with fear.

He stands again, hunched over this time so that his head is barely above the riverbank underbrush. He motions for her to do the same, then points downriver.

Her gaze follows his finger. It takes a couple of seconds to notice what he's pointing to, but when she does, she flinches in surprise, and they huddle together beneath the underbrush.

I know, Santi mouths, back down next to her. *A fucking deer!*

A spike, is what pops into her head. That's what Tyler called it when the antlers were that small, when they just stuck straight up and didn't have any forks in them.

Even though the afternoon breeze is gentle, it's blowing uphill, meaning that they're downwind of the deer, so he can't smell them. Plus, he's focused on drinking, dipping his head down to the water, and the current is so loud that he can't hear them either.

Amelia eases the spear off the ground and hands it to Santi. "You're only going to get one chance at this."

He reaches out as if to grab the spear, hesitates, and then pulls back. "I can't do it."

"It's him or us, Santi. We're going to die if you don't."

"I don't mean I won't. I mean I can't." He shakes his head.

Amelia feels the panic start to set in. The longer they spend arguing about this, the greater the chance that the deer will be gone before they figure it out. She points to her bad arm, but he can only shake his head again.

Okay, she thinks. She looks at her boots and decides that she doesn't have time, that wool socks will have to do. Maybe it will even be better this way. Maybe she'll be quieter.

The deer hasn't moved. It's only about a hundred feet away, but that distance feels like a hundred miles.

It hurts to bend over, keeping the spear low. Her quads scream, her back aches, to say nothing of the fact that she's pinching her bad arm between her thigh and torso.

If I don't kill him, I will die.

She knows this to be the truth. But instead of scaring her, the simplicity of the idea calms her.

Slowly. One step, then stop. Another step. Somehow, the closer she gets to her prey, the less she hears the river. The less her body hurts. When she's thirty feet away, she brings the spear from her side to her shoulder.

Thanks to the slope, she's slightly above her target, which

can only help with the throw. She can see him clearly now, this young buck, his unforked antlers about five inches tall, pointing straight up like twin unicorn horns.

Tyler's voice pops into her head: *He's a beauty, Miels. You can do this.*

How much closer can she get? Each step increases her chances of hitting him. Each step increases the risk of spooking him. Maybe two more? Three? She brings her left foot up, but it gets caught on a bush, and she feels her body leaning forward, too far forward, and she's holding the spear in her right hand and her left arm is tied to her side and she's about to collapse, after all this.

Rather than trying to catch herself, she commits to the fall—an instinct says it will be quieter this way—leading with her right shoulder and letting the spear roll off her open palm. She plops into the bushes on her right side. More pain from her broken arm, and a wave of nausea hits her, but she's able to bite down on her bottom lip until it fades.

Tyler's voice again: *What are you waiting for, Miels? Go get that sonofabitch.*

She curls into a ball and rolls onto her knees and pushes up with her right arm. Once the spear is back in her hand, she crouches up again to see the spike—still there, but wary now, looking out over the river as if trying to figure out what that sound was and where it came from.

She waits. Forever. And when he dips his head for another drink of water, she moves again. One step. Two steps. Twenty feet away, fifteen.

Right there, says Tyler. *Aim just behind the front shoulder. Steady yourself. Breathe.*

She steadies herself. She breathes. Her left leg slides

forward. Her body rotates to the right, the throwing arm back and low.

A gust of wind rattles the trees above.

Now!

She hurls the spear with everything she has, leaning into the throw, following through with such force that she falls forward again. The spear is already halfway to the deer when he looks up, turns toward her, and for a split second, she swears that he's looking into her eyes.

Then she's on the ground again, in pain again, just trying to listen. And there it is. The one sound she was hoping not to hear: the clatter of the spear against the rocks.

"Did you get it?" Santi yells. Of course he was watching her this whole time. Watching her fail.

No, she thinks, rolling onto her side. No, she didn't, and it's time to give up now. Time to give in to the pain and the horror of the last three days, of what happened to Jerry and Rico and Celeste, and there's no shame in it. There's no shame in letting it all go.

***

A hand presses into her back. Gently, right between her shoulder blades. Then a pat. And now Santi's voice, an urgent whisper. "Hey, get up and put these on. We have to hurry."

There's more life in his eyes than she's seen in two days as he helps her feet into the boots and ties the laces.

He disappears downriver, and by the time she stands, he has already retrieved the spear. He's leaning against it with the muddy blade aimed at the cloudless sky. He waves her over and points the blade at the riverside bushes.

"You got him," he says.

"I what?"

"Look!" He points to the bushes again, and once she notices, it becomes impossible to miss.

Blood.

A thin trickle, a crimson line across the bright green leaves. And there, a drop. And another one, bigger. And another.

She got him.

Enough to make him bleed, at least, and a vortex of emotions engulfs her: pride, dread, hope, shame. All at once.

She and Santi follow the trail silently. Downriver, occasionally veering off to the right, toward the water, and then to the left, toward the trees. At first, the spots are spread out, sometimes ten or fifteen feet apart, but the blood gradually becomes more frequent.

"Shouldn't be long now," Santi says ten minutes into their pursuit.

And it isn't. The bloody trail bends away from the river, toward the trees, pools of red the size of dinner plates in some places. They cross a small rock mound, and into the trees, toward a rocky cliff about twenty feet high, there he is. Lying on his side in the shade, halfway to the end of a deep fissure in the cliff wall, his large ears limp, the upper one draped over the small antler. No more than a year or two old.

His throat looks like someone has ripped it out at the neck. Blood, dark red and glossy, spreads down from the wound like an oil slick.

"Nice shootin', Tex."

"I always go for the jugular," she says, not admitting where she was really aiming. She kneels down and puts her hand on his chest. The buck doesn't move, but he's still so warm.

"Now what?" Santi says.

"Can you really build a fire without matches?"

"What about Victor seeing the smoke?"

"I'm more worried about starving to death," she says. "Your stomach already turned nuclear from drinking water. You really want to eat raw deer meat?"

He nods. "Okay. I guess it's been two days since the gunshot."

"I'll see what I can do with this. I'll yell if I need you."

While Santi goes back to get their gear, she sits next to the animal. With the spear on her lap, she unwraps the strips of sweatpant from the business end, then sets about removing the knife from the aspen shaft. It's strange how she can feel both regret and relief so strongly. Knowing that she had to do it doesn't make having done it any easier.

The deer couldn't have picked a more beautiful, more peaceful place to die. She takes some comfort in that. From her vantage point inside the open cave, she can see the river through the trees, the bright green leaves of the riverside bushes, a hint of the ridgeline in the background.

The promise of a venison dinner must have put some pep in Santi's step. She hasn't even dislodged the knife from the shaft by the time he returns. While she contemplates how to cut up the deer, Santi frees the knife himself and makes a bow with a small branch and one strip of Jerry's sweatpants. Then he finds a dry stick about a foot long and two pieces of dry wood and fashions a crack halfway down one of the pieces.

When he's finished with the knife, Amelia wraps the other sweatpant ribbon around what used to be the handle, wishing she'd paid closer attention the last time she and Tyler went hunting. He'd said a woman who could gut a deer was the sexiest thing in the world, and even offered to teach her how, but she told him it was too gross. It seemed like the appropriate response at the time, what she was expected to say.

With the knife handle now properly wrapped for grip, she stands above the deer, thinking. She cleaned a fish once—as a fourth grader, when they lived in Montana, on a daddy-daughter corporate outing she went on with her mom—and what she remembers most is how bloody her fish had been compared to the kid next to her. She'd dug the knife too deep, rupturing the organs inside, and had ended up pulling out a gory mess.

Okay, then. Step one: *Don't rupture the organs.* She stands on each of the hind hooves so that the deer is spread-eagled, and she's about to cut up from the anus, just like with the fish, when she realizes that she's making this too hard.

The easiest way not to rupture the organs is not to go anywhere near them. She and Santi won't pack out the whole animal, so she doesn't have to gut it. She just has to get at the meat. It doesn't even need to be pretty. As long as they can eat it.

She remembers how Tyler peeled the hide away before cutting out the meat, and since the throat is already gashed, she decides to start there. She kneels beside it and tries to stick the tip of the blade into the throat and down. The dead body wiggles as Amelia increases pressure behind the blade, and because she only has one good arm, she has to press her knee on the side of the deer's head. It feels oddly disrespectful, like she's adding insult to injury by smashing his face into the dirt.

Eventually, she's able to get the blade moving down the throat, taking care not to stab too deeply and cause a rupture, but progress is slow. The blade is chipped and dulled, and she has one hand to work with. Cut, put the knife down, peel the hide away, pick up the knife, and repeat.

Though there's not as much blood as she'd thought there would be, the knife's cloth grip has become sticky with it, a magnet for tufts of gray-white fur. Sweat pours down the side of Amelia's face. The hide peels away like a jacket zipping open, and when Amelia hits the end of the sternum, she follows the bottom edge of the ribs to one side.

Twenty minutes in, she sits back on her haunches, realizing that in spite of her progress, all she's done is expose one side of the animal's ribcage. The deer looks like a flasher with half his trench coat open.

She wanders over to Santi, a few feet closer to the river, huddled over a stick and working it back and forth with the Jerry-pants bowstring. A small pillow of wood shavings shrouds the base of the stick, and within arm's reach, Santi's made a pile of twigs. They range in diameter from toothpick to thumb-sized.

"How's the fire coming?"

"Don't rush me," he says without looking up.

"Okay, no problem. I'm just over there trying to skin a deer with one working arm. I could use two more."

His smile is forced, and sweat streaks his sunken face. "I'm getting there."

"I'm taking a break. Maybe you should—"

"No." He focuses back on the fire. "I've got this."

She's about to argue, holding up her hand as if to motion for him to wait, but the sight of her own arm stops her cold. First, the blood: dark red and caked all the way up to her elbow in a kind of swirled paisley pattern. But it's not just blood. Little pieces of deerskin, too. Gristle, maybe, and fat. And clumps of fur. Dirt and blood thick underneath her fingernails.

Amelia drops her arm and shivers a little. With the sun dipping just below the ridge, the early evening air takes on the first hint of a chill, the shade now stretching all the way to the riverbank.

Unable to scrub with her other hand, she plunges her arm into the water and rubs her palm on the riverbed, using the gritty dirt bottom like sandpaper, then does the same thing with the back of her hand. The fur comes off easily, but blood clings underneath her fingernails. She pulls her hand from the river to find that blood has also caked the lines in her palm, highlighting them like the routes on a map.

"Fire!" Santi yells. "I made fire!"

Amelia hustles over to Santi, who's holding his face two inches from a tiny fire. He blows gently and lays the toothpick-sized twigs over the flame one by one. Then thicker twigs, and thicker.

Soon, the flame reaches six inches, then a foot, and Amelia realizes that they're going to be able to cook soon. Skinning the rest of the deer would waste time, so she pushes her fingertips along the back of the carcass as if massaging it, trying to imagine the muscle below, probing for a spot that most resembles the feel of raw steak. She settles on an area between the front shoulder and the spine, and she jabs the knife deep.

There's more blood now that she's digging straight into the muscle, but it's not *flowing*, so she must not be near an artery. The chipped blade catches on the meat as she saws it up and down, but it's still sharp enough to carve out a strip going from the neck halfway down the back of the ribcage. Cut, pull back, cut, pull back.

"Remind me never to piss you off."

Amelia looks up to see Santi watching her with his arms crossed, the fire burning more than a foot high behind him. With one last cut, she frees the strip of meat from the ribcage.

Then she jabs the knife into the deer's shoulder and holds the meat up as if it's a medal. The cut may be uneven, with patches of bloody fur on one side, but it's one step closer to her stomach.

"We still need to skin this piece," she says.

"Should probably wash it a little too, don't you think?"

"What was that you said about not pissing me off?"

Santi laughs and helps lift her to her feet. "My two hands and I will take care of this. You go find some cooking sticks."

"I thought you'd never ask." She wipes her forehead with the back of her arm and goes to wash her hand again. Near the riverside, she spots some shrubs with branches the thickness of her index finger, and they look strong enough to hold the weight of a piece of meat. Plus, they're green wood, so they won't burn as easily as a dead tree branch would.

Using her feet and hand, she's able to break off a few. By the time she returns to the fire with an armful of potential skewers, Santi has cut away the hide and sliced the meat into smaller pieces.

"This is at least a couple pounds here," he says, cradling the meat in both hands. "You're a straight-up badass."

A straight-up badass. Amelia smiles and watches him carry her kill to the river, where he kneels down and hurriedly washes each piece.

He prepares two sticks, spearing a slice of meat for each of them, and he and Amelia sit across the fire from each other. The meat is lean and dark red, and when it touches the flame, it begins to sizzle. It smells so good that she wants to eat it the second it starts cooking. Even though she's spent the last three years in Texas, it's as though she's never been around a barbecue before.

Santi cracks first, pulling his stick back and gnawing on a piece direct from the flame.

"Damn it!" he says, dropping the meat onto the ground. "Too hot!"

He picks it up and makes a brief attempt to wipe the dirt away before biting down again and tearing the meat in half. He closes his eyes as he chews, and though Amelia swears she can hear the crunch of dirt between his teeth, he looks happy.

When she can stand it no longer, she blows on her piece and then lays the stick on her lap so she can pull the meat free. She has never tasted anything like it. Grease collects at the edge of her mouth, drips from her fingers down the back of her hand. By the time she's finished, however, she's hungrier than she was when she started.

"Pretty good." Santi winks at her. "Could use some salt, though."

"More," is all she can say.

So she cooks more.

Without another word exchanged, they cook and eat it all. Amelia's hunger eases after the first few pieces, enough for her to experiment a little, alternating between medium rare and well done, between crispy and slow-roasted. She has no preference. Every bite tastes better than the last.

When the pile is gone, Amelia lies on her back and moans. The sky beyond the treetops has turned a darker blue. Soon the sun will go down, and the temperature will drop, and she and Santi will share an open sleeping bag, as they have for the past two nights.

"We should camp upriver," she says. "In case a mountain lion wants to share."

"Or a bear. I don't know which would be worse."

She sits up and immediately wishes she hadn't. Her stomach is too full for such rapid movements. "Let's cook as much as we can. Raw meat won't keep overnight, and we still need enough food to get out of here—"

"I have an idea," Santi says with a snap of his fingers. He goes to the backpack, and after piling its contents on a nearby rock, removes the garbage bag liner. "Ta-daa!"

They spend the whole evening cooking. Santi finding firewood, Amelia cutting strips of meat from the carcass, eating whenever she senses there's more room in her stomach.

"Here," she says at one point, handing him a strip she cut from above the hind leg. "This must be the rump roast."

"Ha. Rump roast." He threads the stick and holds the meat over the fire, and crackling starts immediately.

She sits down next to him, and he glances at her, the fire reflecting gold off his face, and damned if her heart doesn't skip a beat. Santi smiles, and though Amelia tries to look away, she can't bring herself to. After Santi turns back to the fire, he leans to the side, nudging her shoulder with his own.

"This is crazy," she says.

Santi laughs. "You killed a deer with a freaking *spear*. I built a fire with my bare hands. I'd say crazy is underselling it a bit."

"I did kill a deer with a spear, didn't I?"

"A *homemade* spear!" he says.

Straight-up badass.

44

Because they went to different high schools, Amelia and Tyler had to scrounge weekday time in the evenings, usually at his house or hers, depending on whose parents weren't home. In the last few weeks, though, they'd chosen restaurants and coffee shops instead. Neutral territory. No opportunity for physical contact meant no pressure to pretend they wanted any.

A month into her senior year, they sat in the back corner of the crowded White Horse coffee shop. Even in early October, it was hot enough that they decided to take advantage of the air conditioning.

They were supposed to be doing their homework. Amelia had a college essay rough draft due the next day, and she still didn't know what to write about. She looked at the blank screen, then watched Tyler slowly turn a page of his book, and tried to remember the last time they'd really laughed together. Anything she said was the wrong thing, and anything he said just made her mad.

They'd had rough patches before, and they'd always worked through them. She was his girlfriend. He was her boyfriend. Those were their identities at this point.

"I'm getting a refill," she said, and she realized that it was the first thing either of them had said since they sat down. "Want anything?"

He shook his head without looking up from his book. Her binder fell off the table when she stood up, spreading its contents on the floor: an old essay on *Heart of Darkness*, a college essay topic checklist, some loose sheets of paper, the brochure she'd taken from the Bear Canyon Wilderness Therapy recruiter.

She gathered everything up into a pile and dropped it back on the table. When she returned with her coffee, Tyler was slouched back in his chair, his legs outstretched, with the Bear Canyon brochure in his hand. "What's this?"

"A recruiter came to school today," she said. "They're looking for assistant trip leaders."

He raised his eyebrows. "You're thinking about it?"

"The girls at Bayou Banks would totally flip if I did."

"Yeah," he said with a snort.

"What is that supposed to mean? You don't think I could?"

Tyler glanced once more at the brochure and tossed it on the table. He sat up and went back to his book. "Never mind."

"No, not never mind."

"Let's not do this here."

"Do what? What are we doing?"

"You're right, Miels. What are we doing?" He paused as if expecting her to answer, but she didn't know what to say. "I thought so."

Her silence had apparently been enough for him.

"So that's it?" she said.

"I guess." He shrugged.

"Why?" she said. "I want to know why."

"No, you don't. You say you do, but you really don't."

But she did. She wanted to hear it from him, and she wanted him to hear it from her. If they were going to do this, she wanted to get it all out in the open.

Tyler looked around. Every table was full. He put his elbows on the table. "You think you're different—those families at the club, the debutante parties, all of that. You make fun of it all the time like you're different, but you're not. You're just like them."

"That's not fair," she whispered.

"You used to be interesting."

"Used to be?"

"I don't know if you picked up the brochure because you really want to do this, or because you think it would look good on your resume, or because you didn't want to offend the recruiter."

She knew she should fight back. She knew he was going too far and that she should stand up for herself, but she was just so tired. Yes, she was tired, but more than that, she didn't fight back because she was thinking that maybe he was right.

"You can keep my shirts," he said, standing in such a way that she knew it was pointless to ask him to stay, "but I want my blue hoodie back."

He slung his backpack over his shoulder and turned as if to leave, but then stopped and tapped his finger on the Bear Canyon brochure. "You are who you are, Miels. No brochure is ever going to change that."

Amelia said nothing; she just watched him go. Only after he'd walked out the door and down the street did she notice that everyone in the coffee shop was staring at her.

She leaned back and picked up the brochure and tried to disappear. By the time she took the first sip of her coffee, it was already cold.

The most physically and emotionally demanding experience of your life is also the most rewarding. She knew she could do this. She had to, she realized. Not because she wanted to prove Tyler wrong about her, but because she knew he was right.

She'd go home and tell her parents the news, and she'd fill out the application and send it in before she changed her mind, and then she'd get wasted and try to forget everything she ever felt about Tyler Stafford.

45

Amelia peels away the sleeping bag and sits up. She's alone. The air is cool, and a thin layer of dew coats her face and neck. As has been her habit over the past few mornings, she takes a moment to categorize everything wrong with her body. The arm is still in pain, still splinted and tied to her chest. Her back aches from her waist to her shoulder blades—a newer pain, probably from spending so much time hunched over while butchering the deer.

The outlook is not all bad, though. The bruises on her face seem less tender this morning. The crick in her neck feels better. And amazingly, she's still full after feasting the night before.

When she stands, the top of Santi's head is visible above the riverside bushes. She slides her boots on and tucks the untied laces behind the tongues. Halfway to him, she hesitates. He's sitting on the riverbank with the map in front of him, looking across the water at something in the distance. The ridgeline? Nothing at all?

A branch snaps beneath her boot, causing him to turn back and look at her. His cheeks are less hollow than the day before. He smiles and waves her over.

"Everything okay?" she says.

"With my ass? You bet. Only had to get up twice."

"That's a miracle. Did you eat already?"

"Not hungry, if you can believe it. The food's still there, though. I checked first thing."

"And the deer?"

"Untouched, as far as I could tell." He gestures to the map in front of him. "We're less than thirteen miles away from the access road. Now that I'm feeling better, we might be able to make it today."

Amelia sits next to him and pulls the map over her crossed legs. "I was thinking. We have food now, so that's not a problem. If we follow the river from here, we still run into the access road. It adds . . ." She traces her finger along the blue ribbon and ballparks the distance. "Looks like four miles, but that's a small price to pay in order to guarantee water."

"Seventeen miles? We can do seventeen, no problem," Santi says. He laughs at the absurdity of his confidence.

Amelia laughs with him. "Yesterday morning, eighteen miles felt like a death sentence."

"Yesterday I didn't know you were a warrior princess. A lot can change in a day."

"That's why I think we should stick to the river," she says. "Worst case, the bank is impassable and we have to cross a couple of times, but we've already done that. Maybe it takes another day. Maybe two. But we'll have food and water."

He nods. "They always say the best rescue is self-rescue, but even if following the river keeps us out here a little longer, it gives people the chance to look for us too."

Optimism is sneaky. She didn't see it coming, and it's here before she's had the chance to put her guard up. Making her smile, making her notice the morning sun's rays as they send narrow golden beams over her head.

Objectively, they're still screwed. Amelia's arm is still broken. Santi still has giardia. They're still in the middle of the most remote wilderness area in Colorado, possibly being followed by a lunatic with a rifle. But compared to dying of thirst and starvation, maybe a bout of diarrhea and a broken bone aren't so bad. Even the thought of Victor doesn't dampen Amelia's spirits.

While they pack up their gear, Amelia feels as if they're already reminiscing, as if they're already on the other side of this. As if they've already been found. Oh, here's the deflated air mattress and sleeping bag we shared—pay no attention to the six inches of duct tape. Yeah, that's blood on the chipped kitchen knife, but don't worry—it's not human!

On their way downriver, they check on the carcass, which looks like a whole family of bears ripped it apart: hide shredded and peeled away haphazardly, chunks of flesh missing from the back, one of the hind legs almost entirely torn away, holding on by a few tendons.

"I thought you said it was untouched since last night," she says.

"It is." They stare at it in silence for a minute. "You really did a number on that bad boy, didn't you?"

The deer is way more mangled than Amelia expected, and she can't decide if Tyler would be proud or offended by her work. She knew she wasn't exactly being surgical, but she didn't expect it to look like this. "We were hungry. And I didn't exactly have a lot to work with."

"Either that or the chupacabras came along—"

"Okay, okay."

They stand quietly again, contemplating the remains. Santi clears his throat. "I feel like we should say something."

"I'm pretty sure you've said enough already," Amelia says.

He waves his hand out in front of him, making something like the sign of the cross. "Dominus ominus."

"You're weird."

Another two hundred yards downriver, they stop for the black trash bag, which is dancing erratically against the current, tied to the trunk of a nearby bush with the last remaining strips of Jerry's sweatpants.

Santi kneels and unties the makeshift rope. He hauls the bag out of the river—hand over hand, like a fisherman pulling in his net. "Nature's fridge."

"You dead yet?" Amelia says, watching him load the meat into their backpack.

"Not yet."

"We're going to get out of here, aren't we?" The words feel different in her mouth now that she actually believes them. Empty hope was worse than no hope at all; real hope is better than both.

"You had to go and jinx it, didn't you?" Santi says. He dons the backpack, and with a last glance upriver, they're gone.

Compared to the terrain they've struggled with over the last week, the gentle slope alongside the river makes for an unsettlingly easy walk. Amelia doesn't trust it. Every time they round a bend, she expects to find some new, ridiculous obstacle, like a cliff wall they have to ford around or underbrush dense with brambles and thorns. But while the bushes are a little thick here and there, and they occasionally have to navigate piles of stones along the riverbank, nothing they run across comes close to the dangers in her imagination.

"When I was in juvie," Santi says after about fifteen minutes of solid progress, "I would lie in bed at night and play the 'When I get out of here' game. You know: I'm going straight to Blake's Lotaburger for a green chile cheeseburger. I'm going to study for real this time. I'm never going to do anything bad again."

"I hope you got that cheeseburger, at least."

Santi shakes his head. They reach a bend in the river and start to scale a pile of small boulders. "The only thing that matters now is my sister. I know I can't get us out of Ray's house, but I can be there with her."

"Is it weird that I don't want to go back home?" Amelia says.

Santi's laugh is a sudden, singular *Ha!*, like the pop of a firecracker.

"Don't get me wrong," she says. "I want to get a cast and some painkillers and take a shower and all that. But I'm kind of dreading everything else."

They walk in silence for a minute or two, with the wind occasionally gusting at their backs. The sun has crept entirely above the ridge, and while the morning chill hasn't gone away, the air is crisp. Even the river is calm, having doubled in width; the water moves with a soothing gurgle.

"No, it's not weird," Santi says. "Everything good that's ever happened to me has happened in the mountains."

"Except for the part where you stole that piece of gold."

He stops and glares at her, like he's been betrayed. "Come on, man. I thought we were having a moment."

"Sorry?" Amelia says with a wince.

"I don't even know why I did it, you know? It was there, I took it, and then it was too late to un-take it. I didn't know what I was doing." He shakes his head again. "I don't ever know what I'm doing, really."

"Who does? I think everyone is just as lost as the next

person." She turns to him and holds her arm out wide. "When you see me, what do you see?"

Santi pulls the water bottle from the pack's side pocket and contemplates her as he sips. "I thought you weren't up for sharing circle."

"My dad once told me that I'm the only one in the family he doesn't have to worry about."

"Are you complaining?"

"No, not complaining, but what am I supposed to do when he says that? What if I *need* him to worry about me? I'm about to go to college, exactly what I should be doing, what's expected of me. I'm the easy one, right? But I'm not ready. Not for college, not for life, not for any of it."

"Is that supposed to make me feel better? Because it doesn't. If you don't have your shit together, what chance do *I* have? Private school, country club, oysters—"

"Oysters?"

"Or whatever rich people eat," he says with a laugh.

"Rich makes no difference. There's a girl I went to school with," she says, holding her hand out for the water, "Heather DuBois. Fought with her mom constantly. She went out and bought a $10,000 dress with mom's credit card—"

"No way—"

"Swear to God. She didn't even like the dress. Had it altered right away, though, so her mom couldn't return it."

"What did her mom do?"

Amelia laughs. "More coke, probably."

Santi laughs with her. She's about to put the water bottle to her lips when a gunshot splinters the morning stillness.

Amelia and Santi run to the underbrush, and by the time the echo fades, they're both crouched down for cover.

Santi looks just as afraid as she feels. He whispers, "Was that—"

"A .22?" she says. "Yeah."

"It was really close. Closer than last time. I bet he saw our fire."

Before she can say anything, another shot rings out, followed by another. And another. "What is he doing?"

In answer to her question, a scream fills the river valley. Not a scream of anger—it's one of fear. Of panic. It doesn't make any sense.

She cocks her ear to the sound as it fades. "Why would he—"

Another gunshot interrupts her, followed by a single word.

"I think he just called for help," Amelia says, still confused, still not ready to trust what her ears are telling her.

"What do we do?" Santi says. "He sounds just as crazy as the last time we saw him."

"We have to help him, don't we?"

"What if it's a trap?"

Victor's voice again. *Help.* This time, there's no mistaking it. Amelia glances longingly downriver. "You know we have to go back."

Santi winces but says, "I know."

Uphill takes longer. They move slowly, hunched over to stay hidden, keeping as quiet as possible. She doubts it's a trap, but if it is, she's not about to run right into it.

There are no more gunshots, but Victor's screaming has become a constant. Ragged with a fear that's more apparent the closer they get. They stop to rest at the spot where they'd tied the meat for the night.

"He's got to be at our campfire," Amelia says. She points

to the trees, away from the river. If they stay by the river, they'll be more exposed as they get closer. Better to hide in the trees.

Santi nods, and they zigzag forward quietly, with the trees as a buffer between them and the sound of Victor's voice. They're close now, only fifty feet from the deer carcass. As Amelia starts to run toward the next tree, Santi grabs her shoulder—the one connected to her broken arm—and pulls her back. Somehow, she swallows the yelp as a wave of nausea overtakes her. When she turns to glare at him, the color is gone from his face.

She follows his terrified gaze and can't swallow the yelp a second time.

A mountain lion. Pacing back and forth between the site of their fire and the cliff-side spot where they'd left the deer carcass.

It's beautiful. Light brown with a hint of white along the fur at its belly, its long, thick tail whipping back and forth as it moves. It keeps its head low to the ground, which accentuates the muscles in its front shoulders. The power is evident, even as it stalks.

"He's trapped in there," Santi whispers.

With Santi behind her, Amelia slowly moves toward another tree, parallel to the river, until she can see where Victor has stationed himself: the gap in the cliff. He stands inside at the closed end, his backpack at his feet, holding his rifle by the barrel and waving it like a sword. The only thing between him and the mountain lion is the deer carcass.

"He saw our smoke," Amelia whispers, once again grateful for the noise of the river. "The mountain lion must have showed up just after he did."

Santi's reply is so quiet that reading his lips is the only way she can understand him. "What if it just wants the deer?"

"It'll attack him if he tries to escape," she says. She doesn't know much about how to survive a mountain lion attack, but she does know that running away triggers the predator instinct. "He won't stand a chance."

"We need to distract it, then," Santi says. "Scare it away."

"That's insane. If it notices us, we're dead too."

"How much longer do you think it's going to pace there before it gets bored and goes in?"

"I don't want to see Victor mauled, Santi. But I really don't want to *be* mauled."

Santi removes his backpack. "I have an idea. Wait here."

"What are you going to do?" she says, grabbing his arm.

"He's trapped. He's out of ammo. His only way out of there is if the mountain lion leaves, and I'll bet you a million dollars that Victor panics and does something stupid before that happens."

"That thing could gut you with one swipe."

He takes a deep breath and nods, more to himself than to her. "I never do the right thing." His smile is no match for the fear in his eyes. "I wonder what it feels like."

"Just be careful," she says.

"I love you too." He winks and turns downhill before she can give him the finger.

The next five minutes are torture. Amelia doesn't know where he's going or what he's doing. All she can do is wait. The mountain lion seems to have no interest in leaving. If anything, it's inching closer to the entrance. Closer to Victor, who swings the gun more wildly every time. Santi was right about one thing: panic is taking over.

Victor yells again, and for the first time, the mountain lion yells right back, an angry, high-pitched screech. Amelia expected something deep and menacing, but this is infinitely more terrifying: a shriek that echoes down the valley.

This will all be over soon. One way or another.

Amelia catches a glimpse of movement on top of the cliff. It's hard to see through the tree branches, so at first she thinks her eyes are playing with her. But there it is again: Santi, crouched over, far enough from the edge that he's hidden from below. He shuffles forward, partly out of stealth but mostly because he's struggling to carry a rock the size of his chest.

When he's almost above the fissure in the cliff wall, he eases the rock to the ground and lies on his stomach behind it. Advancing slowly—Amelia can't be sure he's actually moving at all—Santi pushes the rock toward the edge of the cliff, crawling military style behind it, until it's teetering on the brink. He's waiting for something. What is he waiting for?

The mountain lion arches its head toward the sky, but before its screech is fully formed, Santi yells at the top of his lungs and pushes the rock forward. It clatters down the rock face, cracking off smaller stones on the way, making enough noise that Amelia can hear it over Santi's shout.

Then chaos. Ear-splitting chaos.

The mountain lion screams again, and Victor screams, and Santi is still screaming. The boulder hits the ground and keeps rolling, and the mountain lion prances straight up, its back arched like a startled housecat. With one final screech, it sprints uphill and disappears through the trees.

For a moment, there's only the rushing of the water.

Amelia hides behind the tree. Santi lies motionless on the

ground at the cliff's edge. Victor, still in the open cave, spins in circles, looking all around him.

When she's convinced that the mountain lion is truly gone, Amelia steps out toward Victor. He sees her and freezes. He stares at her as she strides closer, his eyes wide as if in shock.

Amelia puts her hand out like a stop sign as she passes by their campfire, then pauses at the entrance to the fissure.

Victor looks ragged, spent. His chest is heaving; his clothes are just as filthy as Amelia's.

"You okay?" she says.

It's as though a spell is broken. His shoulders sag and he drops the gun, and the shock in his face turns to exhaustion.

"I . . . I don't . . . Thank you," he finally says.

"Don't thank *me*."

A rock falls to the ground at Victor's feet, and he flinches backward. Santi swings his feet over the cliff edge above them and sits down. Victor starts to turn toward Santi, but then he notices the rock on the ground.

He squats to pick the thing up, then holds it in front of his face, squinting, and Amelia realizes that it's not just a rock.

"Sorry about the whole 'stealing gold from your stepdad's secluded mountain cabin' thing," Santi says from above.

Victor's chest is still heaving, but he nods, then he nods again. He hunches over. He looks broken. He turns his attention back to the gold in his hand, tossing it up and down as if checking its weight.

Amelia is about to step the rest of the way toward him, to put her hand on his shoulder and tell him that everything is going to work itself out, when Victor squeezes the gold in his fist until his knuckles turn white. He picks his head up and rolls his shoulders back.

He looks back up at Santi and out to Amelia. The anger in his eyes is gone, as is the fear. Victor turns his hand over and studies the nugget resting on his palm, and then he smiles— just a little one; if she'd blinked, she would have missed it—and takes two enormous strides and throws his stepfather's gold out over the river.

His yell thunders through the valley, rippling back to them in waves, as the gold catches the sun and sparkles briefly before the wilderness swallows it whole.

ACKNOWLEDGMENTS

I've been working on this book on and off for so long that there's no way I'll be able to thank everyone who has played a role in getting it this far. I will try to do so anyway.

For early encouragement and honest reads, I want to thank the Antidote Workshop: Alexander Parsons, Colin Tangeman, Greg Oaks, Casey Fleming, Scott Repass, Katy Miner, Ranjana Varghese, and Robert Liddell.

I am indebted to Tyler Stableford and Stableford Studios for a place to work in Colorado and the fine folks at CHMSNA, in particular Sunil Yapa and David Wolman, for their perceptive feedback and unrelenting support. Thanks to Win and Lynn Campbell for being such enthusiastic champions of mine and for continuing to share their Alta Lakes pride and joy.

I am grateful to the American Library Association for selecting my first novel, *The Brothers Torres*, for the Great Stories Club, and to the GSC program coordinator, Lainie Castle, for making it all happen. Thank you for sending me to juvenile detention centers around the Gulf Coast and for giving me an opportunity to meet and learn from the kids. Thanks to the staff members, librarians, and detainees of the centers I visited, in particular: Kathleen Houlihan and Heather Schubert at the Gardner Betts Juvenile Justice Center in Austin,

Texas; Stephanie Wilkes at the Green Oaks Detention Center in Monroe, Louisiana; and Francie Clinton at the Southwest Oklahoma Juvenile Center in Manitou, Oklahoma.

Sara Crowe stayed in my corner throughout, and Greg Hunter gave the book the most thoughtful and thorough reads I could possibly have hoped for.

I could never have written this book had I not spent so much of my childhood in the mountains with my mom, dad, and sister. Thank you for the campfires, the hot cocoa, and the best steak in the history of the world. We all know what Dad is, do we not?

Finally, to Molly, Dayton, and Annie Voorhees: Thank you for believing in me, challenging me, supporting me, and most of all, thank you for being with me every day.

ABOUT THE AUTHOR

Coert Voorhees is the author of the novels *In Too Deep* (2013 Junior Library Guild Selection), *Lucky Fools* (2012 Junior Library Guild Selection), and *The Brothers Torres* (2009 ALA Top Ten Best Books for Young Adults). He holds an MFA in Fiction from the University of Houston, spent time in Chile as a Fulbright Scholar, and taught at Rice University as the Visiting Writer in Residence. Coert is the founding Mayor of Grammaropolis(.com), and his books for children include the Meet the Parts of Speech series and *Storm Wrangler*. When he's not camping or scuba diving with his family, he lives with them in Houston, Texas. Visit Coert's website at www.coertvoorhees.com.